Bad Tommy

A Novel
James Peaton

Pamela,
Thank you
for Cheering me
on with this!

3/9/16

Bad Tommy

Published by James Peaton
© 2016 by James Peaton
Cover art by SP Photography

For information, questions or comments, go to jamespeaton.com or email author at: jpeatonfiction@gmail.com

First printing: March 2016
Printed in the United States of America

First Edition: March 2016

ISBN-13:978-1511722438
ISBN-10:1511722436

10 9 8 7 6 5 4 3 2 1

Bad Tommy

✧

Chapter 1.

Judy peeked around the corner and saw her husband Pete standing in the doorway to the bedroom, pointing his hand gun into the living room. Her heart started to pound and she froze, not wanting him to see her.

Oh God, what's he doing now? He's done too much coke again and having another flip out episode! God, I hope Tommy's in bed!

From the glow of the holiday lights hanging in the doorway, Judy could see that Pete's shirtless body was drenched in sweat and the look on his face either meant he was having one of his worse highs ever or he was terrified at what the gun was pointed at.

"Daddy, come sit wif me. I watch cartoons."

The small voice came from the sofa in the living room. Judy's eyes went wide as she saw the intense look on Pete's face falter for a second. Pete said nothing and continued to point the gun at Tommy.

Without thinking, Judy came around the corner into Pete's view. He didn't look away from his target, but she could see him clench the gun tighter. Tommy was sitting on the couch with a bowl of something in front of him, staring at the television. She inched her way toward her husband.

"Pete, please put the gun down. You're just high again. You're pointing it at Tommy and you're scaring me, Pete," she said, in a whisper.

At the sound of his mother's voice, Tommy looked over at her.

"Mommy, do you want to watch cartoons wif me?"

Judy heard the small voice, ignored it and kept her eyes fixed on Pete.

"What the hell are you doing, Pete? Please, put the gun down!" she whispered, with more force.

The look on Pete's face faltered again and his bottom lip trembled. He lowered the gun slightly and without turning his head, moved his eyes to Judy. They were red, big and familiar to her. She had seen them before. They were the eyes of Pete the junkie, who'd taken too much and needed to sleep, but there was something different in them she hadn't seen before and it scared her.

She inched her way toward him and put her hands out.

"Pete, give me the gun. You're gonna do something crazy. You don't want to hurt Tommy, do you?"

Pete's eyes moved back to Tommy on the sofa. Judy followed his gaze and saw that Tommy was watching TV again, not paying attention to what was happening.

"Tommy, sweetheart, get up and go in the kitchen," Judy said, calmly, not taking her eyes off Pete. She wanted Tommy out of harm's way, but the little boy continued to watch the TV.

At this, Pete regained his determined gaze and brought the gun back up, aiming at Tommy's chest. Judy could see from the muscles in his arm and his white knuckles that he had a death grip on the gun and intended to fire it.

"Please, no!" Judy screamed, as she lunged forward. As soon as she collided with Pete, the gun went off.

At the sound of the report, Judy's eyes went to Tommy, just in time to see his head violently jerk back.

"No, Tommy!" she screamed, looking back to Pete. He was taking aim again.

Judy looked around and caught sight of the snow globe sitting on the end table and snatched it up. A split second of guilt washed over her as she did. The snow globe had been a Christmas present from Tommy and he loved it even more than she did. Judy brought it up over her shoulder and bashed Pete in the head. It made a hollow *thump* sound and he went down, sending the gun sliding across the wood floor. She thrust the globe at him again, this time hitting him square in the forehead.

"No, not Tommy! Not my Tommy! Why, Pete?"

Judy crouched over Pete and continued to hit his head with the globe, despite him not fighting back or moving much after the second blow.

"Ha ha ha, Goofy funny, Mommy."

Tommy's voice made Judy stop suddenly. She dropped the globe next to Pete, as she looked back to her son. He was sitting in his spot on the sofa, pointing to the TV and smiling.

"Tommy!" Judy shrieked. "Oh God, Tommy!"

Without looking back at the mess she'd made of Pete, Judy scrambled up off of him and ran over to Tommy.

"Oh my God, Tommy, you're ok? Oh, please be ok!"

She embraced him, checking him for injuries. There was no blood and he didn't seem to be hurt in any way.

But I saw it! Pete fired the gun and his head flew back.

She hugged him tight and her five year old hugged her back, not taking his eyes off the TV.

"Mommy, look!" Tommy said, pointing to the TV again, smiling.

Judy glanced at the TV passingly and then looked around at their dump of an apartment. The place was usually messy, but there seemed to be garbage scattered around. She looked back at Tommy. He was a mess too, dirty and wearing filthy cloths.

I'm so sorry, baby. I've been working too many doubles at the hospital and haven't been home watching you like I should. I've been leaving you with your worthless, drug dealing father too much.

This thought made her look over at Pete on the floor. He laid perfectly still. A pool of blood had formed around his head and Judy put her hands over her eyes and let out a few muffled sobs.

I've just killed my husband.

A few more sobs escaped from beneath her trembling hands, as she pulled them down and looked back to Tommy. He hadn't noticed what just happened and took another nibble from what was in the bowl, still staring at the TV. Judy tried to gain control of her sobbing.

He doesn't seem to realize what I just did. What am I going to do? Call the police? They'll take Tommy away from me again and for good this time. Aside from what the apartment must look like, I just murdered someone and...

Looking at Tommy, a feeling of dread tickled her skin with goosebumps.

One of the neighbor's probably called the police already! It's after two am, but there's no way they didn't hear that shot. Half of them hate us anyways. They know what my husband sells here. Get a hold of yourself, Judy. What's done is done. At least don't scare your little boy.

She took a deep breath and let it out. Tommy had shifted a little closer to her and took another hand full, popping it into his mouth. Judy looked at him.

Whatever he's eating is making a mess of his face.

Judy looked down at the bowl and her heart took another jolt.

"Tommy, no! Don't eat that!" she snapped at him, as she reached over and snatched the bowl of raw hamburger out of his hands. Tommy shot a look of childish resentment at her, then his gaze followed the bowl, as if she'd snatched his favorite toy.

"Why would you eat that, sweetie? How much have you had? Don't swallow anymore!"

Judy took the back of Tommy's head in her hand and began sticking her fingers of her other hand in his mouth, trying to rid him of the last bite of meat she hoped he hadn't swallowed. Tommy's eye brows tilted together in a slant, wrinkling the skin between them. His face became a sneer and a deep growl started to rise from his throat.

Judy let out a scream as Tommy bit down on two of her fingers.

"Ouch, Tommy! Let go! You're biting my fingers! Stop, that's bad!"

Tommy bit down harder, causing Judy to let out an ear piercing scream. She brought her other hand to the side of Tommy's mouth, with the intent of prying his teeth from her fingers. Before she could, Tommy grabbed her wrist and squeezed, digging his nails into her skin. He pulled her hand back down away from his face with surprising strength. Judy resisted, but couldn't stop him.

Still screaming, Judy yanked hard and Tommy loosened his teeth enough for her fingers to slide out, scraping skin as they went. When they were free, she brought her hand to her chest and fell off the couch, onto the floor. She looked down at the bloody teeth marks on her middle and index fingers and then back up at her little boy.

He was crouched on all fours, with his hands set between his feet, snarling and barking at her with the slightest bit of blood around his mouth, either from her fingers or the raw hamburger.

"No, Tommy! What's wrong with you? Please, baby, stop!"

Without warning, Tommy lunged himself across the sofa toward her, catching her by surprise. Judy kicked her feet against the couch, sliding away from him, across the wood floor, turned and got clumsily to her feet. She made her way across the small living room and to her bedroom doorway without looking back, letting out a desperate scream as she went.

She burst into the room, closing the door behind her, expecting Tommy to slam into it as it shut. The door stopped short of closing and she let out a gasp.

"No, Tommy! Stop!" she screamed, as she pushed her weight against the door. There were no thumps or movements on the other side. It just wouldn't close.

"Oh, please, no!"

She looked down at the floor and saw Pete's hand wedged in the doorway. She opened the door just enough to knock his hand out of the way, while taking a quick glimpse towards the living room.

Tommy was sitting back on the couch, watching the TV contently, eating handfuls of meat out of his bowl.

Judy slammed the door shut and locked it.

•••

Judy sat with her back against the door, sucking in huge gulps of air, in attempts to calm herself. Her throat, dry and raw from screaming, ached with pain. She reached into her coat and pulled out her crappy cell phone, opened it and dialed nine 911, with her quivering finger. The phone rang once and clicked over to a recording.

"Hello, your coverage has been suspended due to non-payment. You are being redirected to our automat—" she snapped the phone shut and threw it across the floor.

"Damn it, Pete! With all the drug money going through here and my paychecks, you can't even pay the damn phone bill?" she mumbled in frustration.

It happened all the time, she didn't know why she was surprised.

"Someone must have called the police. They'll be here any minute."

Judy took a deep breath, quieted and put her ear to the door. She could clearly hear the cartoons and Tommy's giggles. She sat that way for a moment, listening.

EEEEENNNNTTT!

She jumped away from the door, startled.

"God, damn it!" she blurted out.

Judy recognized the sound. It was the dryer alarm. The units were tucked away in a hall closet not far from her bedroom door. She continued to take deep breaths.

Why, Tommy? What's wrong with you? Why would you do that? And why did Pete have to go and flip out?

Then something came to her.

"Oh God, Pete knew. He knew Tommy wasn't right. That's why he went crazy. And I killed him."

She shuddered as her eyes went to the edge of the door where Pete's hand had been caught. A feeling of guilt washed over her.

She slowly stood up and looked around the room. It was messy, dark and gloomy. Judy didn't sleep in the bedroom very often. She usually slept during odd hours on the couch. This room was mostly Pete's and aside from the mess, it was covered in paraphernalia.

She walked over to Pete's desk, scanning the top. It was a messy collage of someone who shot up heroin and smoked crack and pot. She rarely partook in Pete's habits, but she was with him long enough to see he had been busy that day. He had gorged on the stuff in the end.

"Pete, you ass hole. You saw something was wrong with Tommy and shot yourself up instead of going for help. How long has he been like this, Pete?"

It's been days since I really looked at either of them and there's enough stuff laying around in here to put both of us in prison. You didn't want anyone snooping around in here, did you Pete?

She picked up a needle lying on the edge of the desk, looking at it in disgust. She counted five fresh ones on the desk and two on the floor.

"Mommy, come watch cartoons wif me. You in there?"

Judy jumped at Tommy's voice and the needle made a loud clinking sound, as it landed back on the desk. She could see the shadows of Tommy's feet under the door.

She raced across the room and put both her hands around the door knob, holding it in place. She closed her eyes, held her breath and said nothing.

Five seconds went by and Judy sighed in relief. Then the door knob jerked back and forth in her hand, making her let out a loud gasp.

"I hear you in there, Mommy. You hiding from me?" the voice said, playfully.

Judy closed her eyes and bit her bottom lip.

Oh my God, he sounds so normal.

She bit her tongue between her teeth, fighting the urge to answer him. Her hands grasped the knob tighter, remembering how strong he gripped her wrist before.

"Come out and watch cartoons wif me. I hungry too, Mommy."

Judy's mouth opened to answer, when she heard a scraping sound outside the door. She knew what it was and her heart dropped into her stomach. It was Pete's body being dragged across the wood floor. The sound faded and she put her ear to the door. She heard some unrecognizable commotion and then footsteps coming back in her direction. The footsteps were strange, more of a scuttle, short and quick.

Judy secured her grip on the doorknob. The footsteps passed the door and stopped. She heard the sound of the dryer start up. Then the awkward footsteps passed again and faded in the direction of the living room. Soon after, she heard giggles from Tommy, as he continued watching cartoons.

•••

Judy listened to a full episode of Spongebob Squarepants and Tommy didn't come back to the door again. She decided to dare a peek outside.

She reached up and turned the knob very quietly; opening the door just enough to spy into the living room with one eye. Tommy was sitting on the sofa. She had a side view of his head and the light from the TV illuminated what part of his face she could see. She looked down and also saw that Pete's body was gone.

What the hell did he do with Pete? Look at him, Judy thought. *He looks so normal. Could I just be acting silly? Children have been known to bite fingers before. And maybe he saw what I did to his daddy and it confused him. Then again, he has been eating raw meat. Could that make him act crazy? Salmonella or some other poisoning?*

"Oh God, baby, what do you need?" she whispered.

As the words left her mouth, Tommy's head jerked around toward the cracked open door. His eyes stared at her from across the room. His face distorted into a sneer. A shriek escaped Judy before she slammed the door shut.

The second she turned the lock, she heard his voice coming up from the bottom of the door. She looked down and saw his small, bloody fingers curling up from underneath.

"Mommy, pwease come and watch cartoons wif me. You don't like me?"

Judy's eyes instantly started to tear up. She couldn't hold her tongue any longer.

"No, honey, I do. Mommy loves you. I'm just not feeling well, ok?"

She was trying not to cry and her voice sounded like it. She hoped Tommy wouldn't notice and just go back to the couch.

The little boy said nothing back and she heard the scuffle of his feet fade away. She put her ear back to the door and heard commotion in the kitchen.

"Why haven't the police shown up yet? Are my neighbors deaf? It's been too long," she whispered.

She held her breath and listened. It was quiet. She slowly turned the knob and dared another peek into the living room. Tommy wasn't there.

Judy looked around the apartment and spotted the gun. It was lying on the floor beside the couch. Her eyes left the gun as Tommy emerged from the kitchen, heading for the front door. She saw the awkward way he was walking, as if he were wearing ankle cuffs. Short, small steps. The front door opened and hit the adjacent wall hard enough to make Judy flinch. Tommy disappeared out into the corridor.

Oh, great! Now what am I supposed to do? I have to do something!

Judy looked around for a moment and crept out of the bedroom.

The first thing that caught her eye, was Pete. He sat on the other end of the couch, facing the TV. She couldn't see him before and she wished she didn't see him now. Judy approached the couch to get a better look at him. Other than the fact Pete wasn't blinking, he looked alive.

"Pete!" she said, in a forceful whisper. He didn't look. His dead eyes were staring at the TV. Even his pupils were looking directly at it, as if Tommy specifically moved them there.

Judy looked down at the 38Revolver, crouched and snatched it up. It quivered in her hand as she scanned the room. After a second, it dawned on her why the room looked like it was covered in garbage before. There were empty styrofoam meat containers everywhere. Too many of them.

"We didn't have this much meat in our freezer! Oh my God, has he been going out? To the other apartments?" she whispered, covering her mouth with her hand, when a thought came to her.

The neighbors would have a phone.

She looked back to the bedroom, longing to go back in.

No Judy! You have to do it. You have to get out of here before he comes back. You have to bring him some help.

She moved toward the front door, with the gun hidden at her side. She didn't want Tommy to see it. She knew she couldn't use it on him, but it made her feel safer having it.

EEEEENNNNTTT!

Judy almost dropped the gun, startled. She let out a sigh.

That damn dryer again. Why is it going anyways? Pete never does laundry—No, wait. Tommy turned it back on, but why?

Even with the TV blaring, the apartment was quieter with the dryer off. It had been loud, sounding off balance, as if it were stuffed full.

What's Tommy have in there? Is he using it to thaw out all this meat or something? He couldn't be eating it frozen, could he?

She moved in the direction of the dryer, knowing that if Tommy came in she would have to make it past him to get to the front door or run back into the bedroom.

Or sit on the couch and watch cartoons with him.

She cringed at the thought.

As she approached the laundry closet, she noticed how humid the apartment was, like the dryer had been running all day. With the gun shaking in her right hand, she reached out with her left, griped the handle of the dryer door and pulled it open.

The smell hit her, causing her to close her eyes and hold back a gag. When she looked back, the gun dropped to the floor and she filled the apartment with her screams.

Inside the dryer, was a battered and burned corpse of a five year old boy. It was Tommy.

•••

Judy wept, as she attempted to remove Tommy from the dryer. His skin was hot to the touch and felt like it would slide off his bones. As much as she tried, she couldn't stand to move him, scared that he would fall apart in her arms. She left him where he was and sobbed quietly, with her head resting on the opening of the dryer. She didn't have any voice left to scream.

Suddenly, an obnoxious giggle erupted from the other room. Judy raised her head, looking down the hall in that direction, quickly snatching the gun from the floor.

Oh, God! That thing isn't even Tommy. It looks like him, but it's something else. It took part of my little boy somehow and killed him. Pete knew what it did! It played with Pete, like it's been playing with me.

Thinking back, she knew she hadn't been paying attention to Tommy. She usually caught her sleep in the middle of the day, on the couch, with Tommy sitting at the end watching TV. She thought hard and remembered him asking her to watch cartoons over and over lately. She would say 'yes, honey', kiss him on the forehead, cozy up on the couch, tell him she loved him forever and ever and fall asleep.

Oh, God, how many times did I kiss that thing on the mouth?

Judy got up and inched her way down the hall. When she came to living room entryway, she paused, cocked the guns hammer back and emerged around the corner, letting herself be seen.

"Mommy, you came out. Pwease come and watch cartoons wif me."

Judy stared at the thing in disgust. He was holding what looked like a raw pot-roast. Blood dripped down his hands and chin. On the coffee table, were new styrofoam containers of meat. Judy could tell some of them were frozen, with gashes and bite marks on them.

He looks different now. His eyes are sunk back in his skull and his skin looks too pale in the light of the TV. He looks like a sick version of my little boy. My good little Tommy. It's not him, Judy. It's not your good Tommy. That thing is Bad Tommy and Pete was right, Bad Tommy needs to die.

"Mommy, come sit wif me and watch cartoons," Bad Tommy said, grinning as he took another bite of meat. "They're funny!"

Standing in the same spot Pete had stood, Judy raised the gun and took aim at Bad Tommy.

"You're not my Tommy!" she screamed, just before she pulled the trigger.

•••

The shot echoed in the apartment, defining Judy's senses. Bad Tommy's head flew back violently, but Judy saw the bullet miss and hit the couch. She fired again, this time aiming at Bad Tommy's body. In an instant, his body jerked and the bullet missed, exploding into the cushion.

"Oh my God, no! Just die!" Judy screamed, firing the gun three more times as fast as she could pull the hammer back. Bad Tommy continued staring at the TV, as his body convulsed, avoiding each shot.

Without looking at her, he said casually, "Mommy, what's wrong? Are you ok?"

Judy stared at Bad Tommy in dread. Then her eyes flashed to the entryway of the apartment.

Move Judy! Now's your chance! Move your ass and get out of here!

She dropped the gun and ran for the entryway. Before she made it past the coffee table, Bad Tommy leaped over the side of the couch, landing in front of her. His face wrinkled into something that looked nothing like the little boy she loved. It looked rabid.

Judy let out a scream, turned and ran back into the bedroom, slamming the door behind her.

Soon after, she heard the shuffle of feet and the dryer started up again.

Judy flung herself on the bed and screamed into the pillow.

•••

Judy felt like she hadn't slept in days. Morning light was starting to show through the window. She tried to close her eyes and sleep, hoping that she would wake up and this would all be a bad dream. It was useless.

It was the sound of the dryer, accompanied by the *thump, thump* noise of what ceased to live inside. There would be no sleep and no escape. That thump was real.

Judy pried her face from the damp pillow and slowly got to her feet. She walked to the window and gave it a tug upward. It didn't budge. Some long gone tenant had nailed it shut, probably to keep a kid or cat from climbing through.

A lot of good it would do me anyways, Judy thought. *I'm five stories up.*

Outside, snowflakes danced in all directions and the streets were empty and white.

She looked over at Pete's desk and then down at the needles on the floor.

Pete had an escape. Maybe it isn't an escape from this apartment but it's an escape from the horror of what's in it.

She walked over and sat at the desk, eyeing the drugs scattered around. She had never ran a needle in her arm, but she watched Pete fix himself up enough over the years to know how to do it right.

A thought came to her.

But maybe you don't want to do it right, Judy. What do you have to lose? Make it a hot dose and end it, Judy.

It was true, she'd lost everything. Everything she ever cared about was thump thumping away in the dryer.

She started to work with the tools and drugs in front of her, like a woman possessed, almost as if Pete's ghostly hands were guiding her own. For the first time in almost three hours, they weren't trembling and her breath was slow and normal.

"Mommy, come out. Come watch cartoons wif me. I miss you, Mommy."

Judy didn't flinch or look over at the bloody fingers coming in from under the door. She spoke in a calm voice, not taking her eyes off of what she was doing.

"Mommy's coming, honey. I just have to do something first. I'll be right out, ok."

Tommy scuffled back to the living room, excited. He looked at his father sitting at the end of the couch and smiled.

"Mommy's coming, Daddy. She's gonna watch cartoon wif us."

Pete didn't reply.

Tommy reached over and grabbed and piece of chicken off the coffee table. The chicken was raw, warm and had been sitting out too long. The skin looked dry and rubbery. Pink liquid ran out of it and down his chin, as Bad Tommy took a bite.

Judy opened the door to the bedroom, stumbled out and looked across the room at Tommy and Pete; her happy family. The light from the TV illuminated them, giving them an unreal quality. She made her way in their direction, using the wall to keep her balance.

Tommy looked up and smiled.

"Hi, Mamma," he said, patting the cushion next to him, motioning for her to sit down. Judy made her way to the couch, stepping on meat containers as she went. She sat down hard between them, causing Pete's body to fall over against her. She didn't bother pushing him back and sat sandwiched between the two of them.

Bad Tommy moved closer to her and put his hand on her leg, leaving a smudge of blood on her scrubs she was wearing. Judy put her arm around him and hugged him tight.

"What you watching, honey?" Judy said, groggily, as she stared at the TV. It was hypnotizing in the dark room.

"The cat and the mouse ones. His name's Jerry. They're funny, Mommy."

Judy's eyes slowly moved from the TV to the thing that looked like her little boy. She gave him a squeeze and her eyes drifted to the direction of the *thump thump* sound, coming from the hallway.

"I'm so sorry, baby. Mommy loves you, Tommy, forever and ever," she said, creeping her other hand into her pocket.

"I love you too, Mommy," Bad Tommy said, not looking away from the TV.

Judy pulled his small body tighter and brought her hand from her pocket. She plunged the hypodermic needle into the flesh of Bad Tommy's neck and pushed the plunger in. A mixture of cocaine and heroin streamed into his veins.

"Dodge that, you bastard!"

Bad Tommy jerked away, shrieking and clawing at his neck.

Judy jumped up from the sofa and ran for the front door. This time the thing didn't stop her.

•••

Judy ran down the hall to the first door she came to and grabbed the knob. She paused, looking down the hall. She still didn't see him coming, but his raving echoed from her doorway. She turned the knob, started to push the door open and stopped, noticing a small reddish hand print next to the knob.

Then she heard it. Cartoons.

They were blaring from the other side of the door. She quieted her breathing and peeked in.

"Hello, someone, please help me!" she called, trying not to sound too frantic.

Two figures sat on a sofa, motionless in the dark room, illuminated by the TV. They didn't stir at the sound of her voice. Scattered around the apartment, were empty meat containers. Judy gasped and pushed away from the doorway, moving down the hallway again.

She passed door after door without slowing, seeing reddish smears around each knob. When she got to the elevator, she saw small smudges on the buttons, passed it without looking back and went into the stairwell. She started to descend the stairs, sparing glances behind her.

Fourth floor. She hit the landing and turned the corner.

Third floor. The cries were getting louder and closer behind her.

Second floor. She began jumping down the steps, three and four at a time.

Ground floor. Judy stumbled and went sprawling. She picked herself up, crossed the small lobby and burst through the door, into the cold winter air.

"Help! Someone, help me!" Judy shouted, looking around frantically, seeing no one.

Oh God, where is everyone? There has to be someone!

Within seconds her hair and shoulders were coated in white, icy flakes. She quickly moved out further to the sidewalk and looked up and down the street. In the distance, she saw two figures walking in her direction. One big and one small. She rushed to meet them, crossing her arms over her chest, shielding herself from the cold. As she jogged, she looked back over her shoulder at the lobby doors, expecting the thing to be standing there.

Nothing. The door was still shut.

Judy's attention went back to the two people.

"Please, stop! I need help!"

The two figures slowed as she approached them. The man was middle aged and the little girl at his side looked to be about nine or ten. The man's eyes went wide when Judy stopped in front of them and he held his paper sack of groceries tighter.

"Please, you have to help me. I'm in trouble," Judy said, attempting to keep her voice calm.

The man gave Judy an odd look and shook his head quickly side to side. The gesture clearly said, 'no' and Judy's heart dropped.

The way I look, he must think I'm crazy

The next second, Judy looked down and saw that the little girl had her hand out for her to take. The child was smiling. It reminded her of Tommy's smile. Judy unfolded one of her arms and took her by the hand. Surprisingly, the man didn't object when Judy filed in next to them, as they began to walk.

What the hell am I going to tell them or anyone else? No one will believe me. If that thing isn't there when they look in the apartment, it will look like I massacred my family. Hell, the entire building.

"Hey, lady," the little girl said, in a quiet voice.

Judy bent down slightly so she could hear her, past the sound of the chilly wind.

"Yes, honey?"

"Do you wanna come watch cartoons with us?"

The little girls grip tightened, painfully pressing Judy's fingers together.

Judy shot a desperate glance at the man. His lips quivered in fear, as he shifted the paper sack full of meat in his arms.

✧

Chapter 2.

After a short walk around the corner and up the street, the three of them entered the lobby of an expensive looking apartment building. There had been no movement on the street. No people and no cars, as if they were the only three souls in the city. It was strange.

As they exited the elevator, Judy made a mental note that they went up four floors, cringing at the thought. Soon the man was unlocking the door to his apartment, fumbling with the keys nervously. Judy looked down and the little girl smiled at her sweetly. The thing still had a strangling grip on Judy's hand.

A shiver ran down Judy's spine, both from the cold walk outside with no coat and the eerie smile the little girl was giving her. Before, she thought that smile reminded her of her sweet Tommy's, but now she saw that it wasn't his smile. The little girl had the other Tommy's grin; warm, inviting and sinister like a snake.

The man looked to be in his late thirties and hadn't said a word the whole walk over. When he spoke now, Judy was surprised at how deep his voice was. He sounded like the base in a barbershop quartet. It didn't match him and made him seem strange instantly.

"Well, come in and get warmed up." He made a hurrying gesture with his free hand, as he held the door open with his shoulder. Judy hesitated, but the little girl quickly pulled her through the doorway. Before Judy lost sight of the hallway, she made a mental note that the apartment was right next to the elevator they had come up on. After what happened to her that morning, she was already planning her escape.

As they walked through the door, Judy felt relief as the warm air sent shivers through her body. Her hand was release, as the little girl continued into the next room. Judy noticed the short, awkward steps the girl made as she went. Outside, as they strolled along the sidewalks, anyone would've seen those small steps as someone walking carefully, to avoid slipping on the icy pavement, but Judy recognized it now as the walk of something maybe not use to its borrowed feet.

The familiar, whimsical music of cartoons playing on the TV in the next room, drifted through the air. The volume was cranked up and the sound made Judy's heart beat quicken.

She heard the door close behind her, followed by a distinctive snap of a dead bolt. She turned, startled. The man was eying her with a calculating look on his face, still holding the paper sack in his arms. They stared at each other for a moment, when the little girl came scuttling around the corner, dipped her hand into the sack, blindly taking out one of the packages and made her way back into the other room. They both watched her go.

God, Tommy isn't the only one. I wonder how many other children there are.

"Her name is Jamie. She hasn't been feeling well," he said, knowing his daughter's funny walk wasn't normal.

Judy's mind raced. *He doesn't know it's not her. How would he know? I didn't at first.*

It took Judy a moment to gain her composure enough to speak.

"Is she now? That's too bad. I'm so sorry, but as I said before, I really need to use your phone, Mr…" She let the comment trail off, giving him the opportunity to introduce himself.

"My name is Richard and you are?" he said, adjusting the sack to hold his hand out to her.

She paused briefly, looking at it for a moment, cringing at the thought of having her hand touched again after finally being let lose. She held hers out and reluctantly shook his hand.

"I'm Judy." She gave him a fake smile.

"Well then, it's nice to meet you, Judy." He shook her hand enthusiastically. Then without warning, he put the sack down on the counter and headed in the direction Jamie had gone. As he did, the edge of his coat lifted enough for Judy to get a glimpse of a gun tucked into his belt. Her shoulders slumped and she let out a sigh. At that moment she felt like slipping out the door.

Screw this, she thought. *I can find a phone somewhere else.*

She took a step toward the door and stopped. Just above the knob, a hasp was neatly screwed onto the door jam and a thick padlock dangled from it. He must have placed the lock there when she wasn't paying attention.

Oh, shit! Did he put it there to keep her from wondering out or to keep me in? He couldn't know I was coming. He must have it there to keep her from wondering out, like Bad Tommy did.

Judy turned back toward the sounds of the cartoons, swallowed hard and slowly moved in that direction. She peeked around the corner, expecting to see a mess similar to the one in her own apartment, but there was no mess. The place was surprisingly clean and a lot larger than her crummy apartment. An expensive looking leather sofa sat in the middle of the room, across from a big screen TV. The lights were off and the shades drawn, making the only light in the room spill out of the huge screen. Judy could barely see the top of Jamie's head over the side of the sofa. Richard came out of a hallway on the other side of the room, wiping his hands with a rag.

"Come in and have a seat, Judy. Would you like some coffee or tea?" he said, in his deep trombone tone.

He walked over to where Jamie was sitting, picked up a large piece of butcher paper from the coffee table and folded it neatly. Then a spray bottle appeared in his hand and he gave the top of the table a few squirts, wiping it down with the rag.

"No, thank you, really, but I can't stay," Judy said. "I just need to use your phone. I've had some trouble with my son and—"

Richard cut her off before she could finish. "Our phone doesn't work right now and misplaced my cell phone. I'll have to see if I can find —"

Jamie spoke up before he could finish and Judy cringed at her comment.

"Judy, come and watch cartoons with me."

Goose bumps tickled Judy's skin at the phrase and she crossed her arms, feeling cold again. Richard looked at her, as if waiting for a response. Judy flashed him the fake smile. She could hear Jamie chewing sloppily at something and could only imagine what she was eating. She could see her head jerking over the side of the couch, as her teeth pulled on whatever it was.

Shit! I have nowhere to go. I'm trapped, Judy thought. *Should have left when I have the chance. No choice but to play along for now.*

She slowly made her way around the front of the couch, trying not to look at Jamie, but she couldn't help but look.

Richard had a sheet draped across the couch where Jamie was sitting and it was smeared and spotted in places. When they walked in, the little girl's cloths were clean, but now she had quickly made a mess of herself. It looked like she was eating a raw slab of ribs. It made Judy want to gag.

Jamie's eyes didn't leave the screen when Judy walked by her, so she stopped and stood next to the couch, pretending to look at the TV.

"Judy, sit down with me and watch cartoons. They're *so* funny," Jamie's small, muffled voice said, through a mouthful of meat.

"Now, Jamie, don't talk with food in your mouth," Richard said, in his deep voice. It seemed deeper when he talked to his daughter. She kept on chewing, not responding to him.

Judy slowly looked from the TV to the couch. Jamie was smiling at her now, tapping the cushion beside her. Judy looked to Richard and he was watching the both of them, with a grin on his face.

Damn it! Not again! Judy screamed in her head.

She inched her way to the couch and sat at the far edge, keeping her arms folded. Jamie instantly scooted next to her and rested her head on Judy's shoulder, continuing to watch the TV.

Richard stood there for a moment watching them, with a satisfied look on his face.

"She likes you," he said, starting to move out of Judy's view. She watched him go, then her eyes went back to the TV, as the strange man disappeared behind them.

Richard came into the bright florescent lights of the kitchen. "This could work out after all," he mumbled.

I'll have to make it work, he thought. *Can't let her leave now, She's seen too much...and she's kind of cute.*

He peeked back around the corner at the two of them sitting on the couch, smiled and took a large knife out of the butchers block.

"Welcome to our family, Judy," Richard whispered.

•••

Judy sat still, not wanting to disturb Jamie's hypnotic bond to the TV. So still, that she felt her eyes begin to get heavy. It seemed like forever since she'd slept. Her eyes closed and her head started to sag. She caught herself drifting, lifted her head and opened her eyes wide.

Wake up, Judy! Don't you dare fall asleep sitting on the couch next to this thing!

She blinked hard a few times, reviving her eyes. She took her focus off the TV and it helped. In the dark room and the volume up, it seemed to be sucking the life right out of her.

She glanced around and spotted a picture on the side table next to the couch. It showed Richard, Jamie and a woman who must be Jamie's mother. The Jamie in the picture looked slightly different than the one sitting next to her. Better colored skin and her hair seemed thicker. A cute little girl. Judy stared at the picture for a moment.

Where's the mother? Divorced?

She glanced around the room? From the art work and Christmas decorations, it looked like an adult woman defiantly lived here with them. The place was decked out. Huge tree. Holiday figurines neatly placed here and there. It even smelled like pine. It looked like a loving home that would be a nice place for a child to grow up.

My poor Tommy would have loved this. We didn't even get a tree this year.

Then something dawned on her.

Somewhere in this apartment, is a dead body. A dead nine year old girl with good skin and thick brown hair. There's no way he knows that isn't his daughter or he wouldn't be catering to her like this. I have to talk to him. Convince him. I have to get out of here before something bad happens.

As if by fate, her eyes came across a neat row of snow globes sitting on a shelf. She cringed at the sight of them. She didn't think she would ever enjoy looking at one of them again. Not after hearing what it sounded like when it bounced off someone's head.

Judy shifted in her seat to see what Jamie would do. The little girl didn't do anything, just continued to watch the TV. Judy slowly started to rise from the couch.

"Where are you going, Judy? You don't like me?"

Judy froze and bit her bottom lip.

"No, honey, I like you. I just have to use the rest room."

Judy waited for a response. Jamie said nothing, looked down thoughtfully at the bone in her hand, brought it up and began to nibble at it. Judy got up and quickly went around the couch, toward the kitchen where *Mr. Barbershop* had conveniently disappeared.

When she came around the corner, her eyes had to adjust to the bright light. After a second of blinking, she saw him standing in front of the counter, cutting meat with a large knife. The grocery bag was gone and packages of various meats were neatly stacked next to the sink.

Without looking up, Richard spoke. "If I don't cut it up like this, she makes a bigger mess. She's really sick and needs a lot of protein or she gets upset."

The way he said it, Judy could tell he didn't believe it himself. She looked down at the meat. He was slicing it up into small strips, placing the bones neatly in a plastic bowl.

"Are you a nurse?" he said, flatly.

Judy looked down at the scrubs she was wearing. She could see why he would think to ask that.

"No, I'm sorry, I'm not. I'm just a receptionist at Hopkins General."

He let out a sigh and his expression around his eyes changed. She thought he looked more relieved than disappointed.

They were silent for a moment, as he continued to slice the meat.

"Richard, I'm not a nurse, but I can tell you that your daughter isn't sick."

He looked at her with an eyebrow raised.

In fact that isn't your daughter at all— is what she wanted to say next, but from the look he was giving her, she knew it would sound insane.

How am I going to convince him? I'm just some crazy lady who sprung up on him out of nowhere. Hell, I murdered a drug dealer who happened to be my husband this morning. Then gave a five year old child a hot dose.

She closed her mouth and he continued the slice in near silence. In the background, Judy became aware of familiar noise.

Thump Thump Thump

The noise was coming from behind a door across the kitchen. She had heard this *thump* in her own apartment. Now that she noticed it, it was all she could hear. That noise had tormented her for hours.

You've got to be shitting me. It can't be that simple, can it? Maybe if I can't tell him, I'll have to show him. It would be a lot easier to explain if he sees it for himself…as horrible as that sounds.

She peeked around the corner into the living room. Jamie was still fixed on the TV. Judy's eyes went back to Richard.

"Is that your laundry room?"

It sounded like a weird question when it left her mouth.

He looked up at her and then over to the door.

"Yes it is. Why do you ask?"

She started marching in that direction before he finished. He watched her go for a moment, picked up a rag and began wiping his hands with it, turned and followed her. Judy opened the door and the sound pulsated in the air.

Thump Thump Thump

As Judy walked toward the dryer, her heart started to pound in her chest. Her throat started to tighten. Tommy had looked so horrible when she found him in the dryer and the memory flooded back. She blinked and felt a tear roll down her cheek.

Richard watched her inch toward the dryer. She looked like a tigress stalking prey. He could hear muffled sobs escaping her as she went.

What the hell is she doing, he thought. *Is she some sort of nut case?*

Judy stopped and reached her hand out toward the dryer door and paused. The unit was shaking back and forth as the insides spun and her nerves didn't want her to open the door. The knocking in her chest almost mimicked the thumping of the dryer. She could see Richard out of the corner of her eye, standing in the doorway, watching her. Suddenly she was worried what his reaction would be when he saw what was inside.

She took a deep breath, preparing for the smell and forced her hand on the handle. She closed her eyes and pulled. The unit stopped moving and the thumping ceased.

•••

Judy waited for the smell to penetrate her nostrils. She waited to hear Richards's wails of grief. Neither thing happened. She opened her eyes and looked in the dryer.

"What the hell?" she gasped.

She reached down and started shuffling through the warm cloths, ironically hopping to find a dead girl underneath. After a few seconds she began pulling the cloths out and tossing them on the floor.

"Hey, stop that! What are you doing?" Richard said, as he pushed her to the side. Judy stood in the doorway dumbfounded as he began picking up the cloths up from the floor. He reached in and took the rest of the stuff out of the dryer, including a pair of heavy duty work boots that had been thumping around inside.

Judy's heart sank, knowing how stupid she must look.

Richard rose and turned to face her with his arms full. At that moment, Judy caught sight of the gun sticking out of his belt again and imagined grabbing it from him while he had his hands full.

I could make him give me the keys and just get the hell out of here. Maybe even take his money and car if he has one.

Normally she would never think of resorting to armed robbery. Shoplifting maybe, but armed robbery was brutal.

Well, not as brutal as plummeting someone to death with a snow globe and injecting a five year old ghoul with a lethal dose.

Judy gave the gun another glance, trying to muster up the nerve, when, in one quick motion, it vanished as Richard adjusted the load of cloths and his jacket draped over it again. When she looked up at his face, she realized he had been saying something to her.

"What?" Judy said, dumbly.

"I said, are you some kind of nut or something? What's your problem?" he barked. His face looked more concerned than angry. Judy didn't know what to say and stood there with her mouth gaped open.

With no warning, she felt something cold and sticky place itself in her open hand.

"Judy, come back and watch cartoons with me."

Judy shrieked and pulled her hand away. Jamie stood there staring at her, with an eerie look on her face, showing no notice of Judy's dramatic reaction. The little girls hand was still out stretched and Judy could see it was glistening with pink sticky ooze. The same ooze circled her smiling mouth and most of the front of her shirt. Judy absently wiped her hand on her pants, as she stared at the little girl.

Richard made his way in their direction. "I'll go with you, darling. Come on, let's get you cleaned up."

Jamie slowly turned her head to him and smiled sweetly. He smiled back, as he adjusted the load again, placing his newly freed hand on her shoulder. Judy watched as the two of them walked into the living room, Jamie with the awkward scuttle that reminded her of someone wearing ankle cuffs.

Judy sighed and gave the dryer another glace. An image of Tommy's dead twisted body flashed in her mind and she rushed forward and slammed the unit's door shut.

•••

Judy emerged into the living room, planning to put Richard on the spot and simply ask to be let out the front door, when she caught sight of something awkward. Jamie stood in front of the sofa, as Richard pulled her shirt over her head. He'd placed the warm laundry on the couch and Judy watched as he picked out a clean shirt. Jamie stood there staring at the TV, naked from the waist up. Judy blushed and looked away.

When Judy herself, was nine or ten, she never would have allowed her father to see her naked. Seeing Jamie now, with her father dressing her, Judy felt embarrassment for the little girl. Not the thing standing half naked, with the light from the TV glowing on its skin, but the little girl that was hidden somewhere in the house, dead; tucked away like a dirty secret. That little girl didn't deserve for this to happen to her, any more than Tommy deserved to suffer as he did.

Judy looked back as Richard pulled the shirt down over Jamie's body and carefully sat her down on the couch, kneeling in front of her as he did. His hand moved to up pull her long, thin hair out from inside her collar, when in a quick motion, he pulled his hand back suddenly, as Jamie snapped her teeth at his fingers. She was smiling and staring at the TV as she did.

"Now, now, Jamie, you stop that," he said, compassionately, as if he were telling her to behave her table manners.

Nerves rose up inside Judy's gut and before she had a chance to think, she spoke out loud, "That thing isn't your daughter."

The comment sounded thick and hung in the air, like a hook from a chain. Judy, herself was surprised she said it and she waited for a response.

Richard looked at Judy from the corner of his eye and said nothing. He picked up a rag from the pile of laundry and began carefully wiping Jamie's mouth. Judy could hear the clicking of her teeth snapping at his hand, as if she were a teething puppy that hadn't learned not to nibble.

Judy spoke again. "That thing killed your daughter, just like one killed my son. Your real daughter's somewhere in this apartment, dead. We have to—"

Richard cut her off, still using the rag to wipe Jamie's filthy skin. "You sound like her mother. She went crazy and tried to hurt our little girl. I won't let anyone hurt my little girl." His deep voice faltered at the end, in a shudder of emotion.

Judy didn't notice and wasn't paying attention to what Richard said. Something else caught her eye. She could see the bulge moving back and forth under his jacket, as he continued to wipe with the rag. He was on his knees in front of the couch, not looking at her and Judy inched closer. Her eyes went to Jamie, hopping the TV would keep her occupied and the little girl wouldn't see her sneaking. Jamie didn't look in her direction. Judy took a few silent steps, as Richard continued to talk.

"She's just sick. That's all, you'll see. You'll all see. She'll be back to normal and we can just put all this bad business behind us. Isn't that right, honey?" He said the last part to Jamie and Judy froze a few steps away from him, expecting the thing to look in her direction. Jamie didn't look or reply. Judy relaxed and took the last few steps, bent down and reached toward the bulge with her hands. In one quick motion, she lifted his jacket up with one hand and grabbed the gun with the other. For a second it snagged and she struggled to pull it out as he jumped to his feet. Before he could turn to grab for it, the gun came loose and Judy stumbled back a few uneven steps and pointed it at his face.

Richard stopped moving and stared at her. His voice sounded more concerned than angry when he spoke. "Judy, what are you doing? You're acting nuts again," he said, through a grin.

"Shut up, you crazy fuck!" Judy shouted. "Give me your keys! I'm leaving and you can do whatever you want with that thing on the couch!" The gun barrel blocked a little portion of Richards face from her view and she could see it was trembling more that she wanted it too. Judy grasped the gun tighter. It made the trembling worse.

"Leaving? Why would you leave?" Still smiling, Richard spoke in a calm, reasonable tone that made Judy feel nauseous. Richard took a step forward, as he continued. "I didn't want to bring you in here, but Jamie liked you from the second she saw you and here you are. You can't leave now. How can you just leave when we need your help?"

Judy shot a glance at Jamie and wasn't surprised to see her still watching the TV. Next, she glanced at the front door, then quickly brought her attention back to Richard. He was taking small steps toward her with his hands raised, palms out. Judy backed up a few steps and felt her back bump into a bookcase behind her.

"Stop moving or I'll shoot! I m-m-mean it!" Her voice was trembling worse than the gun barrel and Judy felt her nerves begin to falter as Richard Porter moved closer.

•••

Richard took another step toward her and Judy knew he was doing it deliberately, placing his bet that she wouldn't pull the trigger.

Or maybe the gun isn't even loaded! No, if it wasn't, he would have grabbed me already, Judy thought. *And what will Jamie do if it is loaded and I blow his head off. Then what? Is she going to let me go through his pockets, find the keys and go out the front door?*

Something inside Judy told her that Jamie wouldn't even notice if she blew his head off. Bad Tommy didn't seem to notice anything until she tried to leave. That's what worried her. As soon as she got the key in the lock, Bad Jamie might be on her.

The thought made her look past Richard to Jamie's spot on the couch and her heartbeat quickened. The spot was suddenly empty.

Judy's eyes went wide and she dared a few quick glances around the dark room.

Oh God, where did she go?

She remembered how fast Bad Tommy had been and glanced to her side, expecting the thing to be standing next to her, wearing that eerie smile. Richard saw her confusion and made his move.

Judy screamed as Richard lunged forward and took the gun out of her hand. The move was so quick and unexpected, Judy might as well of handed it to him. A second later, he grabbed her from behind, in a bear hug and began pulling her across the room.

"Now, now, Judy. You just need to calm yourself," he said in a calm voice. "I don't want to hurt you."

Judy's arms were pinned at her sides and she could feel the fabric of his jacket at her fingertips. She clawed, trying to get her nails at his skin. She tried to scream again and was cut short as she felt Richard squeeze hard, pushing her wind out and lifting her off the ground. Judy began to choke and her kicks weakened.

Richard carried her across the living room and through an entryway to the hall; the one he had exited earlier. Just before Judy lost sight of the living room, Bad Jamie emerged from the kitchen, holding a tupperware filled with bones in one hand and a butcher package in the other. She calmly scuttled over to the couch and sat down, eyeing the TV, not giving Judy and Richard a glance as they disappeared around the corner.

Judy struggled for a breath as they came to a door at the front of the hallway. Even in the darkness, she could see the same kind of hasp and padlock that dangled from this door as well. She could also see scratches and gouges in the paint, as if something had been trying to claw it was into the room.

Richard's grip loosened enough for Judy to suck in a breath. Disoriented, she heard the jingle of keys and a second later, she was shoved through the doorway. She stumbled and hit the floor, just as she heard the door slam behind her. After a few deep breaths, she quickly got to her feet and stumbled to the door, grabbed the knob and twisted. The knob turned, but the door didn't budge when she pulled.

"Let me out!" Judy croaked, pounding her fist on the door. "You can't just keep me here!"

"Judy, you need to calm down." Richards's deep voice came from the other side. "I can't let you out, you've got it all wrong. I need your help."

"No, listen, she isn't your daughter! She's some kind of monster! We have to get out of here!"

"She's just sick, that's all. She'll get better, you'll see. You'll both see."

She could hear his voice moving down the hallway as he said the last part and Judy pounded on the door in frustration. She tried the knob again, pulled on the door and let her hands fall to her sides. She turned and leaned her back against the door, taking deep breaths.

You've got to be kidding me. I finally escape from one bedroom, just to be trapped in another. How could he do this? He has to be out of his mind. And what did he mean 'You'll both see.' Me and who? Her? That thing isn't going to see anything. He's going to be the one who sees what she really is and I hope I'm not here when he does.

Judy closed her eyes and let her head tilt back, banging it intentionally on the door.

God, I wish Pete were here. He would have knocked that guy's head off. As worthless as he was, he always kept me safe from the lunatics in the neighborhood.

Then after a second, she opened her eyes and thought, *But Pete isn't here. It's just me. I have to take care of this myself. Alone.*

She let out a sigh and glanced around the room. It was nice. A lot nicer than her crummy one around the corner. A big window sent natural light across the floor and she could see it was tastefully decorated. A comfy looking bed. Expensive looking bedroom set. She focused on the window and moved in that direction.

I know we're four stories up, but maybe there's a fire escape or ledge.

As she came closer, she wasn't surprised to see that it was nailed shut. Freshly nailed shut by the looks of it. No paint over the nails like the ones in her bedrooms window.

Bastard!

Outside, it was bright and empty at first glance, with the exception of a man jogging down the sidewalk.

Jogging? No, more like a full out run.

But it wasn't that abnormal a thing to see. There were always people running and jogging around town. She tried to look left and right, but all she could see were trees and the building across the way.

Another expensive apartment with a shitty view. No fire escape and no ledge that I can—

The thought was cut short as a car squealed its tires around a corner, almost lost control on the ice and accelerated quickly across her view, until it disappeared, out of sight to her left. She cringed and continued to look around. A section of grass sat below, but it looked like a long drop. Too long to be worth the risk.

Maybe not?

She gave the window a tug.

"It won't open. I tried already," a quiet voice said, from behind her. Judy jumped and turned, scanning the dark room. She saw no one.

"Hello? Who's there?" Judy said, nervously. For a second, there was no reply. Just when she opened her mouth to ask again, the head of a young girl emerged from under the bed. Judy stared in disbelief.

"Are you normal?" the head asked.

Judy thought about the question for a second. She would have considered herself to be a normal person yesterday, but today she felt very abnormal, so she went with the safest answer.

"Yes, I'm normal."

"Good. Thank God." With a bit of wiggling, the young girl pulled herself from under the bed. For a moment, Judy though it was the other Jamie, the real Jamie and took a step back. As the girl stood, she saw that it couldn't be. This girl was too tall and had piercings in her face.

"Who are you?" Judy asked, as the girl adjusted her clothing. Judy saw the fading color of a bruise on her left cheek.

"I'm Britney," the pierced face girl said. Judy stood there with a questioning look on her face, hinting for Britney to elaborate.

"I *was* Jamie's babysitter." Then after a short pause she added, "But now, I don't know what I am."

✧

Chapter 3.

"Six days?" Judy said, in disbelief. "You've been locked in here for six days? Aren't your parents looking for you? You can't be more than sixteen."

"I'm almost eighteen," Britney said back. She didn't look that old to Judy, sitting cross legged on the floor in front of her. The teen was very animated, with a big smile and her tone sounded like someone who longed to be older. She was clearly relieved to have someone to talk to. She had her upper lip and nose pierced and her hair style was a bit funky for Judy's taste, colored blue and pink in spots. Other than that, she was a very attractive girl.

Attractive and stupid. Look how much cleavage she's showing. She's too young to be dressing like that. The creeps in this town will gobble her up. Her mother must be crazy or a hooker, to let her dress like that.

Britney continued to talk, just as Judy finished the thought.

"Well, I turned seventeen a few months ago and no they won't be looking for me. They have their own stuff going on."

Judy watched as Britney's smile faded when she said the last part and could almost feel her shame by the way she looked down at the floor. Judy knew the neighborhood had its good streets and it bad ones. Good people and not so good ones. After a while you could almost tell which part someone lived in by simply by being observant. A lot of People are like books. If you like to read people, the world is like a big library; no card required.

"Have you tried to get out?" Judy asked.

"Hell, ya. I've tried a few times, but it's hopeless. Even if you get out of here, you have to get past Jamie. She isn't normal. Somethings wrong with her. She's fast, mean and won't let you leave. She acts nice, but it's just a trick or something. He makes me watch TV with her, you know, so he can go sleep or do whatever and one time when he was in the bathroom, I tried to pry that lock off the front door with a butter knife. Jamie saw me and bit me in the back of my leg. I mean, she came out of nowhere. I screamed bloody murder and tried to grab her and she threw me across the room. Like, literally ten feet across the room. I hit the wall on the other side of the sofa and just stayed there, afraid to move. By the time Mr. Porter came back, she was normal again, just sitting there watching TV. He didn't believe me or didn't care."

Britney was rambling, in hopes that Judy would believe her. From the look on the lady's face, Britney didn't know if she was believing her or thinking she was crazy. The scrubs Judy was wearing, gave Britney the impression she was a responsible adult. Someone with a good job and priorities, unlike her dead beat parents. Someone who would be able to help. Someone who might care.

If I'm able to convince her I'm not crazy, that is.

"I'm serious. Jamie's, like, possessed or something," Britney said, leaning forward.

"Oh I believe you, Britney," Judy said. "I've seen it too."

The look on Britney's face relaxed and she let out a sigh, as Judy asked another question.

"How did you end up here in the first place, Britney?"

"Like I said, I was Jamie's babysitter. I've been watching her for the Porters for like…" she paused and calculated in her head, "Two and a half years. They kind of took me in. Everything was fine until about a year ago, when Mrs. Porter got cancer. I felt so bad. She was so cool, like a second mother to me. She was sick all the time, went through chemo and petty much stayed in bed after that. That's when I started coming here every day to help with Jamie. Then it happened."

Britney stopped and looked down at the floor.

"Then *what* happened?" Judy asked.

Britney looked from the floor to the ceiling and started fiddling with her hands. Judy could tell she was stalling.

"Is that when Jamie started acting weird?" Judy asked, nudging the conversation a little.

Britney focused her eyes on Judy and spoke with a sneer, "Ya, she started acting funny and after a while Mrs. Porter noticed. She noticed and said she wasn't her daughter anymore. Me and Mr. Porter just thought it was the cancer, like she was delusional or something like that, because let's face it; she *was* getting a little weird. Anyways, we were all so busy, we didn't see it. Then one night, when I was staying over, I used to stay over if it got late, anyways, I heard some loud noises and walked in on Mr. Porter dragging Mrs. Porter across the floor, toward the bedroom. There was blood all over her and I freaked out."

Judy just stared at her for a moment until the teen spoke again.

"He killed her. Said she was trying to hurt Jamie and he had to stop her. He said 'I didn't mean to do it'. Can you believe that? He killed his own wife and claims it's an accident. There was too much blood for it to be an accident if you ask me."

Judy flushed and her heart skipped a beat. The story brought Pete's face to mind. The scared look he had just before she pummeled him. Years worth of blood shot, wasted looks, angry glares and passionate smiles, flashed in her mind. They all mingled together into a dead man's accusing smirk and she closed her eyes, willing the image away.

Britney continued to talk, looking past Judy at the door. "After he saw me, he grabbed me and tried to make me promise not to tell. He said that if anyone found out what happened, I'd be in trouble too. But I'm not stupid. I knew that was a bunch of bull shit. Hell, I watch crime TV, so I broke free and tried to run out the front door. That was the first time Jamie stopped me from leaving. She jumped up off the couch and blocked the door, barking and growling at me like a dog. It freaked me out and I ran back to the hallway where he grabbed me and that was it. I've been here ever since. I don't even try now."

They both sat in near silence and Judy took a moment to soak it all in. Then Britney spoke again.

"And that's not all. Before all this happened, Mr. Porter seemed to be an alright guy. Kind of a weirdo, but alright. A really good father to Jamie, but after Mrs. Porter got sick, he started to flirt with me a little. Just a compliment here and there. He would talk my ear off, mostly because we were alone a lot, Mrs. Porter being in bed and all. At first I thought it was just him feeling lonely, like he wanted someone to talk to. A lot of guys are that way with me. Some turn out to be creeps, but I felt sorry for him and he seemed ok. But he never crossed the line until…"

Judy looked at her and could imagine how guys acted towards her.

Maybe you should tone down the makeup and crazy hair girly, she thought. Maybe it was partly the way she looked, but mostly it was exactly what she said, 'Some guys are creeps'. Judy knew this to be true from her own experiences.

Her eyes moved to the bruise on the teens face and Britney noticed and brought her hand up, touching it lightly.

"Ya, he hit me. He kept coming in here, sitting with me and talking. Trying to make me feel better about being here. Like, telling me how much he needed me and how if I loved Jamie, I wouldn't tell them what *we* did. Ya, he killed Mrs. Porter and all a sudden acts like I helped him or something. I didn't do anything."

Britney paused. An odd look flashed across her face and Judy's heart beat quickened. Britney looked down at her hands and bit her bottom lip. Judy followed her gaze and saw her own hand was sandwiched in between Britney's. She didn't remember putting it there and had no intent to moving it. She feared what Britney was about to say and squeezed her hand lightly as the teen continued to talk.

"Then he started with the touching. At first, just my leg or my hand. It was creepy, but, I mean what could I do? I would almost rather be sitting in here with him, than in out there with her, you know?"

Judy shook her head and could almost picture it in her mind. His deep voice whispering in Britney's ear. His eyes on her and the scared look her face must have shown.

"Then one day he got brave and tried to slide his hand up my shirt," Britney continued. "I freaked out. I pushed him off me and ran for the door. I didn't care if Jamie was gonna stop me or not, I had to get away from him right then, you know? He caught me before I made it out of the bedroom and I started screaming louder...so he turned me around and slapped me, hard. It hurt like hell and I stopped screaming. He hasn't been back in here bothering me and hasn't made me sit with her since. Of course, he hasn't brought me any food either, but I don't eat a lot anyways and at least I don't have to sit out there and watch her eat. Makes me want to puke, you know what I mean?"

Before Judy could answer, Britney continued to talk. She talked a lot. Judy listened.

"And the cartoons...what's with that? I know Jamie enough to know she grew out of that crap. You know, one time I even got up to change the channel when she was in the kitchen, thinking maybe she wouldn't notice and there were cartoons on every one. Every channel. Weird, hu? It freaked me out, so I tried the power button and that didn't work either. It just stayed on no matter what I did."

Judy thought back to the time she spent trapped in her own apartment. She had listened to cartoons through the crack under her door for hours, nonstop.

What channel has cartoons on at that time a day and for that long? Especially with the big story on the news being a family of some rich guy, lost at sea in that plane crash. The Australian guy, Goldman or Gotham, whatever his name is, it was a big deal. They were talking about that all day and night at the hospital and it was all over the—

Judy lost the thought, as Britney continued to talk.

"I don't think he wants to sit with her either, cause Jamie comes to the door, asking me to come out and sit with her. 'Come watch cartoons with me, Britney', over and over, all day and night, that's all I hear. If I don't answer, she scratches at the door like a damn wild dog or something."

They both looked over to the door and Judy shuddered.

"I hear her at their bedroom door down the hall sometimes too, asking Mr. Porter to come out, but like I said he doesn't like to sit with her. He cleans constantly. I don't know if you noticed it, but I swear I can smell something rotten, like he didn't get rid of Mrs. Porter's body or something. Makes you wonder what the sicko did with it or does with it…or whatever."

Britney stared off into space for a moment, with a disgusted look on her face.

Judy decided to change the subject. "Well, I wish none of this happened. I wish I could go back in time a few weeks and start over."

Then she thought to herself, *Although I don't know what I would change, considering I have no idea how the hell all this happened.*

"I wish I could too." Britney said. "If I hadn't seen what he did, he probably would have been pushing me out the door and I wouldn't be here, but who knows. Mr. Porter's wacko. When you came in, I thought it was him, coming back in here to kick my ass again. Thank God it was you." Britney gave Judy a bright smile, full of white teeth.

Judy returned the smile and slid her hand out from between Britney's as she stood up.

"Well, don't you worry, because we're gonna get out of here."

"How?" Britney asked.

Judy didn't reply, but thought to herself.

If I can get out of that shitty room, I can get out of this one. Mr. Richard Porter shouldn't be a problem. He caught me off guard before. It won't happen again. He's nothing compared to the thing I faced in my apartment. It's his daughter I'm worried about.

Britney watched as Judy scanned the room. There didn't seem to be anything useful. It was just a basic room. Judy opened the dresser drawer. It was empty and there were no lamps or other knick knacks usually present in most bedrooms. The room looked like a prison cell. She checked a few more of the drawers.

"They're all empty," Britney said. "He stripped the place clean after he put me in here."

Judy walked to the window again and peered down.

Britney said, "I told you it's hopeless. Bastard nailed it shut. Besides it's too far a drop. I mean if you go, I'll go, I guess. It'd be better than being stuck in here."

Judy knew she wasn't joking. If she jumped out, this girl would go after her without a doubt. She seemed that desperate.

After what she's seen here, I can't blame her. Plus, I think she's a little wacko herself, Judy thought. *The drop's worth the risk as a last resort, but there has to be another way.*

Judy walked the short distance across the room, put her hands around the knob, turned it and pulled, trying to be as quiet as possible. Britney watched her, letting out a sigh. It was a solid door. Much more well-made than the ones in Judy's building. It didn't budge. The lock and hasp on the other side held it tight.

Judy glanced around the room again, walked back to the dresser and pulled the empty drawer all the way out, until it dangled in her hand. She tested the weight of it.

"What are you gonna do with that, bash him over the head with it?" Britney said, with a smile.

Judy imagined bashing Richard Porter over the head and didn't think she could do something like that again. Thinking back on what she had done to Pete seemed like a nightmare.

"Maybe," she said. "That or use it to break the window out."

Britney's face brightened.

"Maybe if we, like, got his gun, we could shoot him and then shoot Jamie. I hate to say that, I mean, I love that girl, but shooting Mr. Porter would be like a bonus—"

Judy cut her off.

"That thing isn't Jamie. It's something else that looks like her."

Britney's eyes went wide. "You mean, Mrs. Porter was right?"

Judy gave her a nod.

"Then where's the real Jamie?" Britney asked.

"I'm sorry to say this, but she's most likely dead," Judy answered. "That thing in there killed her and is disguised as her somehow."

The room was silent and Judy could feel Britney's eyes on her. Then she heard a whisper from the young girl.

"How do you know that?"

Judy swallowed hard, taken back by the question. It was one of those 'no getting out of it now' questions, where you either had to tell the truth or lie. There was no in between. She didn't know where to begin to answer it. She hesitated looking back at her fellow castaway.

Ya, how do I know? I'm just some crazy lady off the street, wearing dirty scrubs decorated with droplets of blood for God's sake.

Judy let out a silent breath, as if she were blowing out a candle.

No one's ever going to believe me, but if someone did, it will be this girl, right now.

She slowly turned her head and saw that Britney was patiently waiting for a reply.

Judy took a deep shaky breath and exhaled when she spoke, causing her voice to shake. "I know because…one of them killed my little boy."

Judy heard the phrase echo in her mind and her heart started to pound. She felt the strength leave her legs and she dropped the empty drawer at her feet, moving toward the bed.

Britney watched, as Judy sat on the edge, looked down at her hands and continued to talk.

"I thought it was Tommy. But it wasn't *my* Tommy. It looked like him. It tricked me. My husband knew it wasn't him and I…I grabbed this snow globe; one that Tommy had given him for Christmas and hit him until…" her shaky voice trailed off, not finishing the sentence. She closed her eyes and felt the bed flex as Britney sat down beside her. A second later she felt a warm hand slid underneath hers. Her first instinct was to pull away, but it felt good, so she embraced it instead, lacing her fingers between Britney's.

"It's ok, Judy," Britney said. "You don't have to talk about it. But I'll listen if you want to."

Judy inhaled deeply and let it out. She opened her eyes, looked down at the three hands in her lap and started to talk calmly. Britney listened, not making a sound, other than an occasional gasp.

Judy told her everything. Killing Pete. Their joke of a marriage. The drugs. What she found in the dryer. Most of all she talked about Tommy, her good little boy and how much she wished she could have him back.

•••

Scrape Scrape Scrape

"Britney, are you in there? Do you want to watch cartoons with me?"

Judy jerked out a deep sleep and scrambled to move across the bed, away from the voice. She felt week and heavy. Something was stopping her from moving. She looked around the unfamiliar room, then down at the figure draped across her legs and her memory came back slowly. Britney had fallen asleep with her head in her lap. Judy stopped moving and held her breath, looking at the door.

Scrape Scrape Scrape

Judy could picture the things fingernails scratching on the hasp on the other side of the door. She looked down, as the shadow under the door shifted. A second later, Judy heard something that sounded like a dog sniffing through the crack at the bottom.

"Judy? Is that you? Come out and watch cartoons with me, Judy. They're funny."

Judy said nothing and held her breath.

Small fingers curled from underneath the door and it began to flex and creak. Judy stayed silent.

A moment later the fingers slithered back underneath and the door began to shake. The dog-like scratching lasted a few moments and then stopped suddenly. Judy watched as the shadow under the door disappeared. Next, she heard footsteps heading further down the hall. Judy let her breath out and Britney stirred slightly.

When the footsteps stopped, Judy heard Bad Jamie's muffled voice, as well as her fingers scrapping at another door; the Porters bedroom door, she figured. Judy reached down and stroked Britney's wild hair as she listened. Soon she heard the awkward footsteps return, pause slightly outside the door and move on, fading toward the living room.

Judy stared at the crack under the door, thinking of what they needed to do. She closed her heavy eyes and soon her stroking hand went limp.

✧

Chapter 4.

Knock Knock Knock

Richard Porter rapped his knuckles on the door three times, as if he were a UPS driver, delivering a package. He heard movement on the other side.

"Girls, are you decent?"

He chuckled under his breath. "How are you doing in there?" he said, with a grin. "Getting along together, I hope." Richard didn't expect a nice reply. He'd taught Britney her lesson, but Judy still had to be convinced.

Maybe they're sleeping…together.

The thought made a grunt escape his mouth.

Boy, wouldn't that be great. Maybe we could all have some fun. What I wouldn't give to have a peep-hole right here by the door.

It wasn't the first time he had the peep-hole idea. Ever since Britney started staying in the guest room, he toyed with the idea making a peep hole, so he could spy on her, but dismissed the scheme, knowing he would get in trouble with the wife, if she were to find out.

No one's going to fuss about that now, especially not her.

The thought caused him to look to his own bedroom door momentarily. Then his glance went back to the guest room door and he mentally put the peep-hole on his 'to do' list.

"I have some food here for you," he called. "A few bagels, some scrambled eggs and bacon. I know you must be hungry."

He set the tray of food on a table in the hallway and put his ear to the door. He could hear faint whispering, but couldn't make out what was being said. Whatever it was, he didn't like it. It gave him a bad feeling.

He knocked harder on the door and in a louder voice said, "Hello? What are you up to in there? I hope Britney hasn't been telling stories."

He slid his hand into his pocket, grouping for his keys, when he heard glass shatter on the other side of the door. He jumped at the noise and dug his keys out quickly.

"Hey!" Richard barked. "What are you doing?" He shoved the key into the pad lock.

The muffled voices on the other side became louder and more distinct. Richard heard Britney's muffled voice say, "Quick, Judy, go! He's coming!"

"Hey, you stop it!" Richard barked. "You can't!"

I don't believe it, Richard thought. *They're going out the window! They can't do this to me!*

The pad lock clicked open. Richard slid it out of the hasp and dropped it to the floor, turned the knob and pushed. The door opened a few inches and stopped. He shoved harder and it opened enough for him to see that one of the dressers was pushed up against it.

Britney's voice called out again. "Ok, Judy, here I come."

"No, you can't! You can't leave me with her!" Richard growled, taking his gun out. He took a few steps back and hurled himself forward, slamming into the door. The impact shoved the dresser out of the way and the door opened enough for him to squeeze through with his gun drawn. His wide eyes circled the room. The girls were nowhere in sight. He spotted the broken window and bolted in that direction. He peered out it and looked down to the street.

Nothing. No sign of them.

They couldn't have made that jump and walked away so quickly.

He stuck his head further out the window and looked left and right, to make sure they weren't somehow standing on a ledge.

There was no sign of them.

"Shit!" he barked, pulling his head back in. As he did, something else caught his attention. Two apache helicopters flying extremely low between the buildings across the way. The thumping sounds of their propellers echoed down the streets, making them sound like they were a lot closer than they were. He could see uniformed men inside with binoculars. It looked like they were scanning the windows of the buildings. He glared at them in contempt as they disappeared around a corner.

Great! Now what? I have to find them! I have to get them back!

Richard turned, intending to go back out the bedroom door, when he caught movement out of the corner of his eye. Before his brain could register what he was seeing, Judy brought the dresser drawer down from over her head and bashed him in the nose. She had been crouched in the corner of the room beside the dresser he'd pushed out of the way. Britney was nowhere in sight. Richard let out a painful grunt, took a staggering step back and dropped the gun to the floor. Blood started to pour down his chin and he brought up both his hands up to protect his broken nose.

"Hit him again, Judy! Get him!" Britney screamed, as she wiggled her way out from under the bed. She saw the gun on the floor and crawled in that direction.

Judy brought the drawer down again, hitting Richard on the forehead. He lost his balance and stumbled back toward the window, made half a turn and ended up colliding into the wall beside it.

Judy brought the drawer over her head again and lunged at him.

"Please stop!" Richard yelped. He held one of his hands out with his fingers extended, in a pleading gesture. He kept his other hand cupped under his bleeding nose. "We can work this out, can't we? I'm just confused. I need help!" His voice was so deep, it sounded like a boat motor trying to talk, but Judy understood what he was saying and hesitated.

"No, Judy! Don't listen to him," Britney pleaded in a shaky voice. "Knock his ass out!"

Britney suddenly had the gun pointed at Richard, but Judy saw that the barrel was shaking so badly, there was no way to tell where the bullet would go if she fired it. Britney also held the gun sideways, as if she were in a gangster movie.

"Or should I shoot him?" Britney barked.

"No!" Judy snapped.

Britney lowered the gun slightly.

Judy narrowed her eyes on Richard. "Give me your keys and let us leave!"

Richard's breathing slowed and he gawked at her. "You can't leave. She wouldn't like it."

Britney hissed, "We don't give a shit what she likes, you pervert!" Richard glanced at her, then back to Judy. She had the drawer cocked sideways, as if she were standing on home plate, waiting for him to pitch the ball. His eyes focused on Judy's and his deep voice took on a pleading, whiny tone. It made Judy want to look away from him.

"Please, you have to help me. I can't take care of her all by my—"

Just then, a loud noise stung the air and the three of them looked back to the bedroom door. The noise lingered for a moment and they recognized it as a metal bowl or tray twirling round and round on the tile floor, from the direction of the kitchen.

The three of them had the same thought. *Jamie is up and moving around.*

They froze.

The three of them watched the doorway and held their breath. Judy's heart was hammering in her chest and the drawer was getting heavy in her arms. Just when she started to turn her head back to Richard, Britney screamed, breaking the silence.

"Judy, watch out!"

Judy's reflexes triggered and with her eyes closed, she blindly swung the drawer. For a second she thought the heavy drawer was going to swing through the air, hit nothing and most likely throw her off balance, leaving her open for Mr. Richard Porter to rush her.

Would Britney really shoot that gun if she had to, Judy wondered in the span of a second. Part of her mind prepared for the report, but it didn't come. A split second later, Judy felt both her hands scream out in pain, as the drawer connected with something solid and broke into pieces. She released her grip, letting the pieces fall. She opened her eyes in time to see Richard spin sideways and fall, hunched over the open window ledge, hanging half way out. To her dread, his feet rose from the floor and he began to teeter. Judy lunged toward him, grabbed his belt and pulled him back into the room. Richard steadied. Judy stood for a moment, unblinking and breathing hard, with a death grip on the man's belt.

"Holly shit, Judy! Britney exclaimed. "That was bad ass!"

Judy looked at her and saw Britney had the gun back up and pointed right at her.

"Britney, put that gun down. He's out cold."

"Oh, sorry," Britney said, lowering it slightly. It was still trembling in her hand.

Judy let go of Richards's belt and he stayed put on the window sill. She took one step and gently snatched the gun from Britney's hand. Britney let it go as if she forgot she was holding it.

"Check his pockets," Judy said. "We need his keys." Then after a short pause she added, "And his wallet."

Britney nodded and quickly went to work, picking at his clothing with her fingertips, as if the task were a disgusting thing.

Judy glanced at the doorway and moved in that direction. She peeked around the corner and down the hall. It was empty and the noise in the kitchen had ceased.

"Jack pot," Britney said, as she yanked a set of keys out of Richard's right-side jacket pocket. She looked down at them. It was a huge jumble of keys. She couldn't imagine anyone needing so many.

Suddenly, Richard let out a moan and started to stir. Britney froze, clinching the keys tight. Richards head turned and faced her. His expression looked confused and out of sorts for a second, then his eyes narrowed on her.

"Oh, no you don't!" Britney said, as she reached down and grabbed one of his ankles.

Judy heard Britney make a grunting noise and turned in time to see Richard's legs go up and out the window, disappearing over the ledge. Her eyes went wide.

"What the hell, Britney! No, what are you doing?" Judy cried, as she bolted back to the window and peered out.

They both looked down just as Richards's body hit the ground, bounced once and made a half roll. He settled on his back with one of his legs resting in an unnatural angle. Judy glanced at Britney with her mouth open, in disbelief.

Their eyes met and with a smirk on her face, Britney said, "Sorry, I guess I got carried away…but don't worry, I got his wallet. And look…*keys*." She jingled the keys as if she were ringing a tiny service bell and smiled big. "Have you ever driven a Land Rover?"

Judy's opened mouth closed into a smile and she held back a laugh. "My God, Britney, you're out of your mind!"

Britney's expression sagged slightly, then brightened when Judy added, "I like it!"

•••

Judy studied the horrific amount of keys on the ring. It was disheartening.

"How are we ever going to figure out what key goes to what?" Judy said, after a sigh. "I mean, seriously, who the hell has this many keys?"

"I know, that's what I was thinking." Britney said, eyeing the ring in Judy's hands.

The night before, after Judy told Britney her story, they talked, for what seemed like hours, about what they needed to do. The plan, after tricking Richard, was to get the keys and just sneak though the living room and get the door opened before Bad Jamie even knew they were there. It wasn't the best plan, but it was all they'd come up with before falling asleep.

It wasn't a straight shot from the hallway to the front door, but if they crawled across the floor behind the sofa quietly, they would only have about eight feet from there, to freedom. Britney said she knew where the staircase was, so once they were out, she would lead the way and they wouldn't get stuck waiting for the elevator. Then they would take his car and get the hell out of the city. Now looking at the keys, there were at least half a dozen that looked like they could go to a pad lock.

"Crap!" Judy blurted out, in frustration. "It may take a few minutes of fumbling with these before we find the right one."

Britney watched Judy think. She could see that the woman's gears were turning. After a moment, the teen spoke in a deflated voice.

"Even if we have the right one, I don't know about just sneaking in there and trying to leave. She has, like, bat ears. She may not seem like it, but she hears everything. She's gonna notice and try to stop us. Are you sure we just can't shoot her? Like, maybe shoot her from around the corner, where she wouldn't see it coming?"

Judy thought about it for a moment, recalling how Bad Tommy had avoided the shots.

"No, that won't work. Like I said, the thing in my apartment wasn't even looking at me when I shot at it. It was staring at the TV and I still missed. It avoided the shots without even trying."

Britney let out a sigh. "What are you doing?" she asked, watching as Judy began plucking keys off the ring and setting them on the floor in front of her.

"I'm taking off the ones that I'm sure aren't for the lock; that way we'll have less to shuffle through."

When she was done removing keys, there were eight keys left on the ring. One was the key to Richards Land Rover. One was the key to the regular front door lock, Judy hoped. That left six keys of varying styles and sizes. She scooped up the loose keys in her hand.

"Here, put these in your pocket, just in case," Judy said. "I'll hold on to the ring of keys and be the one to try them in the lock."

Remembering how Britney's hand was shaking holding the gun, Judy felt more capable of finding the right key and sliding it into the lock quickly. Of course, her own hands had been shaking a lot in the last twenty hours or so, but she didn't want to leave it to Britney. As much as she liked her new friend, Britney had already shown she was a little 'wacko'.

"So..." Britney said. "We're seriously going to just go in there and try to make it past her and all the way to the door?"

"Yes," Judy replied. "We just have to be quiet and if she does see us, just tell her something she wants to hear and act normal. Shit, I had to finally sit with one of them...with my arm around it." Britney gave her a sour look, as Judy continued. "But it distracted it enough for me to get out. The TV is the best distraction, besides meat."

"Hey, maybe we should try to unplug the TV. Then she would be distracted trying to figure out how to turn it back on?"

Judy thought about it. Remembering the layout of the room, there wouldn't be an easy way to unplug the TV without being seen, even if she thought it was a good idea, which she didn't.

"Britney, I wouldn't even want to know what it would be like without that TV on," Judy said. "There's something about it that keeps them tame. Without it, I think she would be on us in a heartbeat."

Judy cracked the door open and peeked out.

Britney let a pouty sigh escape her lips. "This sucks. Going out the window seemed like a better idea," she mumbled sarcastically.

"Whatever we do, we better do it before she comes back scratching on the door again," Judy said. "And it would be better if she were eating, so she doesn't stumble on us getting up for more food." Then, after a short pause, Judy added, "You ready?"

Britney's eyes went wide and her breathing quickened. Judy looked back at her. The teen didn't look ready at all.

Judy snapped the door shut again.

"Come on now, you got this, girl," Judy said, as she turned back to face her. "Just let me go first. We stay low and quiet. When we get to the edge of the sofa, you wait for me to creep over and unlock the door. As soon as it's open, we bolt out of here. If she sees us, I'll think of something."

Britney was nodding her head up and down, taking deep breaths with her eyes closed. Judy looked down at the useless thing in her hand.

"Here, take the gun if it makes you feel better," Judy said, holding it out in front of her. Britney reached out and took it, looked down and gave it a pitiful smile.

"Just don't shoot me," Judy added with a smirk.

Britney let out a snort and held back a laugh. "Ok, I'll try. Let's do it! Let's go, before I lose my mind."

•••

From the dark hallway, Judy took a quick look around the corner and saw Bad Jamie sitting on the couch, staring at the TV.

Her face was a mess and her jaw slowly moved up and down, as if she were tonguing a piece of gum or hard candy. Judy was sure it wasn't gum or candy and didn't want to think of what was rolling around inside the things mouth.

From here, Judy could see that the floor of the kitchen was littered with pots, pans, bowls, condiments and only God knew what else. It looked like someone had ransacked the place, looking for whatever scrap of food they could find.

I hope she didn't eat everything already. Judy thought. *It would be better if she were eating.*

"Is she there?" Britney whispered. "What's she doing?"

The sudden break in the silence made Judy jump in her skin. She glared back at Britney.

"She's just sitting there, staring at the TV. She isn't eating and I don't see anything in front of her, but it's hard to tell, there's stuff everywhere."

It was amazing how quickly the place turned from a nice, neat, upper-class apartment, to a dirty, garbage littered shit hole. Richard Porter must have been constantly cleaning it to keep up with her. It reminded Judy more of her own apartment now.

Britney was crouched on the floor with one knee to the tile. She looked longingly back to the open door of the spare room prison cell she had been tucked away in and wished she was back inside, under the bed.

"Well? Are we going or what? I can't take just sitting here," she said, in a whisper.

Looking at the room now, Judy's nerves were fighting with her common sense. The distance to the edge of the sofa, looked like a quarter mile instead of four feet. She didn't want to make it half way and see Bad Jamie's eyes fix on them or look up and see her spot on the sofa suddenly empty again. The thought was nerve racking.

"Damn it! I wish she was eating!" Judy whispered in frustration.

"She probably already cleaned the place out," Britney murdered. "Mr. Porter was going to the store like, every day, sometimes twice."

Judy didn't respond and Britney shifted to her other knee, glancing back at the bedroom doorway again. As she did, she spotted the tray sitting on the table by the door and quietly moved over to it.

On the tray, was a plate of scrambled eggs, a few bagels, and a second plate covered with half a dozen strips of bacon. She picked up the bacon and made her way back to her spot behind Judy.

"Judy, look. Will this work?" she whispered.

Judy glanced back at what Britney was holding and smiled. "It's not raw, but maybe. Only one way to find out."

Britney smiled and said, "It'll work. Who doesn't like bacon...am I right?"

•••

"Daddy, come sit with me and watch cartoons," Bad Jamie mumbled to herself, as she stared at the TV. The room was dark, just the way she liked it and a hypnotic glimmer of colorful lights danced across her face. Her eyes shifted to the hallway for a split second, then back to the TV, as her nostrils twitched. Her stomach made a deep gurgling sound, louder than a ten year old girl's stomach should.

On the TV, a cartoon cat was smashed in the face by a small mouse yielding a baseball bat. The mouse was dressed in a baseball player's uniform and Bad Jamie let out a gale of laughter.

Before her laughter tapered off, her nostrils twitched again, cutting the giggles short. Her gaze shot to the edge of the sofa, as a piece of bacon landed on the cushion. Her eyes narrowed on it and she sniffed at the air toward it. She quickly slid across the sofa, blindly picked it up and shoved it in her mouth without giving it a second look. Her attention barely left the TV.

After a moment, Bad Jamie caught another whiff. She shot a glance at the end table, just in time to see another morsel land on the top and slide off the edge. She shifted and looked down over the arm of the couch. The leather creaked as she reached her hand over the side, stretching her small arm as far as it could go. Her fingertips hovered above it for a moment, before she gave one final stretch and plucked the morsel off the floor. Before she popped it in her mouth, Judy threw another piece. Bad Jamie saw it land on the carpet in front of the end table and quickly slid off the sofa after it, not noticing the two females crawling across the floor toward the back of the sofa. She snatched it up and crammed it into her mouth with the other two pieces as she chewed.

Just as Judy and Britney made it around the back of the sola, Judy tossed the rest of the bacon on the far side of the couch, not wanting Bad Jamie to follow its scent. They both heard the leather of the sofa creak, as Bad Jamie jumped back on the cushion, then a sloppy chomping sound, as she discovered the rest of the bait. They held their breath until they heard her adjust herself again and giggle through a mouthful.

They inched their way across the carpet behind the couch, trying not to make a sound. Ahead of them, Judy could see the front door, with the pad lock dangling on its hasp. She clutched the keys tighter in her hand as she crawled and looked behind her. Britney was crawling along, with her hand up to her face, covering her mouth and nose. When Britney noticed Judy's glance back, she lowered her hand and mouthed the silent words 'Do you smell that?'

Judy gave her a questioning look, then the smell hit her. An awful smell. The smell of rotten meat. She shot a glace up at the top rim of the couch, expecting to see Bad Jamie peering over them with rotted meat hanging out of her mouth. Nothing hovered over them and after a moment, another giggle drifted through the air and the couch creaked again, confirming the little monster hadn't moved from its spot.

Still watching the TV. Good...But what's that awful smell?

Judy inched along, holding her breath, trying not to take the smell in. She approached the end of the couch and stopped. She looked up at the door across the dark room, started to turn back to Britney, when her hand snagged on something soft and startling. Judy didn't have to look down at it, to recognize what it was. She jerked her hand back and paused. She looked to Britney and saw that she had stopped and was giving her a questioning look.

Judy ignored the look and glanced down at the floor along the back of the couch. Britney followed her gaze. The light in the kitchen radiated just enough to make out a thick strand of dark hair sticking out from under the couch. Human hair.

Judy looked at Britney and saw the confused look on her face as she stared at the hair. Then, realization flashed in her teenage face and Britney looked up to Judy, holding back a scream.

Judy moved to her quickly, placing her hand over her mouth, prompting her to keep quiet. Britney relaxed and took deep breaths under her palm. Judy removed her hand and Britney whispered, a little too loudly.

"Please tell me that isn't..." she trailed off, squeezing her eyes shut.

Judy crept back over to the spot where the hair draped out. She could feel her heart thumping in her chest as she looked at it.

The sofa was the type that had legs, with a skirt around the bottom and Judy took hold of the leather flap with the tips of her fingers, hesitated, lifted and peered under. It was dark underneath, but she could see the shape of a head. After her eyes adjusted, she saw the dead stare of a ten year old girl looking at her. A girl named Jamie Porter, who had thick brown hair and had grown out of cartoons. Judy quickly dropped the flap and closed her eyes.

Images of Tommy's dead, burned body flashed in her mind and she willed them away.

Come on Judy, get ahold of yourself. You can do it. Just calm down and go. We've lingered here too long as it is.

Judy looked back to her fellow escapee. Britney still had her eyes squeezed shut and her mouth was moving silently. Judy reached her hand over and touched her on the shoulder. Britney startled and her eyes shot open wide.

The leather of the sofa creaked and Bad Jamie let out a deep grunt. Judy could imagine her looking around the room, feeling bored and lonely.

Or maybe she's already hungry again, Judy thought. *We don't have much time.*

Judy silently shushed Britney's, placing her finger to her own lips. Britney looked scared, but nodded. Judy made a movement that told Britney she wanted to whisper in her ear; to tell her a secret, so Britney brought her ear to Judy's lips.

"You wait here and don't make a sound. I'm going for the door. When it opens you run for it, ok?"

Britney was shaking her head 'yes' before Judy even finished whispering. Judy looked down before she pulled away and saw the gun in the young teen's hand trembling. Judy covered it with her own and squeezed.

•••

As Judy stood, she noticed how shaky her legs were. It made it hard to keep still. The back of Bad Jamie's head came into view and Judy imagined her face jerking around and sneering at her. She tried to think of what she would say if that happened; what she would do, but her mind was blank. She took a step toward the door. As she did, the side of Bad Jamie's pail face came into view. She knew the thing would be able to see her out of the corner of its eye, if she wasn't carful. The TV was loud and the lights were a blinking cascade of colors and Judy tried not to look directly at it.

She couldn't help but recall what Britney said earlier. That she was thrown across the room, when Bad Jamie saw her fiddling with the door. At first, it seemed like an exaggeration, but just past the sofa, on the wall under a collage of hanging Christmas decorations, Judy could make out a dark crack in the drywall near the floor. Britney had said, 'I hit the wall on the other side of the sofa and just stayed there, afraid to move.'

Bad Tommy was fast, unnaturally fast and strong enough to move Pete's corps onto the couch. And that was a five year olds body. What can these things do with a ten year old's body?

Judy didn't want to think about it. She turned her head and focused on the door, taking long quiet steps. She looked back at the TV, to the sofa, then to Britney, in a nervous triple take. She had her hands out in front of her and startled when one of them made contact with the door lightly. She reached up and took the lock in her hand, fumbled the keys as quiet as she could manage and brought the first one up to the lock. It didn't slide in and she picked for the next one, sparing glances over her shoulder at the thing on the couch.

Crouched down on one knee, Britney watched Judy fumble with the keys. It seemed like it was taking forever. Britney cringed at every jingle the key ring made.

Does she know how loud she's being with the keys? Please just hurry, Judy!

She began mumbling to herself as she watched.

"Please, Judy, open the door. Open the door; I don't wanna be here anymore. Please, Judy, open the door. Open the door; I don't wanna be here anymore."

It was a simple rhyme that just popped into Britney's head, but it was keeping her focused and relaxed. It was also distracting her from the sound of the keys and the dark clump hair on the floor at her knees.

Judy failed with the second key and pick at the ring for the third one. Britney closed her eyes, took a deep breath and started to whisper the words again.

The third key didn't work either. Judy let out a puff of breath and shuffled for the next key. She spared a quick glance over her shoulder. Bad Jamie was lounging on the couch, with her legs crossed in front of her. Her jaw was working up and down. Judy looked at her small hands and could see a few pieces of the bacon sticking out from between the things dirty fingers.

When she finishes those, she's going to get up and go toward the kitchen. She might not look at me, but she will defiantly see Britney. I have to hurry!

Judy looked down at Britney during the thought and saw her mouth moving slightly, as if she were praying, although she didn't look like the praying type with the gun in her hand.

No better time to start then now, Judy thought. *Please God, let the next key work, for Christ sake.*

As if God answered Judy's prayer, the forth key slid into the lock. It went in easier than the others and felt as if it fit. Judy's tense muscles relaxed. She flexed her hand to turn it, when suddenly the room exploded in noise. She jumped and her hands instinctively went to her ears. The key slid out of the lock and the ring dropped to the floor. She turned, with her back to the door and saw that the TV had changed from a colorful array of cartoon characters, to a screen full of static and the room buzzed with the noise. Her eyes flashed to Britney's terrified face, then to Bad Jamie in an instant.

Oh shit! Oh God, please no!

Bad Jamie's head tilted sideways for a moment. Then she uncrossed her legs, reached forward and plucked the TV remote from under a pile of discarded butcher's paper on the coffee table. The TV burped a few times as she hit the buttons, but the static remained. She let out an animal like snort and launched herself from the couch. Her body soared over the coffee table and landed in front of the TV. She instantly started slapping the screen with her palms, grunting and growling with each swipe.

Bad Jamie's sudden burst of movement startled Judy and for a second, she stared at her, not believing something could move that fast. The thing that looked like her son had been quick, but nothing like this.

Judy looked down and spotted the keys on the floor, bent down and grabbed them. The keys jingled lightly. As soon as they did, Bad Jamie's attention shot to the woman standing by the front door.

In a deep voice, Bad Jamie said a single word.

"Judy!"

The grumble in the things voice seemed to tower over the noise of the static and Judy felt the floor under her feet vibrate. She froze.

"Hurry, Judy! Open the door!" Britney screamed, rising from behind the couch with the gun drawn. Bad Jamie's eyes shot to Britney, her head tilted sideways again, as if she were a dog hearing a tiny noise. Britney screamed, took aim and before Judy could prepare herself, the gun went off. Bad Jamie's body jerked to the side and the bullet exploded into the wall behind her. The sound was defining. Before the blast of light from the report dimmed in the dark space, Judy saw Bad Jamie bolt across the room in two more leaps, before disappearing from view. Disoriented by the shot, neither Judy nor Britney saw where she went and they both looked around the room in a panic. Their eyes met for a split second before Britney's feet were jerked out from under her. She hit the floor hard with a *thud* and the gun flew out of her hand. Judy watched as her body slid feet first, behind the couch and out of sight.

Britney let out a muffled scream, as Bad Jamie barked and growled.

Judy gasped, turned and fumbled with the keys. At that moment, if the door had magically opened, she would have ran out without a second thought towards Britney or anything else.

She lost her place on the ring and had to start over. She slid the first key into the lock and it wouldn't turn. She pulled it out and put the next key between her fingers—

"Judy, where are you going? Don't you like me?"

The voice made the skin on Judy's arms prickle and she screamed out. She turned and bumped her back against the door, leaving the keys dangling in the lock. Bad Jamie was standing inches away, looking up at her, smiling sweetly. Her jaws were moving up and down, as if she were chewing on a large wad of gum. Judy couldn't look away from her, but could see Britney out of the corner of her eye, crawling across the floor toward the hallway. Even with the loud static buzz in the room, Judy could hear her choking, trying to catch a breath.

Before Judy could reply, Bad Jamie playfully jabbed her fingers into her gut. It wasn't a hard hit, more of a poke, but it hit just the right spot and was enough to knock the wind out of her. Judy went to her knees, gasping. She closed her eyes and fought for a breath, anticipating another blow. When it didn't come, she opened her eyes and saw Bad Jamie's small feet on the floor in front of her. The toes wiggled playfully. Judy looked up slowly, until she saw Bad Jamie's eyes looking down on her. They had a hint of worry in them.

"Is something wrong, Judy? You don't look too good."

Judy gasped for air, glanced past her and saw that Britney had regained her breath and was on all fours, approaching the hallway. It looked like she was going to go back into the bedroom.

Judy looked back to Bad Jamie, parted her lips to reply, when a warm wad of greasy goo shot out of Bad Jamie's mouth, hitting her in the face. Judy's eyes screamed in pain and she let out a cry. She brought her hands up and began wiping her face with them, spitting out bits that had made it into her open mouth. It was greasy and salty and it only took Judy a second to recognize what it was. A wad of chewed up bacon. She gagged and wretched onto the floor. While she did, she heard Britney begin to scream.

Just when Britney thought she would make it to the bedroom, her knees were jerked out from under her and she was pulled backwards across the floor again. She grasped the wall at the entrance to the hallway and held on, screaming, as she was tugged. It felt like she was being toyed with, as if Bad Jamie could yank her legs right off, leaving her with two bloody stumps. And Britney knew she could. Her eyes went to Judy and saw that she was upchucking on the floor by the front door. The teen screamed and her eyes went back to the bedroom doorway.

"Jamie, no! Please, stop! I'll watch cartoons with you! Anything, just stop!" Britney pleaded, attempting to kick her feet, "Get off me, you b-bitch!"

A gall of child-like laughter erupted from behind her and Britney felt the grip on her ankles tighten.

Judy dry heaved one final time and wiped her eyes with her dirty, slimy fingers. She looked across the room just in time to see Bad Jamie pull Britney loose from the wall, sending her flying through the air in a half spin. Judy watched Britney soar, in what seemed like slow motion. A second later, Britney collided with the sofa, tipping it backward and rolled off gently onto the floor.

Judy rose to her feet and watched as Britney scrambled to her knees. Before Judy had a chance to think of what to do, her eyes went to the dead body lying on the floor where the sofa had sat. The little girl's corps was twisted and bent, as if it were crammed underneath with a lot of force. It was wearing pajamas, similar to the ones Bad Jamie wore. It could have been Bad Jamie, if not for the dead look in its eyes. Now, in the dim light, Judy could see a dark purple bruise on the left side of dead Jamie's neck and knew the other side would have a similar mark. She saw marks like them a lot over the years working at the hospitals. A city this size had a lot of domestic violence cases. At that moment, Judy knew the little girl had been choked to death.

And shoved under the sofa, like a dirty secret.

Up until now, Judy thought Tommy died in the dryer, spinning in the heat filled space until his small body gave up. A horrible way to die. Now looking at these marks, she imagined hands around his neck.

Was he choked to death first? Maybe the dryer was just a hiding place. Maybe my little boy was choked first!

The thought seemed to drain what fight she had left in her and she had to lean against the door to keep from going to her knees again.

Judy slowly looked back at Britney and saw that she was gazing toward the hallway, with a blank look on her face. Judy's eyes moved in that direction and saw Bad Jamie, looking down at the body as well. For a moment Bad Jamie seemed to have a look of sorrow and thoughtfulness on her face, but it didn't last long.

Her eyes slowly moved to Judy, then to Britney and then back to the body. Bad Jamie let out a cackle of laughter that echoed in the room and childishly pointed at Jamie's body, mocking it. She looked back to Judy and Britney with a sinister smile on her face and continued to laugh.

Britney looked down at the body for the first time and shock filled her face. When she glared back to Bad Jamie, Judy could tell that some of the fear had left the teen.

"Don't you laugh at her?" Britney screamed, "You don't get to laugh at her, you nasty bitch!"

Bad Jamie's laughing ceased and she glared at Britney with her head tilted. Before Britney could continue, Bad Jamie's face turned into a sneer and with no warning, she took a leap across the living room towards Britney.

Judy clenched her hands. At that moment, she felt the fear leave her as well. It was replaced by rage.

•••

Judy pushed off the door in a run, trying to collide with Bad Jamie as she cleared the coffee table, but the thing was too fast. Its feet landed inches from the dead body on the floor, leaped again and cleared the sofa, colliding with Britney. By the time Judy stopped moving, Bad Jamie had Britney by the throat against the wall on the other side of the room. Judy bolted in that direction.

"No, get off her!" Judy shrieked.

Britney's eyes turned to Judy as she came around the side of the sofa. The teen was gasping for air. Her face had turned red and her eyes looked like they were going to pop out of their sockets. Judy took a hold of Bad Jamie's hair and yanked. Its small head moved back slightly, but she didn't seem to be fazed. Judy pulled harder and her hand started to slip. The hair was wet with sweat and had a slimy feel to it; plus Judy's hands were a greasy mess from the bacon facial Bad Jamie had given her. Judy backed off, twisted the hair around her fist and yanked as hard as she could. The hair came loose in her hand, sending her staggering to the floor. Judy's ass hit the floor hard and she felt pain shoot up her spine. She looked in her hand, confused for a moment and saw she held most of the back of Bad Jamie's scalp. She looked up and saw a bloody, pink bald spot where it had been.

Judy tossed the hair to the side and got back to her feet, advancing on Bad Jamie again. Britney's eyes were rolling back in her head and Judy knew it was only a matter of seconds. She reached out and groped for Bad Jamie's shoulders.

Before Judy even touched her, Bad Jamie jerked her head around and clamped her teeth on the meaty part of Judy's left hand, just below her thumb. The speed of the action was eerie and Judy let out a painful scream. It felt like the things teeth went right to the bone, causing pins and needles to shoot up her arm. Judy let out an angry cry, tried to ignore the pain and put her other hand around Bad Jamie's head, pulling her forehead back. Britney was released and she slid down the wall to the floor, choking and gasping for air.

With little effort, Bad Jamie slipped from Judy's grip and twisted around to face her. She released Judy's hand from between her teeth and before Judy could react to the sudden shift or look at her wound, Bad Jamie grabbed her throat with both hands. Judy grabbed her wrists and struggled, but it was no use. The thing was too strong.

Bad Jamie may have been stronger than a normal ten year old, but she was no heavier. Judy grasped under her arms and picked her up off the floor. Bad Jamie thrashed and buckled until the two of them toppled over the sofa, rolling over dead Jamie's body. Before the roll stopped, Judy felt the fingers digging into the flesh of her neck ease up enough for her to croak out a few words.

"Britney, go for the door! Get out of here while you ca—"

Britney stood up just as they stopped rolling, gawked at them and then glanced to the door. The keys were handing in the lock. She moved in the doors direction, looking back over her shoulder. Judy's legs kicked weakly, as Bad Jamie straddled her.

Bad Jamie barked and growled, squeezing her hands tighter around Judy's neck. Droplets of spit sprinkled down on Judy's face. From behind Bad Jamie's horrid face, Judy saw the dimness in the room brighten, as Britney opened the door, letting light from the hallway spill in. A feeling of relief washed over her as she gasped for air.

She's safe! She got away! I saved her, Tommy! Mommy saved her!

Tired and out of breath, Judy let her hands fall from Bad Jamie's wrists, dropping them to the floor. One of them bumped the arm of the real Jamie's body next to her and her fingers took notice of the fabric. It was thin and as soft as velvet. It reminded her of something her good Tommy would have worn to bed. She closed her eyes, rubbing it with the tips of her fingers, as she pictured hugging Tommy again in the afterlife.

Mommy loves you, honey, Judy thought. *Forever and ever and ever.*

As soon as Judy had the thought, there was a flash of light.

A second later, everything went silent and she felt the grip around her neck loosen. She sucked in a gulp of air, with her ears ringing.

Judy opened her eyes and peered up at Bad Jamie. Her face was frozen in a blank sneer and slowly started to fall forward. Judy put her arm up and pushed the limp body to the side, sending it most of the way off of her and toppling to the floor, like a dead animal. Confused and gasping for air, Judy looked from it, to a dark silhouette in the doorway. When her eyes adjusted, she saw Britney in front of her, with Richards's gun trembling in her hand.

Britney's eyes went from Bad Jamie's body, to Judy and she quickly lowered the gun, realizing she was pointing it at her new friend again. The nervous look on her face faltered and turned into a weak smile. Judy raised into a sitting position and coughed, clearing her throat.

"I thought I told you to get out of here," Judy said, in a croaky voice, with the hint of a smile on her face.

Britney grinned back, pointing the gun at the floor. "Oh, I was about to run my ass out the door, until I looked down and saw the gun. Besides, I couldn't just leave you here." Then, in a sarcastic tone, she added, "I thought you said these things couldn't be shot?"

Judy pushed Bad Jamie's body the rest of the way off of her and struggled to her feet. Britney quickly came forward, putting an arm around her, eyeing the body cautiously. Judy welcomed the help.

"I guess you're a better shot than I am," Judy said.

"Well, it helps if you press the gun barrel against the back of the head." Then after a short pause, Britney added, "Do you think that's, like, cheating?"

Judy smiled at her, brought her arm around and hugged her tight. "Yes it is. It most defiantly is. Thanks for sticking around."

"Well, you'd of done it for me, right?"

Judy nodded, briefly recalling the fact that she almost didn't. If the door had opened, she would have left Britney, in the spur of the frightening moment. It would have been a mistake, one that she would have had to live with and she wondered if she would have stopped in the hallway and had the nerve to come back.

I guess I'll never know, but I like to think I would have stopped. That I am the type of person that would have come back.

They both moved toward the door and looked back at the two nearly identical bodies lying side by side. It was an eerie sight. Britney stared at the good one. The one that hadn't tried to kill her. The one that was just starting to talk to her about boys. Jamie Porter, her friend.

"Good bye, Jamie. Sorry this had to happen to you. I'll miss you," she said, into the dark room.

Judy let Britney linger for a moment, until she couldn't stand to be there any longer. She didn't want to look at either of them.

Giving Britney's arm a tug, Judy said, "Well, come on, let's get ata here before something else happens."

Judy took ahold of Britney's hand and pulled her towards the doorway. Britney didn't move, as if her feet were glued to the floor.

"Wait, Judy!" the teen whispered. "Holy hell, look at that!"

Judy slowly turned her head, not wanting to know what would make Britney want to wait. *Whatever it is, I don't care, I don't want to see it*, Judy thought. *I just want to get the hell out of here.*

Regardless of the thought, Judy followed Britney's gaze back at the two dead figures.

A fine, green mist started to rise from Bad Jamie's dead body, surrounding both corpses. It hovered and shifted as if it were alive. It moved fast enough that the clothing the bodies were wearing rippled, as it swirled around them. It made it look as though the bodies were moving.

"Holly shit! She's coming back!" Britney said, as she moved toward the door. "Let's go!"

"No!" Judy shouted, letting go of her hand and moving back, deeper into the room.

Britney sighed, glancing down the hallway, in the directions of the stairs, then back to Bad Jamie's corps.

"Come on, Judy!" she pleaded. "Let's leave while we have the chance."

Judy acted as if she didn't hear the comment. Something else caught her attention. She inched her way toward the mist, staring not at Bad Jamie, but at the good one. The mist danced over the body, moving its clothing and hair. As it did, the big purple burse on dead Jamie's neck start to fade. Suddenly the TV static faltered and a split second of horrible moaning filled the apartment. Judy didn't flinch or look away from the body.

Britney's eyes shot to the TV, then back to Bad Jamie.

"Come on Judy! Seriously, let's go! I'm freaked out!"

"No! Look at the bruises," Judy sputtered. Before she finished the words, the bruises were gone and most of the green haze moved back to the bad thing on the floor, as if its job were done and it was going home.

Judy stared at Jamie in disbelief.

Did that really just do what I think it did, Judy thought. *Oh please, little girl, be ok. Please be normal.*

Jamie's eye lashes fluttered a few times, before the little girl slowly opened her eyes. The color had come back into her skin and she looked around the room, as if waking up in a strange place, after a long nap. Judy crouched down on one knee and whispered to her.

"Jamie, Jamie Porter? Is that really you?"

Jamie looked at her, rising up into a sitting position. She licked her lips before she spoke. "Yes, it's me." She looked at Judy and back at the silhouette in the doorway. "Are you two normal?" she said, in a shaky voice.

"Yes we are," Judy said, without hesitation.

Britney moved up beside Judy and dropped to her knees. Jamie smiled at her friend, putting her arms out.

"Britney!" she cheered, as the wide eyed teen embraced her.

"Oh my Lord! Jamie? It's really you! I can't believe you're ok! I never thought I would see you again," Britney cried, hugging the ten year old and rocking her side to side. Judy watched them in silence and noticed a few strands of mist lingering around them. The bruise on Britney's face, the one Richard porter had given her for not letting him fondle her under her shirt, started to fade. After a second, it was gone.

Judy looked down at her hand Bad Jamie had bitten. It was a gnarly mess of a bite and looked like an infection waiting to happen.

I wonder...

Judy put her hand out in front of her and the mist moved to it and began to circle her hand, as if it knew it had a job to do. It tingled and had a chill to it, as it were drifting out of an open freezer door. Within a few seconds, the wound began to heal before her eyes. Even the bite marks Bad Tommy left on her fingers vanished. She turned her hand over a few times, looking at her skin. For no reason, other than curiosity, she brought her fingers up and smelled them. The smell was familiar and pleasant. As she did, more of the mist moved in her direction, as if it saw her interest and welcomed her curiosity. It danced in front of her face, moving enticingly, the way a belly dancer would for a crowded room. Judy followed it with her eyes, mesmerized by its motions. It seemed to call to her and without thinking, she leaned forward and took its scent in. She inhaled deeply and her eyes shot open with her pupil's dilated. It smelled like peppermint and she was taken back by a feeling of adrenalin. Her head cleared and she could think straight. The pain in her back faded and she felt energy well up inside of her. It was a rush, better than any drug Pete had shown her. She quickly shook her head, part of her regretting taking it in.

That can't be good. Anything that feels like that has to be bad. What was I thinking?

She backed away from it and the mist moved from her, back to the dead thing on the floor. It swirled faster. The static on the TV shuddered again with a painful moan. Judy, Britney and Jamie looked up at it briefly, then back to Bad Jamie's body, engulfed in the mist. The green haze seemed to thicken, making it hard to see the body and Judy felt a ting of nervousness. Britney took Jamie in her arms, stood up and moved toward the door. Judy lingered for a moment, watching, mesmerized.

The TV let out few more burps in a rapid succession and the mist started to flow in its direction. As it did, Judy saw the thing on the floor slowly start to disappear. The mist continued to hover toward the TV, until Bad Jamie vanished completely, leaving only a damp spot on the wood floor.

Judy stared at the mist circling the screen. The picture continued to burp and moan for a moment, then in one swift motion, the mist flowed into the TV screen, as if were smoke being sucked through the back of a fan. Britney cringed and looked at Judy. Her new friend looked as if she were in a trance.

As the last of the mist rushed into the screen, there was one final pulse of moaning. The next second, the screen cracked down the middle, leaving the apartment in silence. Judy stared at the dark screen for a moment, blinked her eyes and took a few deep breaths. For a split second, during the final flash, she saw Bad Jamie for what it really was, as if it were looking back at her from wherever it came from. The image imbedded itself in her mind. All at once, a thought popped into her head.

Britney's voice stung the silence, although Judy barely heard it. "Judy, come on, let's get out of here while we can. I mean, before someone comes along and starts asking a bunch of messed up questions. They'll think we're crazy!"

Judy said nothing in return. She sat, staring at her hand, turning it slowly in front of her face.

"Judy! What is it?"

Judy turned toward Britney, with a strange look on her face. A look that scared Britney a little. A wild look. After a few seconds Judy sputtered a single word.

"Tommy!"

✧

Chapter 5.

As they approached the exit to the lobby, Judy, Britney and Jamie slowed. The doors were glass and the light outside had dimmed more than they expected. It was already dusk and the streets were alive with activity.

"My God, now what? What's going on out there?" Britney asked, through a puff of breath. They had come down the four floors using the stairs, like they planned. Even though there was little risk of anything coming after them, they didn't have the nerve to pile into the small elevator.

"I don't know. When we came in yesterday, it was like a ghost town out there." Judy looked down at Jamie and gave her an awkward smile. It was still hard to remember that this wasn't the thing that had a death grip on her hand when she first entered these doors.

Britney walked to the glass and looked out. There were people everywhere and the streets were packed with cars.

"It looks like the shi…." Britney paused and glanced at Jamie before she continued. "The *crap* has hit the fan," she finished, with a smirk on her face.

"Nice, Britney," Judy replied, giving her a look that was both comical and stern.

Outside, people were moving around every which way. Some were walking with confused looks on their faces and a few were running. The ones running looked terrified. The place looked close to a riot.

Judy's eyes fixed on something she wasn't at all surprised to see. A soldier eyeing the activity from the top of a building. He had his rifle out and appeared to be scanning the crowd with the scope. She looked down the block and saw people pouring out of an apartment building. Soon after, a group of soldiers wearing gas masks exited as well. One of them gave another soldier the thumbs up and they moved to the next door and quickly disappeared inside. Suddenly noise erupted overhead, as a huge helicopter came into view, flying low, blowing dust and debris in all directions. The pilot didn't seem worried about disturbing the crowd. People ducked and gawked at it, as it hovered for a moment and moved on down the street, tilting forward slightly.

"Holy crap, look at those guys!" Britney said, pointing to a brawl going on near the side walk. It looked like someone had gotten out of their car and was fighting with a pedestrian. Another soldier stood nearby and watched them with little interest. Judy looked around and saw that a few of the other cars were vacant as well, the doors standing open, abandoned by people not wanting to wait in traffic, she supposed.

"When we go, stay with me," Judy said. "It looks a little crazy out there, but my apartment building is just around the corner, not very far at all."

Britney cringed. "I can't believe we're going back there, I mean, what if the other Tommy; I mean the bad one…" Britney stumbled over her words and continued. "you know…isn't there anymore. You said you heard it chasing you, right?"

Judy thought about it. She did think it was chasing her when she went down the stairs, but she was frantic. It could have been her terrified mind playing tricks on her.

Britney watched Judy for a moment. When Judy didn't reply, she continued timidly.

"I mean, I don't know that much about drugs and shooting up and all, but if it was a hot dose, like you said, shouldn't that have killed it?" After a short pause, she added, "Maybe it's just too late?"

Judy's eyes focused on her and Britney quickly looked away. By the way Britney was talking, Judy could tell she was struggling with the idea of going to the apartment. For a split second, Judy's eyes narrowed, resenting the words she was hearing. Then she took a deep breath, in attempt to control herself.

I can't blame her. I wouldn't want to go either if I were her. She doesn't have kids and can't know what it's like. She's just a kid herself.

"Well what if it did die," Judy asked. "What if it died, brought Tommy back and now he's just in the apartment alone?"

Britney continued to stare blindly out the window and thought, *Ya maybe, but God damn. Going back there seems risky…almost suicide.*

Judy glanced down at Jamie. She was holding Britney's hand and looking out the window. She looked kind of out of it, but

James Peaton • Bad Tommy

she was alive. She was ok. They hadn't asked her many questions and she hadn't given them many answers. Looking at her now still gave Judy the creeps.

She looked back to Britney and caught her looking up from Jamie as well. Their eyes met and Judy adjusted her face, knowing it must have had a sour look to it. Before Judy could speak, Britney did.

"Whatever you want to do, we're with you." she said. "I mean, if it weren't for you, I'd still be stuck in there and she'd still be…you know. I just don't know what you're expecting."

Judy gave her a weak smile. "I don't know if I expect anything. I didn't expect any of this to happen." She motioned to Jamie. "If we can bring her back, then we can bring Tommy back. I have to try. I'm sorry, but that's it. I have to try."

Then, Judy's own voice whispered in her ear. *Even if you have to drag another one of those things into that apartment and kill it for its mist, you will, if it can bring him back. If you have to kill a dozen of them, by yourself, you'll do it. You know you can.*

Judy's lips tightened at the thought. The way she felt, she did think she could. Whatever was in the mist, was still lingering in her body, giving her some kind of raw energy.

I'll get my son back, if it kills me!

Britney's lips cracked into a smile, as if she'd heard the thought. "Ok then, lead the way, Judy."

Judy eyed both of them. They looked tired. Judy should have been tired too, but she wasn't. She felt fine. More than fine. If she didn't have them with her, she would be tempted to sprint back to the apartment, full speed and take care of this nasty business. Whatever that mist had in it, Pete could have made a fortune with it.

The little girl brought her hand out for Judy to take. Judy glanced at it for a moment, feeling a nauseating case of Deja vu. Then she looked to Jamie's smiling face. The smile was grim, but alive and normal, different from the eerie smile the other Jamie wore. Judy hesitated for a moment, then reached out and took Jamie's hand, half expecting it to clench down on her own. It didn't. It was as warm and as week as it should have been. Judy smiled at her and spoke.

"Ok, remember, stay together. We don't have far to go."

Judy opened the door, letting the noise and cold air drift in and they stepped out onto the busy sidewalk.

•••

They walked as fast as they could, more or less pulling Jamie along, but the people around them were moving faster. Several people whizzing by, gave Jamie an uneasy look, as if she were a wild animal. Judy glanced down at her and saw what they saw. A little girl with wild hair, wearing dirty pajamas and no shoes.

We didn't put shoes on her, Judy thought. *Its freezing and we didn't put shoes on her.*

The cold concrete didn't seem to be bothering Jamie, but Judy stopped and grabbed her up, putting her across her chest. She was heavy, but the weight of her felt good. Britney filed behind them and they moved faster through the crowd.

Around the first turn, the three of them jumped at the sudden sounds of muffled gun shots coming from inside a building ahead of them. The people mingling around suddenly shifted, bumping and shoving with no regard for each other. Judy looked at the crowd moving in their direction. It looked like a wave of people coming at them. Soon they were being pulled back in the direction they had come from. She spotted an alley and quickly ducked into it. The chaos seemed to dim as they stopped and took a breath. Jamie had her arms around Judy's shoulders and felt limp, as if she had fallen asleep.

"Dang, were never gonna make it through that crowd," Britney said, out of breath. "And what were those shots? Did the army guy's actually shoot one of them?"

"I don't know. I hope so," Judy mumbled.

Britney reached around and fingered the gun in the fold of her jeans.

A machine gun would be a lot better than a crummy revolver.

Judy scanned the crowd blowing by them. Across the way, she could see a soldier standing by a mail box. He was looking blankly at the crowd with a bull horn in his hand. It dawned on her that he should be barking into the thing, telling people to 'keep calm' and 'move in an orderly fashion', commands he would be trained to say, but he was just looking at them, as if he didn't care. Just then, a woman about Judy's own age, came up and began to talk to him. Judy saw his hand go to his side arm, as the woman seemed to plead with him. She looked desperate. After a moment, the soldier relaxed and turned his attention back to the crowd, ignoring her. Clearly angry, the woman yelled something at him. From where Judy stood, it was just a mumble in the noise of the crowd, but the body language and look on the ladies face said it all.

She was begging for help; demanding it. The soldier pointed in the direction of the street and Judy saw his lips say 'move along', with a few more unrecognizable words. The look on his face was very stern and the woman took a step back, flipped him off and walked away, disappearing into the crowd.

"Judy, hello! Are you listening to me?"

Judy looked to Britney. She hadn't noticed she was talking.

"What?" Judy said, dumbly.

"I said, maybe we should ask someone for help. One of the army men. I mean, we only have one or two more bullets in this gun. I don't even know how to open it to check." She held up the gun in her hand. "Or maybe we can snag one of their machine guns?"

"I don't think they are going to be much h—"

Before Judy had a chance to finish, a man staggered into the alley with them. He was out of breath and looked scared. He stood there, breathing hard for a moment, before noticing he wasn't alone. When he did, his eyes went wide at the sight of Jamie, as if she were bearing fangs. He quickly merged back into the flow of people, gawking back at her over his shoulder before disappearing.

Judy and Britney looked at Jamie, then at each other. "Britney, keep that thing put away," Judy said, calmly. "We don't need any more attention."

"Ok, sorry." Britney tucked the gun back into the fold of her jeans. "But I don't think he was scared of the gun though." They both looked at each other and Britney eyes flashed to Jamie. Judy knew what she meant. The man was clearly spooked by Jamie. Judy looked back at the horde of people moving about and scanned the crowd. It was hard to tell, but she didn't see any children right off hand. Not a single one.

Are all of these people going to look at Jamie that way? We don't need that kind of attention either.

"Maybe we should walk that way," Judy said, gesturing to the alley. "If we walk to the end and take a left, it will bring us most of the way to my building."

Britney gave her a nod, clearly relieved not to be going back out to the street. Judy adjusted Jamie's limp body in her arms, turned and started to walk down the dark alley.

•••

The alley was disgusting and narrow. Trash and grime littered the ground. Judy walked it a few times in the past with

Pete. It was a good alley to take if you didn't want to be seen and also didn't mind the smell of cat piss. Muffled gun shots and distant screams tainted the air, making her nervous and glad to be off the street despite the smell.

"Judy?" Britney said, quietly.

"Yes?"

"Why do you think the picture on the TV went off like that in the apartment? I mean, it seemed kind of weird, right? Like I said, I tried to change the channel before and they were all cartoons. I couldn't even *turn* the damn thing off."

Judy opened her mouth to respond and before she could, Jamie's small voice spoke up.

"I think it was the army. They must have shut down all the networks thinking it would kill them or draw them out."

Judy and Britney shot glances at each other.

Britney cleared her throat and asked, "How would they do that?"

"They're the army, they can do whatever they want," Jamie answered. "Besides there are only fourteen TV networks here. We went on a field trip to one of them last year for school. There is a button you can push that shuts it down. Usually they would play a jungle or show a sign off picture when they go off the air." Then after a short pause she added, "I don't think they knew what it would do, but I bet it didn't work the way they wanted it too."

"Why do you say that?" Britney asked timidly. The little girl seemed like she knew a lot.

"Because they didn't come out. They thought it would be like poking a stick at a hornets' nest. The kids would come out and they could grab them or whatever. But they aren't coming out. Now they have to go door to door and check every apartment."

A burst of muffled shots came from somewhere in the distance behind them and Britney's attention jerked in that direction.

Judy spoke up. "Jamie, do you know what these things are? Do you remember anything? Maybe right before you went away?"

Jamie was silent for a moment and Britney slowly turned her attention to back to them and waited for her response.

Jamie spoke slowly, as if she were pulling at the words. "I kind of remember some stuff…being in a dark place. It seems like I could see the living room some of the time after…"

"Like, from under the couch?" Britney blurted out. Judy felt Jamie's body tense and she looked at Britney wide eyed. Britney's expression deflated and she looked down at her feet as they continued to walk.

Judy's tone softened. "Go on Jamie, just tell us what you can. It's no big deal if you can't remember."

Jamie replied quickly, "No, I can remember some stuff, just not everything. It's just...I could only see the living room. I think I was looking back through the TV screen or something...but not a TV. It was in, like, a cave or something and the picture was shining off the rocks." Then after a short pause, she added "I saw bad things. Things I didn't want to see."

Jamie stopped talking and the look on her face tensed. Judy realized why she was having a hard time talking about it and what she probably saw, but before she could say anything, Britney spoke again.

"What bad things did you see?"

Judy gave her another look, but this time Britney was focused on Jamie when she said it.

Judy felt Jamie's heart begin to pound against her own chest.

"I saw my mommy and what she was about to do to the other me...the bad one. She knew it wasn't me, but no one would believe her."

Britney instantly regretted asking the question and looked back to her feet.

Jamie continued, breathing faster. "Then I saw my daddy come in and...do what he did. It was so scary and it was like I couldn't look away." Then after a short pause, she added, "I saw everything."

Judy squeezed her slightly and rubbed her back with her palm. She felt the little girl tighten her grip around her shoulders.

"I saw Britney come in and start screaming," Jamie continued. "My daddy grabbed her cause she saw it and he didn't want her to tell on him." Jamie looked at Britney. "I saw what he was making you do, sitting with her. You looked scared and I know you didn't want to be there. He was making you do it."

They were silent for a moment, until Jamie spoke again.

"He's not a very good guy, is he?"

Before either of them could answer, Jamie whispered, "I don't ever want to see him again."

Judy squeezed her tight and whispered, "You don't have to, sweetie. I don't think he's gonna bother you or anyone anymore."

Jamie gripped Judy tighter and pushed the side if her face into her neck. After a short silence, Judy spoke again.

"Jamie, do you remember how this happened to you? How the bad thing got you?"

Jamie shifted a little, before she spoke. "I remember it started out as a voice. A little voice in my head. My mommy and daddy couldn't hear it and didn't believe me when I told them about it. It was only me and I thought I was going crazy."

Judy and Britney slowed their pace as the little girl continued to talk. Britney's mind flashed to a time a few weeks ago when she overheard the Porters taking about Jamie hearing things. They thought it was just her coping with her mother's sickness. An imaginary friend kind of thing.

"What did the voice say to you?" Judy asked. Britney was about to ask the same question, closed her mouth and listened.

"I don't remember. It asked me all sorts of questions about being a little girl, about my parents and what I ate for food. Some of the questions seemed silly and it asked them over and over. I remember it never said anything, unless it was asking a question. It didn't answer any of mine. Then one day, I saw my reflection on the TV was something else. It was turned off and when I walked by, the reflection stood still. I stopped and knew right away that it was her. It didn't scare me. She was almost like my friend by then. Mommy was sick and daddy was always busy and I didn't have any friends. I tried to talk to it and it just stared at me. It looked sad."

Jamie stopped talking. Judy and Britney glanced at each other briefly, before Judy spoke.

"Why would it look sad?"

"I think she was sad that she wasn't me. She wanted a mommy and daddy to sit with, like I had. She even asked about Britney."

Judy looked over at Britney and saw her swallow hard.

"And she really wanted to eat. That's mostly what she asked about. I think she was starving." Then, after the slightest pause, she added, "I feel sorry for them."

Judy stopped in her tracks, causing Britney to nearly bump into her back. "*Sorry* for them! Honey, why would you feel sorry for them? One of them *killed* you!"

Jamie could hear the contempt in Judy's voice and without hesitation, she said, "I know, but it just wanted to be loved, like I was. I think they miss being loved. They live in a dark place, with no colors or sounds. I think that's why they like the cartoons and the music. They want to come here, even if it means they have to do bad things. To them, bad things are normal things. Maybe they don't know they're being bad."

Judy's ears were burning. She couldn't believe what she was hearing. She spoke next in a cold voice. "Well, one of them killed my son and I don't feel sorry for them at all. I hope the army blows them all up."

The comment hit the air like a brick and the three of them were all silent for a moment, as more gun chatter went off in the distance. The rifle blasts were behind them and sounded more distant. It made Judy hope they hadn't already been through her building. Something told her it wouldn't be the only building full of death in the city. There had to be more. Of all the people moving about the streets, there weren't any children, so that meant they were left behind, hidden away, waiting to be found.

I bet the military doesn't know they can be saved, Judy thought.

She started to walk faster.

They came to a corner and made a left turn down a similar alley way. This one was narrower, but a little cleaner. It didn't smell much better. Britney took advantage of the new surroundings and was the first to break the awkward silence.

"So Jamie, you say it was your friend. Was it ever mean to you, before it...you know?" Britney brought her hands up, as if to choke an invisible neck in front of her. Judy shot her a glance and Britney quickly lowered them. Jamie didn't seem to notice the crude gesture.

Nice subtlety, Brit, Judy thought.

Jamie answered, "No, not really. But I think it got upset when I didn't want to keep answering it, especial in front of my parents. They already thought I was crazy and I did too."

"So how did she take your place?" Britney asked.

"I don't remember. The next thing I knew, it was me looking at her through the TV. Before that, it's all kinda foggy."

Judy adjusted Jamie in her arms again. It dawned on her, how far she had carried her. Jamie had to weight twice as much as Tommy and she could remember how her arms hurt when she carried him half as far. Her arms didn't feel soar at all now. In fact, she felt great. As Britney would probably say, she felt *amped*.

It's the mist, she thought. *I can still taste the peppermint flavor in my mouth. Whatever it is, I hope it stays with me for a bit longer. I might need it.*

Judy flexed her hand. The one that Bad Jamie bit. It felt normal. If someone came into the hospital she worked at, with an injury like that, it would have required stitches, inside and out. There was no way the muscle of her thumb hadn't been severed.

Whatever the peppermint mist is, it could change modern medicine, she thought.

"Jamie, do you know what that mist is?" Judy asked casually, trying not to sound too interested.

Jamie shifted a little, nervously. "I don't know, but I know it's not good."

Judy slowed her stride. "Not good? How could it not be good? It brought you back!" She said it with more enthusiasm than she intended and felt Jamie shift again.

"The mist is part of them," Jamie murdered. "It's a bad thing. Maybe I shouldn't have been brought back. I don't know, it just doesn't feel right. I don't feel right." Then Jamie looked Judy in the eyes and said, "It's bad, I just know it. I wouldn't mess with it if I were you."

Judy wondered briefly if the military knew about the mist yet. If they'd shot any of the things, they would have had to of seen it. She didn't want to think of what they would try to do with it, if they realized what it could do. An evil part of her surfaced and the hairs on her arms prickled. Greed is the best word to describe the feeling.

I don't want them to have the mist. God, what I wouldn't do for another whiff. Or even a cigarette would hit the spot right now. A menthol.

Pete smoked them. Judy only had one every now and then, usually when she was really happy about something and wanted to celebrate or if she were really sad about something and wanted to die. She couldn't remember the last time she had one. Happy had been far in-between these last few years. And well, sad had sort of become the norm, not worth smoking for.

Judy's mind wondered for a moment, until she looked over saw Britney giving her a look. Judy knew the expression and what it meant. It meant Britney didn't think they should be doing what they were about to do, that maybe it was *too late* for Tommy and Jamie just basically said the same thing.

Judy gave Britney an unintentional dirty look as she turned her head back to the alley in front of them.

It can't be too late! Tommy wasn't supposed to die by the hand of one of those things. I don't care what they think. They don't have to come with me. I can do this myself.

Judy could still feel Britney's eyes on her, so she changed the subject.

"So, they're not aliens then, right?" Judy asked Jamie.

Before the little girl could answer, Britney spoke up.

"No, they aren't aliens. They're demons."

"Why do you say that?" Judy asked passively, as she looked up at the windows above them. As Britney spoke, she could see faces in some of the windows. Children's faces, small and innocent at first glance, but sinister the way they didn't take their eyes off of her. As her eyes moved from one to the other, they stared and pawed at the glass, as if they were starving for her. It was the first time she noticed them.

"They just don't seem like aliens," Britney continued. "Aliens wouldn't need to do this and if they did, they would be smarter about it. From what I know about demons, this has them written all over it. Demons can shape shift, taking the forms of people or animals. They can enter your mind and cause you to believe things that aren't true. They are liars and thieves. From what Jamie says, it seems like they want what they used to have before they were cast away. Before they fell from heaven to the smoky realm of the damned."

Britney finished with a far-away look on her face and didn't notice the other two staring at her. When her eyes went to them, she blushed. "Sorry, a few years ago, I went through a faze. Me and my friends were a little Goth."

Jamie tilted her head slightly. "Ya, that's it. That sounds like them, kind of… Demons," she said, staring off into space. After a few seconds, she added "What's Goth mean?"

Britney's mind went blank and before she could think of an explanation that didn't sound stupid, Judy interrupted the conversation.

"Ok, *shhhh*. Give the gibber jabber a rest, Britney!" Judy snapped harshly. They had come to the end of the alley and were approaching the corner. They would be able to see Judy's building if they peered around it.

Britney stared at Judy for a moment with a deflated look on her face, then down the alley, the way they had come. It looked like a long way and she fought the urge to sit down on the dirty ground at her feet. Her legs felt week and her stomach was growling. She glance back at Judy.

I wondered how she's able to carry Jamie this far. She seems like she's freaking amped and rearing to go. I would be too, I guess, if it where my son…but she doesn't have to be a bitch about it. After all, who saved who back in the apartment?

Then after a moment, she thought, *I don't know if I can be that brave again.*

Britney stared at the back of Judy's head for a moment and then caught sight of Jamie's eyes on her. She quickly adjusted her face and smiled at her young friend.

It's crazy, I can't believe we got her back.

After a second of staring at Jamie, Britney thought *Judy's right. We have to go back and try to save Tommy. If we didn't, it would probably drive Judy insane.*

Britney took a breath and joined Judy, peering round the corner.

Though what seemed like a sea of people and parked cars, they saw the door to Judy's building. Judy looked up and down the street. It didn't look like the military had gotten to her building yet. She let out a sigh of relief.

Judy spoke. "Ok, let's go. It's not too far and there are a lot less people. Stay together. Ready?"

Both girls nodded.

With Jamie still in her arms, Judy made her way in the doors direction, with Britney close behind her. The cars were a little less packed together on this street and a lot of the people darting about were walking between them, giving more space on the sidewalk. Judy stopped as they approached the steps to her building. She gazed up at the door and a shiver ran up her spine.

"Here Britney, can you take her?" Judy said, adjusting Jamie in her arms. Britney nodded and prepared herself for the load, when Jamie spoke up.

"No, I can walk. I feel better now."

Judy set Jamie down on the sidewalk. "Are you sure?"

"Ya," she said, stretching her arms over her head. "I just feel all stiff; maybe if I move around it'll get better.

Britney and Judy glanced at each other, both thinking the same thought. How they would feel if they had been strangled and shoved under a couch for over a week. 'Stiff' seemed like the right word.

Judy looked back at the door and then down the street. There weren't any soldiers in sight, just lots of people. She looked back at the door as she spoke.

"Do you guys want to wait here or what? I don't know what's it's gonna be like in there."

Britney looked down at Jamie, then around at the hundreds of people roaming about. "No, we'll come. Better than staying out here. What if you need help? Besides I have to pee really bad," she finished, with a comical cringe on her face.

"Well I don't think you're gonna want to pee in here."

"Well then I'll hold it, but let's hurry." Britney reached behind her and plucked the gun from the fold of her jeans. She glanced at it for a moment and held it out to Judy. "You lead the way. We're with you."

Judy smiled and took the gun. Britney watched as she opened the cylinder and peered down at it.

"So that's how you open it," Britney mumbled, as Judy flipped the gun sideways, causing the cylinder to snap back into place. Britney and Jamie looked at each other in awe. The calm look in Judy's eyes when she did it, made her look like a gunslinger, straight out a Steven King novel.

"One bullet left and I hope we don't need it," Judy said, as she slid the gun into the front pocket of her scrubs.

She turned and started up the four steps. The other two girls followed her.

"When we get in there, try to keep quiet," Judy said, calmly, not looking back at them.

They got to the top and without hesitation, Judy put her hand on the knob and before her nerves knew what she was doing, she pulled the door open.

A gust of foul oater hit them in the face and they brought their hands up to block it. It smelled like rotten meat and sewage. They pushed through the doorway and stopped in the lobby, looking in all directions. It wasn't much of a lobby, more of an entryway. Nothing like the lobby of Jamie's building. This one consisted of some mail boxes along the wall on both sides and an elevator straight ahead. The staircase Judy had come down was through a doorway just to the left of the elevator. The door had been missing for years and Judy was glad not to have to open it. Dryer doors. Locked doors. Doors with blood on the knobs. Doors with fingers sticking out from underneath and retched smells waiting to gust in her face; God only knew what on the other side of each one. Judy was sick of opening doors. Other than some newspapers swirling around in the breeze the lobby door let in, it looked the same as she had left it.

Slam!

The noise obliterated the silence in the small room, causing the three of them to jump. Judy and Jamie turned and saw Britney looking at the lobby door, with her hand on her chest. She looked to the both of them with a pitiful expression on her face. The noise echoed up the stairs and faded in the distance.

"Sorry. The wind blew it shut," Britney said, in a small voice.

Judy smiled at her and let out a breath. "Well, so much for being quiet."

"Ya, well, I don't have to pee anymore either," Britney whispered, glancing down at her jeans. Judy looked to the staircase, not needing to look back at Britney's crotch to know she probably wasn't joking.

Judy walked toward the stairs and the other two girls filed in behind her. She glanced up the steps to the first landing. There were no windows and a light fixture on the wall at the top of the steps provided the only light. She started to climb.

Before Judy knew it, she was at the top, glancing around the next corner. It looked identical to the first flight and she glance back at the others as they neared the top.

Panting, Britney whispered, "Do you think there's any more of those things in here? I mean, Tommy couldn't have been the only kid in the building, right?"

Judy dismissed the question. They'd lived in the building for four years and had never seen another child. Some older teens, ya, but no children close to Tommy or Jamie's age.

Before Britney could elaborate, Judy started taking quick steps up the next flight. Britney took ahold of Jamie's hand and continued to follow at a slower pace. Half way up this section of steps, she looked ahead and saw Judy make the next turn without looking back. Britney's heart dropped and she fought back the urge to yell for her to wait.

Did she just leave us? No, she wouldn't do that, would she?

Britney's legs throbbed with pain, as she climbed faster, with one hand pulling on the railing and the other pulling Jamie. When she reached the top, she looked around the corner at the next flight. It was empty and she broke her silence.

"Judy! Wait for us!" her voice echoed up the stairway.

There was no reply from Judy and Britney swallowed hard and continued to climb, cursing her new friend, silently in her mind.

•••

On the fourth flight, Judy saw it. The bulb on the wall was flickering, but it still gave off enough light to see a dark red smear on the wall about half way up the steps. Judy's heart started to beat faster, as something familiar caught her eye on the steps below it, next to a mess of cigarette butts. A hypodermic needle. *The* hypodermic needle. She picked it up and turned it in her fingers.

It wasn't in my mind. He was chasing me.

Judy snapped out of her thoughts, as the sound of Britney's voice echoed up the stairway. Judy looked back toward the voice, then shot her glance up to the doorway at the top of the stairs ahead of her, expecting to see it standing there, with its eerie smile. The doorway was empty and she looked back down at the needle. An image of it sticking out of Bad Tommy's neck flashed in her mind and she dropped it to the steps, wiping her hand on her scrubs. She turned to head up the stairs, when she heard Britney's voice again. Her voice had a rough growl to it this time.

"Judy! Wait up, damn it!" Britney barked.

Judy looked back and saw Britney pulling Jamie up the stairs toward her. She watched them come for a moment and then looked back at the doorway above without responding. Britney was sucking in gulps of air as she approached.

"Judy, what the hell! Why'd you take off like that? What's the—" Britney stopped when Judy quickly shushed her. Britney gawked at her for a second, then continued at a near whisper.

"What do you mean '*shhh*'? I'm scared shitless here and you left us. If that things alive it probably knows we're here anyways."

"It is alive. It made it down the stairs this far at least," Judy said, in a calm voice, pointing at the blood smear on the wall, then to the needle on the floor. Britney looked at it with little interest, then back to Judy, opening her mouth to complain again. When she did, she saw Judy was making her way up the steps already. The teen closed her mouth and followed with her jaw clenched.

When they entered the hallway, the sounds of static filled the air. Nearly all the doors were open just enough to see the apartments were dark inside, with hints of a flicker of light radiating from the static of each television. Jamie's face puckered and she grabbed Britney's hand tighter. As they walked Britney noticed small smears of blood around the doorknobs they pasted. She could just make out the tinny fingers and her heart started to beat faster.

So small. Its hands are so small. Seeing Jamie like that was bad enough, but I can't imagine seeing a little five year old... I don't want to see it.

Britney looked at Judy ahead of her. The gun had appeared in her hand and she could see that it wasn't shaking. She instantly regretted silently cursing her before.

She looks pissed. Poor Judy. This must be so hard. I can't imagine.

Before Britney finished the thought, Judy stopped in front of doorway. The door was ajar and Britney swallowed hard, knowing they had reached the one they came for. Before she could take a breath, Judy walked through the door without a look back at them.

Britney stood there for a moment listening. She looked at Jamie. The little girl gave her a pitiful smile. One that seemed to say 'Here we go again'. Britney looked past Jamie, down the hall. The smell was awful and the opened doors were creeping her out.

It could really be behind any of those doors, staring at us right now.

She couldn't stand the thought of waiting in the hall, while only God knows what was happing inside. She looked back at Jamie. For a moment, the little girl was looking down the hallway as well, then her gaze went to Britney, almost as if the ten year old knew what she was thinking.

"What the hell. We came this far right?" Britney whispered. "Should we follow her?"

Jamie shrugged her shoulders and looked to the open door. A second later, they walked through it, holding each other's hands tight.

✧

Chapter 6.

Judy crept into the apartment and stopped, standing in the same spot she was when she had seen Pete pointing the gun into the living room. That had been a little over a day ago, but it seemed like weeks to her now. She clinched the gun tight in her hand and poked her head around the corner, scanning the room.

It was almost as Judy had left it, other than the brain numbing static crackle that replaced the sounds of cartoon hijinks. It made it hard to concentrate, but she thought she could hear another sound. A dripping sound, accompanied by a slow, rhythmic raspy sound.

Drip Drip Drip

She knew she shouldn't have been able to hear this, but for some reason she couldn't ignore it. She wondered briefly if Britney and Jamie would have heard it if they were there. The raspy sound, reminded her of breathing, but Bad Tommy was nowhere in sight. An eerie feeling told her he was in the room. Judy could sense it somehow. Sense that he was staring at the TV. She looked at the couch, where Pete was hunched over, as if he had fallen asleep, drunk or high. Her ears told her that the sound was coming from the floor at his feet, in front of the couch. She stepped into the room with the gun drawn and made her way in that direction.

Judy's eyes fixed on the hall entryway. At the end of it, across from his own room, her little boy, her good Tommy, was tucked away in the dryer, dead, but not for long. The *thumping* sound was absent, telling her that the dryer wasn't running. A feeling of relief washed over her.

Mommy's here to get you, baby, Judy thought. *Don't worry, Mommy's here. I just have to take care of something first.*

Judy came around the side of the couch and her eyes went to Pete again. It was hard for them not too. She never thought she would see him again. Until this moment, she didn't think she would want to.

He didn't really deserve any of this either.

Her eyes left Pete and drifted down to the thing lying on the floor at his feet. Bad Tommy lay sprawled out flat on his back, with his head unnaturally propped up against the bottom of the couch, in an impossible looking position. The dripping sound stopped as soon as she looked at him, but the raspy breaths continued, as his chest moved up and down. The breathing didn't sound like a little boys breathing and the thing didn't look like Tommy anymore.

His skin had taken on a grey color and seemed to be hanging off his bones. He didn't see her yet. His swollen eyes were glued to the TV and his finger was franticly pushing buttons at random on the remote control at its side. She could see the spot the needle had gone it his neck was swollen and red, with something leaking out of the center of the wound.

You strong little bastard. I'm so glad you're not dead...yet. After all you've put me through, you're going to help me now.

In the bad light, Judy saw something that made her skin crawl. To the left of Bad Tommy, Pete's feet dangled over the couch, nearly touching the floor. One of his feet, the left one, had been gnawed at. The meat looked like it had been eaten off clear to the bone in places. The fabric of his jeans was shredded up to his calf. The sight made Judy shiver.

Ran out of food, did you? Too weak to move, you little shit?

For some reason the thought of the thing suffering should have pleased Judy, but she exhaled deeply, as a feeling of sorrow surfaced for a split second. Judy closed her eyes and something in the handle of the gun made a cracking sound, as she clamped down tighter on it.

Judy saw Britney and Jamie enter the room out of the corner of her eye. Her concentration on Bad Tommy broke as she looked over at them. Britney's hand went up to her mouth as she let out a loud gasp. Despite the noise from the TV, Bad Tommy took notice he wasn't alone and rolled his eyes to Judy, turning his head slightly. A horrific smile came across his face.

"Mommy, you came back! I thought you didn't like me anymore," he said, in a deep, groggy voice. The sound reminded Judy of Richards baritone voice. It seemed too deep for the small body it was coming from.

Judy returned his smile. "Oh, I came back for you alright. Came back to finish what I started," Judy said, in a cold voice.

Britney stared at the grim scene, not knowing what to say. Jamie put her arms around Britney's waist and brought her face close to her hip. Neither of them could take their eyes off the thing, until Judy spoke. Her next words snapped their attention from Bad Tommy, to her.

"Watch that thing, I'll be right back," she said, flatly.

Britney and Jamie's eyes widened.

Judy moved to the other side of the room, sliding the gun back into the pocket of her scrubs. Without warning, she disappeared around the corner and down a hallway. Britney watched her vanish and looked back to Bad Tommy. His eyes met hers and he smiled sweetly. One of his eyes had a glazed over appearance, foggy and whitish. She looked away for a second, then back to the eye again. It was impossible not to stare. The eye seemed to call her back and hold her gaze.

What is she doing in there? God, you couldn't have given me the gun, Judy, Britney thought. *Wait, that thing can't even move. It looks like its dying. I think we're ok.*

Britney's eyes were locked on Bad Tommy when she had the thought and her tense body relaxed a bit. Without warning, he began to move and her eyes widened. He partially turned on his side and groaned involuntarily, as if the change of position squeezed air out of his body. Britney's heart jumped and she felt Jamie's hands clench on to her tighter, as the little girl buried her face into her hip.

"No! You stay there, T-T-Tommy!" Britney stuttered out. "Don't move!" A second later, she called Judy's name across the apartment, as she took a step backward. Bad Tommy clawed the floor in her direction and Britney thought about bolting out the way she had come.

This is bull shit! Where the hell did she go?

Britney stood her ground another few seconds, until Judy came back into the room. She opened her mouth to say something; to complain about being left again, when she saw what Judy had in her arms. The sight made her mouth shut and her jaw clench tight.

In Judy's arms, she held a small body. Even after the story Judy had told her, it looked worse than Britney could have imagined. How Judy had picked Tommy up without him falling apart was a mystery.

Bad Tommy stopped reaching toward Britney when he saw Judy walk into the room. The smile brightened on his face. Then, he noticed what she was holding and the innocent smile turned into a sinister one. All it took was a narrowing of its eyes and a curve of its lips for the smile to transform.

Judy walked carefully to the middle of the room, took her foot and placed it under the edge of the coffee table, still littered with Styrofoam meat containers. In one swift motion, Judy kicked the table out of the way. It made one spin in the air and collided against the wall with a bang that made Britney jump.

The table left a gouge in the wall. Britney couldn't believe how easily Judy kicked it away, as if it were an empty cardboard box. She looked back to Judy, just in time to see her settle Tommy's burned body gently on the floor where the table had sat.

"I have to get this just right if I want to bring you back, honey. We may only have one shot," Judy said, calmly to her son. Judy never gave Britney nor Jamie a second look since fist seeing them come in, as if they weren't in the room. It made Britney wish they had waited in the hall. This all seemed very personal, as if she and Jamie were crashing a candle light dinner between two lovers.

Britney's thoughts were interrupted, when Judy unharnessed a back pack she had slung over her shoulder and tossed it in her direction. Britney barely caught it by the straps, with a surprised look on her face.

"Here, hold on to that!" Judy said, flatly.

Britney thought, *What's she gonna to do? I mean, I know what we came to do, but this seems so unreal.*

Britney eyed her suspiciously for a moment, until Judy turned and took a step toward Bad Tommy. When Britney realized what Judy intended to do, her eyes went wide.

Without hesitation, Judy grabbed Bad Tommy by the left foot and yanked hard, pulling his body across the floor. A blood curling squeal escaped Bad Tommy's lips and Britney watched as he clawed at the wood floor with his nails, as Judy pulled him a few feet. Britney cringed and brought both her hand up to plug her ears and she felt Jamie tense up against her hip. Bad Tommy continued to squeal and grunt as Judy struggled, pushing and pulling, until the two small bodies were lying side by side. When she was done, she stood up straight and looked at the two of them, with her hands resting on her hips. Britney noticed she wasn't even breathing hard after the chore. Britney was breathing hard just watching it.

What's she doing? Let's just get this over with and get out of here, Judy!

Before Britney could open her mouth to convey the thought out loud, she saw the gun appear in Judy's hand. She watched as her new friend pointed it at the thing moving on the floor. Judy pulled the hammer back. Britney heard the click, closed her eyes and prepared for the shot.

The shot didn't come.

Instead, she heard Judy's voice whisper something. Under the static of the TV and groaning of Bad Tommy, Britney couldn't hear what it was and she didn't care. She kept her eyes closed and waited for the shot she knew would come.

"You killed my little boy!" Judy whispered to the thing. "You tricked me! I didn't see you before, but I see you now."

There was a moment of silence, before Bad Tommy let out a croak of laughter that echoed in the small apartment. He smiled and focused his eyes on Judy, while continuing to laugh. It was a hard thing to listen to and the gun twitched in Judy's hand as she winced.

"You see me?" Bad Tommy said, in a childish tone. "She sees me, she sees me!" The voice seemed to be coming from every corner of the room and Judy looked around the apartment, lowering the gun slightly. Bad Tommy continued to laugh as the voice faded. Suddenly the laughter stopped, as if Judy's ears vanished from her head and she looked back to the thing.

He was staring at her, with an odd look on his face. She could see its eye, the fogged over one, jiggling around in its socket, actually moving the skin as if it were about to explode. A feeling of terror clawed at her and the gun started to slip out of her hand. She caught a grip on it at the last second and brought it back up just as he spoke again. This time the voice was coming from its lips and the eye continued to shake.

"You don't know what you're seeing, Judy. You have been blind for years. You have neglected your little boy in favor of that prick drug dealer. You lost your mind a long time ago! And now you have lost your son! "

For some reason, what the thing said, hit Judy in the guts like a fist and she fought the urge to go to her knees. It was almost as if the thing were pulling its words out of her own head. A feeling of guilt washed over her.

He's right! I have neglected Tommy. I even got him taken away from me a few years ago and barely got him back. I swore then that I would leave Pete. Leave Pete and the drugs, take Tommy and disappear. But I didn't. I stayed and now I've lost Tommy again.

Judy tried to squeeze the trigger of the gun, but she found she couldn't. Like the eye in Bad Tommy's socket, the gun began to shake in her hand. She lowered it and gawked at the eye. Suddenly, it felt as if her thoughts were plucked from her head and she glanced around the room.

Oh my God, what's going on? Where am I? What's happened?

"Why look there, Judy. Look what you did to your *precious* little boy," Bad Tommy grumbled to her. His eyes went to the couch when he said it and Judy's followed. There on the couch, Pete's body had been replaced with Tommy's. The little boy had blood dried to his head and his eyes were rolled back deep in his skull.

"Tommy! No!" Judy screamed, dropping the gun. She took a few unsteady steps toward the couch.

Judy's scream caused Britney to open her eyes. She saw Judy go to her knees on the couch cushions and take Pete's body in her arms. Judy began to sob and she wiped the hair from Pete's forehead, as if he were a child and not the man Judy had described to her earlier. The bad man with a hot temper and worse habits. The tuff guy. Britney looked at her confused. She hadn't heard what was being said. She looked back to Bad Tommy. He was chuckling as he watched Judy. Britney scanned the room and her eyes fixed on the gun lying on the floor at its feet.

Judy continued to sob, "Oh my God, Tommy, what have I done? I'm so sorry, baby, Mommy didn't mean to!" She continued to rub Pete's forehead. Images of her bashing Tommy in the head with the snow globe over and over, flooded into her mind.

I have gone mad and killed my little boy! My good little Tommy!

Britney could barely hear Judy's over the static of the TV and the sinister chuckle, but could hear enough to understand what was going on.

Oh, shit! She thinks that's Tommy. It's tricking her. It's messing with her mind somehow.

She pried Jamie's arms from around her hips, dropped the pack on the floor by the wall and moved toward the gun on the floor, eyeing Bad Tommy as she went.

Jamie ducked behind the wall and peered back around the corner just as Britney snatched the gun from the floor. She saw Britney raise it in front of her and point it at the bad thing.

Without taking her eyes off Bad Tommy, Britney spoke in a shaky voice. "Judy! That isn't Tommy! It's Pete! It's all in your head, Judy! Please wake up!"

In an instant, the sinister chuckle ceased and Bad Tommy's attention focused on Britney. Its eyes seemed to slice into her like a knife and she gasped. Her hand started to tense up and before she knew it, she was squeezing it so tight, droplets of blood started to run down the handle. She glanced at it and back to Bad Tommy. One of his eyes shook in its socket.

Suddenly, it was as if the gun were burrowing itself into her hand and she couldn't stop squeezing it. Then, to her horror, the gun tilted away from Bad Tommy and made its way towards her own head. A second later she felt the barrel push against her temple and her finger started to pull the trigger back. Britney tried, but couldn't stop it. She let out a shriek and attempted to duck her head away from the barrel. Bad Tommy smiled and began to giggle.

Jamie watch this with wide eyes. She looked back at the front door, then back to Judy, Britney and the bad thing on the floor.

Oh my God! I have to do something! Or should I run? Mommy and Daddy would want me to run.

Jamie stared off into space, thinking, when something came into focus. On the ground, half way across the room, lied a snow globe. It was rocking back and forth, making the snow inside move like a wave. Her mother collected them and had them scattered about their apartment, but here was something about this one. Something she couldn't put her finger on. Something that made her skin crawl. Jamie stared at it for a moment, when suddenly there was a gun shot and the drywall next to her head exploded. She fell back on the kitchen floor, stunned by the noise. Without thinking, Jamie scrambled to her knees and headed for the front door.

Britney opened her eyes. Her ears were ringing. The gun had jerked away from her head a split second before going off. She glanced at Judy. She was sitting on the couch, holding Pete's dead body, rocking back and forth silently. Next her eyes moved to Bad Tommy. He was smiling at her. She had control of her hands again and quickly dropped the gun and backed up a few steps.

He did that on purpose!

Before she finished the thought, Bad Tommy's voice creeped into her head. Its lips weren't moving and she could feel her mind being probed.

Of course I did. You don't think I would let you die that easily do you? Besides, you have company, Britney!

Bad Tommy said the last few words savagely and the room shifted before Britney's eyes.

•••

Britney tried to move her arms and couldn't. They were bound behind her. She looked around and recognized where she was instantly. She was back in the Porters spare room, sitting on the bed.

Oh my God...what is this? This can't be. I was just... I mean, I was with...

She struggled to remember where she had been and who she was with, but couldn't. Slowly, she started to hear footsteps approaching the other side of the closed door. Britney recognized the clunky sound. They were Mr. Porter's work boots. Suddenly she knew what was about to happen, but didn't know why she remembered. Mr. Porter was going come in and sit next to her. He was going to talk to her gently in his creepy deep voice and then try to try to fondle her. She wasn't sure why she knew this. It was almost as if it had happened before and terror struck her. She glanced behind her and saw a pair of hand cuffs around her wrists. She looked down and saw a similar pair were around her ankles.

Knock Knock Knock

The three distinctive knocks on the door made Britney eyes squeeze shut. She had heard this knock before as well.

"Britney, you ok in there, honey? Want some company? I'm awfully lonely," The deep baritone voice asked.

Britney's eyes opened and went to the door, as she heard Mr. Porter fiddling with the pad lock on the other side. She began to pull on her wrists, trying to slide them out. It was no use. She was trapped this time and nothing would stop Mr. Porter from doing whatever he wanted with her.

A feeling of claustrophobia ripped through her and she let out a scream. She could feel the scream vibrate in her throat but couldn't hear it in her head. She squeezed her eyes shut, trying to will whatever was happening away. She heard footsteps enter the room; they seemed to echo in her mind, then the bed shifted as he sat down next to her. Before she could think, she felt his breath on her neck and she let out another silent scream.

As silent as they seemed in the Porters spare room, Britney's scream weren't silent in the apartment. Jamie stopped half way down the hallway when she heard the first one and peered back at the opened door.

I can't leave them. Mommy would have wanted me to go back. Daddy would have told me to run, but Mommy would want me to be brave, like she was.

Jamie took awkward steps back in the opened doors direction. When she heard the second scream, she started to run.

"No Mr. Porter! Please no!" Britney's voice echoed down the hall. Jamie entered the doorway at a run and stopped just inside the kitchen. She crept to the wall and looked around it, into the living room.

Britney was on her knees, with her hands behind her back. She was mumbling between her sobs, with her eyes squeezed shut.

"Please don't Mr. Porter. Please don't do this! I love Jamie. How could you do this to me?"

Britney slowly maneuvered, without the use of her hands, until she was lying on her back. It almost looked to Jamie as if she were being laid down by an invisible pair of arms. Next, Britney's shirt began to move as if there were a pair of hands caressing her from underneath. Her mouth was clinched shut, tight enough to turn the edges of her lips whitish. A few muffled sob escaped them.

Jamie looked past Britney to Judy. The woman had the body of a man in her arms and she was rocking back and forth. Her lips were moving and Jamie knew she was singing to him. She could almost hear the song in her mind. She stared at them and without knowing it, moved out from behind the wall and stood partially in the room. Her attention on the two woman broke when a deep voice said her name.

"Jamie."

The little girl's eyes snapped to the thing on the floor.

"Jamie, come in. You've been a good girl and I want to show you something."

Jamie couldn't take her eyes off the thing and could feel him trying to go into her thoughts.

He's tricking them! And now he's gonna try to tick me, but I won't let him...I can stop him...I think?

Images flashed in Jamie's mind, but she could tell they weren't as bad as he wanted them to be. She could feel his frustration and her body relaxed. Her heart slowed down and a smile crossed her lips. At that moment, she knew what it was trying to do to her and why it couldn't.

Bad Tommy let out a deep breath he had been holding, sucked in another gulp and pushed harder. Jamie could see the strain on his haggard face.

"You can't trick me like your tricking them," Jamie said, in a calm voice. "Nothing you can show me could be worse than what I've already seen."

Bad Tommy snickered at the comment.

"What have you seen, girl? Please, try to remember. I want to see these thing *you* say are worse!" Bad Tommy closed its eyes, waiting for her thoughts to enter his mind. It waited for her trivial memories to flow.

Jamie focused her eyes on Bad Tommy. She knew it would be able to see her thoughts. She didn't know why she knew, she just knew. Images started to flash in her mind. More important than the images, were the feelings that came with them. Some of it was hers, but most of it was the other Jamie's; the bad one who came from the same place as this thing. Somehow Jamie had retained some of its memories, like ghostly glimmers on the top of a deep dark pond. When you look close, you can see what the bottom looks like from the top of the water, but it's hazy and unclear. When you dunk your head in, it looks different, more real. That's what she was doing now, dunking her head in and the images and feelings started to flow through her and into Bad Tommy's mind, like a VHS tape playing in fast forward. When she saw something coming she wanted to emphasize, she concentrated on elongating it, if only for an extra second.

Bad Tommy flinched, clawing the floor with his out stretched hands. He saw the catacombs under the earth and felt the loneliness and fear he had festered in for too long. A hundred years' worth of dread and longing. Hunger and boredom. He had already forced these memories out of his head and replaced them with whimsical music, bright colors and the mineral taste of blood. Seeing them now, was like reliving them all over again and all at once.

"No! Stop! How are you doing that?" Bad Tommy tried to break the bond and let out a horrible screech when he failed.

He saw the darkness and could smell the unending stench. Bad Tommy's eyes and nose started to run. Without warning, his stomach clenched and a howl escaped his lips. An unforgiving feeling of hunger bared down hard, as if all he had eaten was ripped out of its stomach, leaving it empty and hollow.

"No! Stop! I don't want to feel that again!" Bad Tommy cried out. "How can you know this anguish, you have not felt this pain! You can't know it!"

Jamie focused harder. "You forgot what it feels like, you mean thing, but I can show it to you because I was there, where that little boy is now," Jamie said, in a flat voice, motioning to the body lying next to him. "You need to go back where you came from. It's where you belong. It's what you deserve."

Jamie focused harder, pushing the images forward like a nasty gift. Bad Tommy saw himself, alive and happy, just as Jamie had been. Then Jamie ripped it away, just as it had been taken from her. It was a feeling so bad, that it made Jamie afraid to live again, but she kept it fresh in her mind and sent all of this to the thing lying on the floor. It howled in pain.

Bad Tommy felt what it was like to have something as beautiful as life jerked away from him. Jamie let up for a moment, giving him a brief second of relief. She needed to take a breath and Bad Tommy sucked in a gulp of air as well. Then, the next second, Jamie focused on ripping the good feelings away again, replacing them with hunger, sorrow and pain. She did this over and over, causing Bad Tommy to heave and retch into the air. Mucus and blood shot from its mouth and came down with a wet splat on the floor. Jamie ignored the horrid sight and continued to stream images into Bad Tommy's brain. She could feel its bond on Judy and Britney weakening.

"No! You can't!" Bad Tommy screamed. "Jamie, you stop that right now, young lady!" It sounded like a woman's voice and Jamie recognized it as her mothers. Hearing it gave her a moment of doubt. Just enough for Bad Tommy to gain a moment of leverage.

Jamie cringed, as a series of images and feeling rushed back at her. She saw Judy take the snow globe she had noticed earlier in her hands and bash a man in the head with it. Judy hit the man over and over until he stopped moving and blood started to pool around his head. The next second, Jamie saw Judy bashing her father in the face with a dresser drawer. She saw his body fall through the air. She saw him thump to the ground and gasped, "No, Daddy!" These images were quick and sharp and Jamie let out a grunt as she tried to push them away.

The feed of images slowed down and Jamie saw Britney in her parent's bathroom, calmly taking money out of her father's wallet, as his voice sang behind the shower curtain. The next instant, Jamie seemed to be looking through her fathers eyes, as he snuck up behind her mother with the butt of his gun raised in the air. Jamie had seen this before, but not from this angle. The gun came down and she felt the vibration in her own hand, as it collided with her mother's scull.

"No! Oh, Mommy, I'm sorry!" Jamie cried out. It was the worst of the images and did the job Bad Tommy wanted it to do. Jamie struggled to gain control. With her teeth clenched, she felt anger well up inside of her. Her eyes shot open and she bared down hard on Bad Tommy. She focused on the fogged over eyeball wiggling in its socket. Bad Tommy let out a shriek and Jamie felt his control begin to slip away again.

Jamie spared a glance at Britney. She was still lying on the floor. The cloth of her shirt was motionless, but twisted and folded, showing part of her stomach and a bit of her bra. Whatever was happening to her had stopped and Jamie could see her chest rising and falling peacefully.

Oh please, wake up! I don't think I can do this much longer!

More images were rushing by in Jamie's head, as if she were looking out the window of a fast moving train. She started to feel overwhelmed.

After a quick glance back to Bad Tommy, she looked to Judy. She had stopped rocking and was glancing around the room with a blank look on her face. Jamie took a relieving breath at the sight and her eyes lingered for too long. She felt Bad Tommy start to slip away from her. She shot her eyes back to the thing on the floor and focused, stabbing his mind deeper. When she did, she noticed the fogged over eye had stopped jiggling in its socket and she knew its bond to her friends was weakening. She knew she was winning.

•••

Judy looked around the room. Her body was caked in sweat and she could feel weight on her body. She looked down and saw

Pete's dead eyes looking back up at her. She shuttered and pushed his body off of her lap. There was a lot of noise coming from the TV and it was hard to concentrate. The room was dark and she felt half asleep; groggy, as if she had been on an all-night drinking binge. Her head was pounding. She glanced around the room and focused on the first person that caught her eye. A young woman lying on the floor. Her hair was wild and had streaks of pink and blue.

I know you.

Judy struggled to bring a memory into the blankness in her head.

You name is Brandy, Judy thought. *No, that isn't right.*

"It's Brit…Britney. Your name is Britney," Judy said, to herself. She glanced at the other bodies, turning her head carefully. They were just silhouettes in the bright static of the TV. It hurt her eyes to look at them, but she could see that one of them was standing and two were side by side on the floor.

Jamie?

The name popped into her head easily. Then before she knew what she was saying, she blurted "Tommy!"

Her memories came flooding back into her head like a thimble being filled with a tea pitcher and she sprang up from the couch. She started to move in Jamie's direction and stopped.

Oh my God. What is she doing?

Under the static of the TV, Judy could hear that Bad Tommy was groaning in pain. He looked like he was dying. Judy squinted her eyes and looked at Jamie's face. The little girl was focused on the monster and somehow hurting it.

She's killing it, Judy marveled. *How is she doing that?*

Judy didn't say the thought out loud, but heard Jamie's voice answer her.

"I'm not really doing it, he is and I don't think he can stop! It hurts," Jamie said, through a whimper. "Hurry, do something!"

Judy looked at Bad Tommy, as he started to move. Blackish liquid streamed out of his mouth as he turned over and started to pull his way across the floor. He looked like a zombie from one of those old horror movies Judy hated. The horrid thing looked up at her and gargled a few words.

"Mommy, help me! She's hurting me, Mommy. I didn't mean to be ba—"

Jamie pushed hard and the gargling words stopped. Bad Tommy's movements slowed. Judy just stood and gawked.

Jamie's strained voice pleaded, "Hurry, Judy! It's getting really hard! I can't hold him much longer!"

Judy franticly scanned the room.

Come on! Where is it? There's one bullet left!

The thought prompted Jamie to speak again. "There isn't a bullet in it. Britney fired it already. Hurry, I feel dizzy!"

Then an unknown voice whispered in Judy's mind.

Use the snow globe!

The voice sounded strangely like her own and Judy's skin crawled at the thought of using it to bash another skull in. She would never forget the *thump* sound it made against Pete's head. She looked around the room before spotting it on the floor at her feet. She reached down and snatched the snow globe up. The weight of it felt familiar in her hand and she moved in Bad Tommy's direction with her fingers clenching it tight. Bad Tommy laid face down on the carpet, breathing deeply in and out. Jamie's feet were just out of his reach.

Judy went down hard on her knees beside the things quivering body. She took the snow globe in both hands and started to raise it over her head. She could hear Jamie groaning now as well. As the globe past in front of her face, it looked as if something inside the glass moved. Judy stopped and gaped at it in the darkness. It was her reflection, but it didn't have the haggard cringe she felt was on her face. The small distorted Judy in the glass was laughing hysterically. Judy's eyes grew wide and she felt an urge to throw the thing across the room, ridding her hand of it. Just when she started to think it was just her eyes playing tricks on her, the reflection stopped laughing and gazed at her in a terrifying stare. It seemed to look right through her. Without thinking, Judy closed her eyes, raised the globe above her head and brought it down on the back of Bad Tommy's skull with all of her strength. The glass exploded in her hand, sending a mixture of water and blood in a spider web shaped splatter across the carpet.

Jamie convulsed, snapping her eyes open as she took a few steps back. She lost control of her legs and went down on her butt, turned and quickly crawled to Britney's motionless body.

Judy watched Jamie flee and wanted to ask if she was ok. Could feel the words trying to come out, but her throat wouldn't make a sound. Remembering how Jamie heard her thoughts a moment ago, she sent one to her instead.

Jamie are you alright? Can you hear me?

Jamie looked at her, with a slight smirk on her face. It seemed to say 'Yes, I'm alright, thanks to you'. Before Judy could smile back, Jamie moved her attention back to Britney. She proceeded to tilt Britney's head up with one hand and lightly tap her cheek with the other. Judy saw Britney's eyelashes flutter, a split second before the teen's eyes jerked open. She looked around the room, as if she had been somewhere else. For all Judy knew, maybe she was.

Judy eyes went back to Jamie and she sent another thought in the little girl's direction.

Did you hear me a moment ago, Jamie. Or was that smile just a coincidence?

Her eyes narrowed on the little girl. *I kind of need to know if you're in my head.*

Judy watched her carefully and didn't see a response from the little girl. Not even a flinch. She slowly moved her eyes back to the thing lying on the floor next to her. It looked like something out of a child massacre scene. The back of the skull was cracked and blackish liquid was oozing out, seeping into the carpet. Next to it, was her son, Tommy. He still looked worse than the oozing corps at his side.

Judy watched, with an intense look on her face, waiting for the mist to come and bring her boy back to her. Her heart beat quickened. Her mouth began to water and a sinister part of her; a part that was new to her, not only wanted her boy back, but also wanted the peppermint taste in her mouth again. She wanted to feel the adrenalin. For a moment, part of Judy's mind raced at the thought of the mist and Tommy was forgotten.

Just one more hit. I may never get another one.

Her mind toyed with the thought for a moment and her attention crept back to her little boy.

No! I can't. The mist is for him, not me! How could I even think of that right now?

Then after a few deep breaths. *What's wrong with me? I still want it!*

Judy continued to stare at the mist.

Jamie had her arms around Britney's neck, making it hard for her to catch a breath. Despite that fact, she hugged back until the little girl let her loose. When she did, Britney slowly sat up, took Jamie's small hand in hers and scanned the scene. Judy was still on her knees over the two small bodies in the middle of the room.

In a groggy voice, Britney said, "What happened? Did we do it? Is it over?"

Before anyone had a chance to reply, the mist started to seep from Bad Tommy's corps. It instantly started to swirl around the two small bodies at Judy's knees. Britney quickly scrambled to her feet, absently rubbing her soar wrists. Jamie watched as she turned them in her hands. There were red scratches around them as if she had been tied up or cuffed.

Judy watched the mist build up and start to engulf both bodies. She could smell it. The tangy peppermint scent invaded her nostrils and her heart started to race. She wanted her boy back, but it seemed impossible. Looking at him now, she couldn't see how he could be healed. Sure, Jamie had been healed by it and Judy's own hand had been miraculously healed, but Tommy's whole entire body was a wound, red and pink, with the skin cracked and hanging loose in places. It seemed impossible, but as the mist circled him, twisting and curling around his limbs, she saw the skin begin to tighten. It was like watching a body decay in reverse.

The static on the TV started to burp and flicker. Britney jumped at first, having forgotten how it did it in the other apartment. She stared at it for a moment and then back to the two small bodies on the floor. Just in the short amount of time she glanced away from them, the real Tommy was starting to look better. More like a person than burnt corpse. She could see now that he was blond, just like his father and probably cute as a button. She smiled, knowing how this must be making Judy feel.

Good for you Judy. You got your son back.

Then after a moment. *We got him back. You were right, Judy. Even if it was a little freaky and we almost got killed again, I'm glad we came back for him. We saved him. We did it!*

As she looked at Judy, Britney's smile began to quiver and a tear rolled down her dirty cheek. She looked down at Jamie. The little girl was looking to the center of the room and Britney couldn't tell if she was smiling or not. She pictured that she was and gave her quivering hand a comforting squeeze.

Jamie didn't squeeze back and she wasn't smiling. She was focused on the back of Judy's head. She knew she shouldn't be, but she was listening to Judy's mind race back and forth. It scared her. She didn't know how she was doing it and she couldn't stop. Her eyes went to the little boy they had come to save, in hopes it would stop if she looked away from Judy. The thoughts dimmed, but she could still hear them whispering.

Tommy was almost back to his normal self and the bad one had taken on a transparent look. The mist made them both hard to see, but sitting as close as she was, Judy could see them just fine. It was only a matter of time before the horrid thing would be gone, either dead or sucked back to where it came from. Judy's breathing slowed and her week muscles relaxed as she stared at the mist twirling in front of her eyes. It seemed to be teasing her and her mind continued to swirl with it.

It's almost over and the mist will be gone. Maybe one more sniff won't hurt. I may need it to get out of here.

No, I can't! This isn't the reason I came here. I don't need it. Jamie said it was bad stuff.

What does she know, she's only a kid!
I should be a good mother and let it alone, but I want it.
I need it.

The mist seemed to understand her thoughts; seemed to sympathize with her dilemma. Judy watched as part of it, a very small part, swirled around and formed what looked like a three fingered hand. The hand beckoned her, curling one smoky digit into a 'Come here, have me if you like' gesture. Judy took a look out of the corner of her eye and saw that Britney and Jamie couldn't see it from where they were standing. She turned her eyes back to the mist and leaned forward.

Behind her, Jamie looked down at the floor, with a frown on her face. *Please don't do it, Judy,* she thought. *It's bad! Please don't do it. It's bad, stay away from it.*

Jamie repeated this over and over in her mind, but she could feel that Judy couldn't hear it. The mist had her and its voice was more enticing than her own.

Judy remembered what Jamie had said; that the mist was bad and to stay away from it. She could almost hear the little girl's voice now, whispering in the background 'It's bad, stay away from it', but she couldn't help it, she wanted more. A devilish smirk filled Judy's face and she leaned further forward ever so slightly. As soon as she did, the mystical fingers joined and swirled in her direction. Judy closed her eyes and inhaled deeply, letting the sweet peppermint flavor in. It didn't stop at her lungs, but seemed to race through her whole body until she could actually feel a minty tingle it in her fingertips. All the hairs on her body fluttered, tickling her skin and her muscles tensed up. Her body quivered in delight.

Oh my! Yes, oh yes! More! I can feel every inch of my body screaming in delight. Oh my, this is better than an orgasm!

After a moment she knew she needed a breath, but didn't want to stop. For what seemed like minutes instead of seconds, it was just her and the mist. No one else existed.

"Mommy, no!" a small voice erupted from in front of her. "Don't do it, Mommy!"

Judy's eyes snapped open and saw Tommy sitting up, with a horrible look on his face. Other than being a little dirty, he looked good; alive and alert, but close to tears. Judy stopped inhaling abruptly and struggled for air. She gagged and cleared her throat as Tommy's arms came up and wrapped themselves around her neck. His face pushed into her bosom as muffled words escaped his lips.

"Mommy, pwease no! Don't let the bad thing get in you!"

Judy opened her mouth to speak and couldn't make any sound come out. She attempted to clear her tingling throat again. It felt raw and had an overwhelming taste of peppermint, as if it were saturated in mouthwash. Her arms felt like rubber bands about to snap and she couldn't bring them up to hug him back. They trembled with effort. She felt paralyzed, as if her little boy were hugging a stone statue of a bad mother. She could do nothing to comfort him.

Oh God, what did I do? Why did I do that!

Tommy eased his hold around her neck and brought his face away from her body. In a small, mousey voice, he said, "Mommy, are you ok. You not talkin to me? Pwease, Mommy, pick me up, I don't want it to get me again!"

At that, Judy took a deep breath, focusing on her limbs and her body seemed to relax. She brought her arms up and around him, squeezed and picked him up. She managed to spit out a few words as she moved them away from the mist. To her, the words sounded like croaks coming from a frogs mouth and felt like it too.

"I'm ok, honey. Don't you worry, everything is gonna be fine now."

"But Mommy, you let the smoke get in you," Tommy said. "Now they're gonna come for you. And you're talking funny, Mama."

Judy tried to collect every drop of spit in her dry mouth with her tongue and swallowed hard. Her mouth was as dry as a wad of peppermint sawdust. She stared off into space for a moment, thinking. *If they do, they do, at least you're safe now. So just you hush now and don't worry about what you don't understand...Boy!*

A shiver ran across Judy's skin.

Boy? Why did I just call him 'Boy'? I never call him 'Boy'. Pete called him 'Boy' all the time and I hated it!

The thought perplexed her. He was her 'sweet Tommy' or her 'honey boy', but never just '*Boy*'.

"Mommy, you're hurting me. You're squeezen me too much!" Tommy's voice sounded raspy and forced. Then after a short pause, he pushed away from her chest to look at her. "You're okay, right Mommy?"

It didn't feel to Judy like she was squeezing that hard, but she eased her hold on him. He squirmed in her arms slightly.

Judy cleared her throat one final time and felt the croakiness ease up. When she spoke again, her voice wasn't quite normal, but close.

"I'm sorry, honey."

Tommy eyed her suspiciously and after a short pause, she added, "I just missed you so much! Mommy's been looking everywhere for you, honey boy!"

Judy saw relief in his eyes and she could tell his mind was at ease for the moment. He buried his face into her bosom again and she looked across the room at the others. They were both standing wide eyed, watching the mist do its dance. Judy made her way in their direction.

Judy could hear the static on the TV sputtering like it had before. At that moment, she didn't want to look back at the mist for two reasons. First; she knew what Jamie had said was right, the mist was bad stuff and she shouldn't have messed with it. Second; she didn't want to see it go. She still wanted it and knew she may never see it again.

"Ok Let's go, before anything else happens!" Judy said, picking up the backpack from the floor. Britney and Jamie looked at her, then back to the mist. Judy gave them an evil glare.

Why are you both just standing there? Don't you see I got my boy back! We did what we came to do, now move!

"Well, come on! We're done here!" Judy snapped. The rough sound of her voice made the two girls take notice and Britney brought her hand up, pointing to the other side of the room.

"I don't think we *are* done yet, Judy. Look at that!"

Judy rolled her eyes and glanced behind her. The mist was still swirling around in the middle of the room and at first she didn't know what Britney meant. Then she saw it and her muscles tightened.

Bad Tommy's body was vanishing and the mist was flowing away from it, in the direction of the TV, but some of it was flowing to Pete's body on the couch, as if it were a small creek splitting off from a misty river flowing across the living room. Judy's eyes went to the right foot, the one that had been nibbled away at. The flesh was red and blistered, but it was quickly starting to resemble a foot again. She looked up at the dead stare of Pete's eyes and a moment of terror struck her.

Oh God! If he wakes up, I'm in for it. Will he remember what I did? He won't understand why I did it and might flip out and try to hurt Tommy again. He might try to hurt us all. Besides, I don't want to deal with—

Judy nervously thought of what was in the bag hanging from her shoulder and her mind started to race, until it settled on one thought.

You can't come with us, Pete.

After a moment of gawking, Judy's face relaxed and she said, in a quiet voice, "We need to go, now."

Britney was the only one that heard it over the noise erupting from the TV. She looked at Judy with her head tilted.

"What did you say?"

"I said lets go, now, while we still can."

Britney looked at the body on the couch and then back to Judy. She spoke at a near whisper. "You mean you don't want to bring him along? We can't just leave him, can we?"

Judy looked her in the eyes and tried to put on a sympathetic face. "Believe me, we don't want him with us. We need to go." The look of sympathy started to fade on her face. Judy felt it happening, so she looked away, took Jamie by the hand and started to walk out of the room. On their way out, Judy spotted a pack of cigarettes on the counter. They were Pete's brand, the cheapest full flavor menthol you can buy. Next to them was the Zippo lighter Tommy had given him for Christmas. Tommy picked it out at a gas station because it had Pete's name printed on the front of it. Pete had pretended to like it a lot, which of course made Tommy very happy.

"Something to remember you by, Pete...you asshole," Judy said, quietly to herself. She snatched them up without stopping, put them in the front pocket of her scrubs and walked the kids out the door.

Britney looked back to the shirtless body on the couch. She remembered what Judy had said about Pete when they were locked up together in the Porter's spare room. He was mean, unreasonable, a drug addict and kind of a dick. But still, she felt guilty leaving anyone behind.

After all we just did to save Tommy, we're gonna just leave this guy behind?

Then after a moment, she thought, *maybe he'll be ok.*

Britney shrugged.

Good luck Pete.

After a moment, she realized she was by herself in the room and she quickly walked out, not sparing a look back.

✧

Chapter 7.

Britney stepped out of the apartment and saw that Judy and Jamie were at the end of the end of the hallway already and just entering the stairwell. She jogged in the middle of the hall, eyeing each doorway she past.

"Hey wait up!"

They didn't slow. She jogged faster, entered the stairwell and carefully started down the steps. Her legs were throbbing already. She caught up to the others just as they were nearing the bottom of the first flight.

"Thanks for waiting up, turds!"

This got a smile out of Jamie and a chuckle out of Tommy. It was the first smile she had seen on either of their faces and it seemed to relieve some tension.

As they came to the first landing, a popping sound echoed down the stairwell. It was the sound of the TV in Judy's apartment ceasing to function. They paused for a second and listened for any other noises. Jamie and Tommy glanced at each other with a questioning look. Judy and Britney didn't say it, but they were both listening for the same thing. A male voice. The sound of Pete's voice.

Judy had a thought.

Maybe he was so strung out when he died that he won't wake up, not right away anyways.

Then another thought invaded her mind. *Don't you mean; when you killed him. Just say it like it is, Judy. You killed him and you hope he doesn't ever wake up.*

Judy tightened her jaw, hard enough to make her teeth creak. *That's not true. I killed him to save Tommy. I didn't know…I mean, I loved Pete, but I thought he'd gone mad!*

Then why aren't you waiting for him now that you know he was sane? And why did you take all of his money and drugs?

Judy glanced at the strap of the nearly empty back pack slung over her shoulder.

We need the money and...well it's probably two grand worth of drugs. Maybe we can sell it to someone? I don't know, I just took it in case we need it.

She waited for a response and got none.

After a moment, no other sound followed them down the stairwell and they turned and continued downward, Judy carrying Tommy tight with one arm, Jamie close behind her holding her other hand and Britney at the rear.

They neared the bottom level and Britney let out a sigh of relief. Her legs were screaming. As they filed into the lobby, she looked down at Jamie. The little girl's eyes were lazy and she looked nervous.

Britney leaned toward her and whispered, "Are you ok, honey bunny?"

Jamie looked up at Judy for a split second, then to Britney, as if she didn't know who the whisper had come from. Britney didn't get the smile she expected from her. 'Honey bunny' usually got some sort of smirk out of her. Jamie just stared at her until Britney spoke again.

"Jamie, what is it? What's wrong?"

Jamie's eyes briefly flashed to Judy before she answered. "Nothing. I'm-I'm ok, just tired."

Britney watched her for a second, until Jamie's eyes left hers and went to the floor.

Britney thought, *She's been through a lot. I'm not even sure what happened in there, but I think she saved us all.*

She looked at the little girl for another moment.

But something's bothering her. She isn't acting like herself. Of course, who could after everything that's happened to her, I guess.

Next Britney watched as Judy opened the lobby door a few inches and peeked out. Britney noticed that no light was shining in through the crack and the cold wind was howling as it skipped across the opening. Just thinking about the cold gave her the chills.

How long were we in there I wonder? It can't be dark already, can it?

She looked around for a clock as the thought came to her, but quickly realized this lobby was too crappy for a clock. Her attention went back to Judy, when she heard the door snap shut.

Judy stood facing the door and let her forehead bump it lightly. She stayed that way for a moment before Britney spoke.

"Well, what is it? Are those things everywhere out there or something?" Britney said, in a deflated voice.

Judy looked over at her. Britney's eyes were like big, brown, trembling hubcaps, which seemed to say 'now what?'

"No, it's not that," Judy said, in a forced, scratchy voice. The peppermint flavor in her mouth was stronger than ever, as if her throat was coated in candy canes and the trek down the stairs strengthened it.

Britney looked down at Jamie. She was watching Judy wide eyed as well, as if the little girl knew what she was about to say.

I bet if I could read Jamie's mind, she knows what Judy's about to say. They're both acting so strange, that I wish I could.

Before Britney could finished the thought, Judy cleared her throat and continued.

"The military is everywhere and I don't see very many people out there. The ones I do see are being loaded into buses."

"What? Why?" Britney said.

"Maybe they're evacuating the city," Judy said, in a fake optimistic tone.

Jamie looked at her, narrowed her eyes and said, "Or quarantining it."

Judy looked at her as if a naughty word had escaped the little girl's mouth. Britney moved toward the door and Judy stepped to the side, putting her head down obediently. Britney opened the door just enough to see down the street, where there was in fact not only one bus, but a line of them that went around the corner. They were normal city buses, but the soldiers standing around them made them look very stern. The area was being illuminated by huge lights, but she couldn't tell where they were coming from. High from the top of one of the buildings she supposed.

Oh shit! It could be that or, like, from a space ship. Maybe they are aliens after all.

Her heart raced at the thought.

A small crowd of people were lined up along the side walk, leading up to the bus in the front. Most of the people were standing quietly, but some were putting up a fuss. A few of the soldiers had their rifles casually drawn, keeping the trouble makers in check. Most of the people weren't dressed for the cold weather and Britney could tell they'd been jerked out of whatever warm place they were in, suddenly and without warning.

Or they ran out because their kids started to freak out on them. When the TV went off and the other Jamie started to freak out, I would have ran outta there nude if I had too.

Britney jumped as something bumped the front of her jeans. She let out a whisper of a gasp and looked down. The top of Jamie's head had appeared in front of her and the little girl was fighting for an eyes view from the crack.

Britney whispered "Jamie, be careful, you scared the crap out of me!"

Jamie ignored her and peered out at the commotion. Her ears were better than Britney's; in fact they were better than they ever were before. A lot better. She could hear a dozen conversations, all mingled together in one noise. She saw one soldier talking to another and focused on them. The rest of the noise faded and she caught a little of their conversation.

One soldier said to the other, "We're never going to get all these assholes out before they wash the place. Half of them don't know what's going on."

The other soldier answered "Maybe it's better if they don't. Hell, I don't even know what's really going on. If what I was told is true, then we must be in some Twilight Zone episode or something. Who knows, maybe it's just—"

After a hiccup of static, a robotic voice interrupted them.

"Sarge, we just found another one. Looks like it could be a keeper. Kinda calm. Should we bag it and tag it?"

One of the soldiers took a radio from his belt and brought it up to his mouth "Negative. They said we have enough Eaters, just put it down if you need to and get out of there. You're only looking for adults, no kids. If you see a kid, I don't care if it looks like the little girl with dimples in the coke commercial, leave it and move on. Clear?"

After another static hiccup, the robot voice replied "Roger, we're sending eight more Normies to you."

The soldier harnessed the radio and turned back to the other man. "Great, more assholes on their way. Oh well, in another hour, every asshole better be on these buses or their ass gonna be Kentucky fried."

This got a chuckle out of the other man and the first man continued. "I don't even know why they're still checking buildings. I mean honestly, where do you move a whole city? It's like trying to move all the scum out of the ocean. Anyone who doesn't know to get on these buses by now, has got to be dumb or dead."

Jamie lost interest in the conversation, as commotion in the crowd erupted. A man was taken down to the ground by a third and fourth soldier. The disorderly man was cursing at the men in uniform and Jamie looked away with a cringe. Her eyes went back to the first couple of soldiers. They were looking at the commotion as well.

"I don't know why these jerks have to try to run, like we're not doing them a favor, letting them on these buses. After all, it's the only way out of here, except for the airport, that is."

"The airport? I thought they grounded all the planes," The other soldier asked, digging into the front pocket of his uniform. He pulled a cigarette from a pack and the other soldier watched as he lit it.

"No, they did. Zero flights in and zero out, but some of those rich bitches in Snobsdale didn't want to leave their Porsches. Threatened to sue. Someone caved and they're letting some folks out that way in their own cars, right off the end of the runway. As long as they scan clean, they're through, but they better have four wheel drive, cause there isn't anything but forest for miles and miles out that way."

The other soldier smiled, as he let out a smokey breath. The smoke drifted sideways in the chilly wind and Jamie watched as it disappeared.

The first soldier continued, "After we get the rest of these assholes wrapped up, we're out of here. I'd hate to be one of the poor suckers that get left behind. I don't care how nice a car I had, I'd be on those buses quicker than a rabbit's pecker."

This got a smile out of the second soldier, as he took another drag off his smoke. Both men stopped talking and Jamie's attention moved on.

She looked at the crowd of people and focused on the front of the line.

In a whisper, Jamie said, " Look at that. They are making them look at a machine before they get on the bus."

Britney's eyes went directly where Jamie's were and she saw the little girl was right. The people were being scanned by some device before being let on. They watched for a moment to see what happened in anyone was rejected. No one was.

Britney turned and looked back just as Judy was adjusting Tommy in her arms. He was lazy eyed, but watching everyone as they moved around the small lobby. Britney spoke in a tone that wasn't like her. A serious one.

"Do you think they will be able to tell that the kids are…" she paused and struggled for the right word. Judy finished the sentence for her.

"Infected?" Judy spoke in a cold tone. "Probably. What else would they be looking for, Britney?"

The voice spoke up in Judy's head.

You know what else they might be looking for, Judy. You don't think they know what the mist does to people? All those gun shots before. How many do you think they shot? One of them must have seen it or tasted it, Judy.

Despite the unwelcome voice in her head, Judy kept a straight face as Britney continued to speak.

"Do you think they *are* infected? I mean, I thought they were ok now."

Judy stared at her, but before she could answer, Jamie spoke up "No, it's not the kids. Look, there are no kids. One man told the other man that they were leaving all the kids. He called them Eaters."

Britney asked, "How do you know that?"

"Because I heard them say it," Jamie said, timidly.

"Honey, they're too far away for you to hear them talking," Britney said, looking out the crack. It only took a second for her to see that Jamie was right again. There were no kids in the line.

"She's right though. There are no kids and they're scanning the adults. Why would they be doing that, Judy?"

A chuckle erupted in Judy's head and it took some will power for her to keep a straight face, when the voice continued to badger her.

They aren't looking for the brats, but they'll kill them if they see them. I doubt if they even know what you two fool's stumbled on to when you brought them back. They want you! You're the infected one. We need to ditch these others. They are slowing us down. We don't need them. Especially the little girl. She knows you're not right, Judy.

Judy tried to ignore the voice, but it was harder now. It was taunting her, as if her own thoughts weren't hers anymore, but someone else whispering to her. She fought the urge to scream at it to shut up so she could think. The worse part was, it wasn't wrong and she knew it.

Britney waited for an answer, but Judy had her eyes squeezed shut and looked like she was concentrating.

Judy could feel Britney's eyes on her and anger bubbled up inside her. An anger that felt strong, bitter, and wonderful.

Judy took a deep breath, calming herself before she spoke.

"I don't know Britney, but whatever they're doing out there, we don't need any part of it. I say, let's get the Rover and get out of here while we can. We've lingered here too long," Judy said, making a slight gesture with her eyes, toward the stairs.

Britney followed her gaze, remembering what was up there possibly waking up. She looked back to Judy and gave her an unsteady nod.

•••

Britney looked up and saw what she thought looked like lights from a spaceship shining on the city, were actually spot lights the soldiers had set up on tops of various buildings; the big Hollywood premier kind. They were making huge circles around the streets below. She squinted her eyes now and could see tinny figures standing on the roof tops around them. She could even see they had their guns drawn.

After leaving the lobby, Judy led them across the street and to the alley they had come from, making sure not to be seen by the soldiers down the block. They were far enough away for this not to be a problem, but Judy warned them to be on the lookout for any stray soldiers and to avoid the lights.

The four of them entered the alley just as a light crossed their path behind them. Judy peered down the alley and cringed at the windows. When they had come through the alley before, there were faces in them. Horrible faces. For a brief moment she pictured the parents of those children on the buses.

My god, they must be in anguish. I can't imagine how they feel, even after all I've been through.

When Judy had to leave Tommy behind, even after she realized he wasn't the sick little boy on the couch, but the dead little boy in the dryer, she had the warming thought at the time that it was all in her head. A whisper in the back of her mind that none of it was really happening and she was going crazy. All those people on the buses, who had to leave their little boys and girls behind didn't have that luxury. By now, they would all know that they aren't crazy, that this is really happening. That their children are gone.

The ironic thing is, Judy thought, *the children can be saved and they just don't know it.*

As Judy walked past the first window, she couldn't help but look over at it. She remembered the window from before. It belonged to the parents of a little red headed boy. His face had an abnormal amount of freckles on it and his brows, when turned in, came together in a wrinkly mass that gave his face a particularly nasty look to it. He was one of the children in the windows that made her look away before. Now she approached the window and was unable to look away from it. As she inched closer, she prepared herself for the gruesome sight. Her feet slowed directly in front of the glass, but there was no boy, only the reflection of a middle aged woman staring back at her. The figure was wearing scrubs and holding little boy in its arms. Judy stood still, but the Tommy in the reflection was being rocked back and forth.

The Judy in the window spoke.

You're never going to get them out of here, the shape they're in, Judy. Maybe they should have taken their chances with the buses. At least they would be protected.

The reflection looked down at the child in its arms and goosebumps tickled Judy's arms. She continued to walk, passing the window. As she approached the next window, she wasn't surprised to see the figure appear in the next pain of glass, looking back at her, still rocking the bundle in its arms. Judy pushed a thought as hard as she could.

You shut up! I don't want to hear any of your crap right now! I can handle this. I've gotten this far. I saved my good Tommy and the rest of them and now we're going to get out!

The Judy in the window stopped rocking the little boy and looked at her in a sneer. It opened its arms and the little boy in the window dropped. Judy let out a gasp and fumbled Tommy in her arms, clenching on to him tight. For a second, she thought he was slipping out of her grip.

"Ouch, Mommy! That hurts me!" Tommy wined in a groggy voice.

It was a petty trick and Judy narrowed her eyes, feeling stupid for falling for it.

The figure in the window let out a cackle of laughter, which made Judy want to scream.

See, you can't even keep yourself together, Judy! You're going to fail and they will all suffer.

The reflection continued to laugh and Judy focused ahead of her and marched, not looking at the windows.

Behind her, Jamie brought her hands up to her ears and squinted her eyes shut, as if something loud and obnoxious were hurting her ears. Britney watched her for a second, then turned her attention back to the windows. Most of the children were still there, pawing at the glass absentmindedly.

"Jamie, keep walking, sweetie. They can't get at us," Britney said. A second later she had a thought, but kept it to herself.

Well, I guess they could break the glass, I mean, why couldn't they. They could probably rip the whole window pane out, jump down and start chasing us right now.

Britney's body tensed and she took a few swift steps, catching up with Jamie.

Without warning, Tommy spoke. "Mommy, my tummies hungry."

Maybe it was the sound of someone else saying it out loud, but as soon as the words left his mouth, Britney felt her stomach make an angry sound, loud enough to embarrass her on any normal occasion.

Judy stared at Tommy for a moment, then Jamie spoke up as well. "Ya, me too. I can't remember the last time I ate. And my legs hurt."

Judy cringed.

Oh please don't start with this. We don't have time for this crap. We have to keep moving.

In a timid tone, Britney said, "Maybe we should try to go into one of the stores and get some supplies."

See, I told you. They're weak! You're not hungry are you, Judy? No, I bet your fine. You should just ditch them and get yourself out. Maybe bring the boy if it makes it easier for you, but ditch the rest. They're just going to drag us down. If you take off running right now they'll never catch you, the shape they're in.

Judy clenched on to Tommy tight and closed her eyes tighter, willing the voice away. As she did, she heard the little boy whisper in her ear. Her eyes jerked open at what he said.

"Mommy, don't listen to the mean lady. Pwease, don't leave me again. I don't wanna ride on the bus."

Judy brought her hand up and stroked his back. "What mean lady, honey? There's no mean lady."

"The mean lady from the partment. She got you Mommy, just like the mean boy got me. I wouldn't let him in…and that's why he…" Tommy's voice trailed off. He didn't have to finish the sentence for Judy to understand what he meant.

You didn't let him in you, so he killed you and took your place. There couldn't be two of you after all, could there?

Judy looked back at the others. The windows were dark now and Britney and Jamie were both peering at them as they walked by, not paying attention to her and Tommy's quiet conversation.

"How do you know about the mean lady?" Judy asked Tommy, in a whisper. "Can you see her?"

"No, but I can hear her talk-in to you. The mean boy talked to me too. And when I didn't want to talk to him no more, that's when he grabbed me up. He wanted me to do bad things, but I didn't do it. I was good, Mommy."

Judy's heart swelled, then a thought came to her.

Can he only hear the mean lady or everything I'm thinking too?

She didn't say the thought out loud, but she felt Tommy's head move up and down against her shoulder. "I can hear the bofe of you, Momma."

Judy pushed another thought to him.

You were very good, baby. Now don't worry about anything. It's gonna be alright.

"Ok, Mommy," he said, quietly, with the hint of a pout in his voice. After a second, Judy sent another thought his way.

Honey, can you talk to me in my head too, like I'm talking to you now?

Tommy hesitated for a moment, then shook his head from side to side as he spoke. "I don't know."

"Ok baby, hush now," she said in a whisper, giving him a carful squeeze.

Judy looked back at Jamie and wondered again if she was in her head too. Judy pushed lightly.

Jamie can you hear me?

Judy watched for a reaction from Jamie, but there was none. The little girl continued to walk, peering into the dark windows lining he alley.

Suddenly, the voice of the 'mean lady', as Tommy called her, invaded Judy's head again.

She can. She just can't control it. None of you can. She will always be in your head, feeding on your thoughts, your desires, your deepest most private secretes, unless you get as far away from her as possible.

Images of Judy's past invaded her mind, as if the voice opened the side of her head and poured them in. The times she shoplifted. A rare night when she partook of Pete's habit and stuck a needle in her arm. A dark period of her life when she reluctantly dabbled in bondage with and old boyfriend of hers.

Judy squeezed her eyes shut.

"Ok, ok, just stop! I get the picture!"

She said it out loud by mistake and felt Tommy's body perk up a bit.

The boy can do it too and he will see what you did to his father, if you think of it long enough.

A thought flashed through Judy's mind. In it she saw the way Tommy looked at Pete, as if the dirt bag were a God. The little boy didn't know any better. Pete was his father. The only male figure in his life and Tommy loved him.

But I was only trying to save Tommy. I didn't know…I mean, I thought Pete had gone mad.

You tell the boy that then. And tell him why you left poor innocent Pete back in the apartment. I'm sure your boy will understand.

Judy cringed, knowing Tommy was probably catching every word. She tried to change the subject.

What about you? How do I get you out of my head? Do I have to get far away from here before you go back where you came from?

A chuckle engulfed Judy's mind, causing her to squeeze her eyes shut again for a second, until the voice spoke.

You conjured me, you greedy bitch. I'm stuck with you just as you are stuck with me...for now. Couldn't get enough, could you? It felt good, didn't it? It made me notice you. You've been bad. The bad ones are so easy; so...open. I'm here to stay until you give me what I want.

There was a moment of silence, as Judy waited for the voice to continue. When it didn't, she let out a sigh and asked the question it wanted her to ask.

Who are you and what do you want?

I am Sumonk and I want a body. I need one, but not like the adolescent ones they chose.

Judy could feel that the voice was gesturing to the kids in the windows and she turned her eyes to look at them for a moment as the voice continued. It was getting dark and the windows were fogged with frost, but the children were there, watching.

They were easily taken, weak and naive. The others only wanted to feel pleasure and the taste of blood on their lips; a vacation if you will. They are mindless and wouldn't last long in this place. They know this and yet still they settle with no real agenda. They took the place of adolescent creatures that can not survive on their own, hopping they would be cared for. Loved, if even for a short time. They should have known it wouldn't last long, but they are fools, not unlike yourself. I am older than them, by more years than you can imagine and in no need for a vacation. I want a place to stay, a good strong host I can take over. Unlike them, this host must be alive and willing. After all, a dead host isn't a host at all.

Judy almost spoke out loud and caught herself before she did. She sent the thought as hard as she could.

Well, I won't be your host! I have a son and a long life ahead of me, so go find someone else and leave us alone! I've been through too much to end up being your puppet!

Judy heard a taunting snicker.

I do not want you as a host. I need a strong host, not a weak, reckless creature such as yourself. I need your help finding a suitable body. One that will last a long time, help me and I will leave you alone to your pathetic life.

I will never help you! My son was killed by your vacationers and shoved in a fucking dryer! I brought him back and now I'm done. Find someone else to do you favors.

Judy's breathing quickened and the taste of peppermint doubled in her mouth and nostrils. The voice didn't reply and she could feel that wouldn't, for now. She let out a sigh to slow her breathing, looked in front of her and continued to stroke Tommy's back as she walked.

Jamie glanced ahead at Judy and let out a sigh. It took a lot of effort to ignore the thoughts Judy was sending to her. She didn't want Judy to know she could hear her what was in her head; not while the bad thing was listening.

Now she knows Tommy can do it too. It's the mist in her that's letting us do it, I think.

Jamie was sure Judy couldn't hear her own thoughts. When Bad Tommy was in her head, it felt like fingers were fondling her eardrums. She didn't feel this now, but hearing Judy's thoughts made her feel guilty, another reason she didn't want to admit it. The Bad Judy terrified Jamie. She wanted nothing to do with it.

Having Bad Tommy in her head had opened something up. Something Jamie didn't want to use.

I can't hear what Britney's thinking, but she didn't smell the mist or go to the other place. The caves. Maybe I am infected. Maybe Bad Judy is right. Maybe they should get away from me. Am I just a freak now? What good is it hearing their thoughts anyways? It's not like they would listen to me. I'm only ten. Once Judy knows, she won't want to be around me.

Jamie looked down at her feet, continuing to walk. Suddenly the things in the windows weren't bothering her anymore. Too her, they seemed less like monsters and more like victims.

Maybe I shouldn't have been brought back. Maybe they should have let me be.

Jamie's thoughts were interrupted by a curse from Britney's mouth.

"Oh shit!"

They turned the corner, entering the scummier alley, when Britney saw them. Judy was marching at a faster pace than Britney and didn't seem to be paying attention ahead of her or she would have seen them sooner.

"Judy, stop!" Britney said, in a hushed tone, not wanting to draw too much attention. Judy didn't respond and continued to walk. She almost made it past the men before she was stopped.

"Hey there, where *you* off to in such a hurry?" a tall, bearded man said, in a teasing tone. He quickly put his arm out, blocking Judy's path. Without thinking, she slapped it aside. The force in which she did, surprised the man. The look on his face tensed as he took his forearm in his other hand, rubbing it lightly.

He glared at her.

"Whoa, this one's a fire cracker. Watch out, Ben," another man said from the shadows. Judy looked in his direction as he came into view. He was a well-built, Hispanic male. His shirt was open at the top and she could see his muscular chest was covered in a variety of tattoos. To Judy, they looked like prison tats. With the exception of the tattoos, Judy, on a normal day, would have found his smile, smooth voice and muscular physique very attractive, but not today. Today she found him an inconvenience.

As soon as she made eye contact with him, five more figures came into view behind him, all a variety of race. Two Hispanics, three white guys and a black guy wearing the biggest smile full of white teeth she had ever seen. His smile kind of reminded Judy of the actor Chris Rock, except in a thuggish sort of way. Judy could tell that a few of the men didn't look like they were regular members of this crew. They looked nervous and out of place, probably just looking for protection. Judy thought of them as *nervous nellies* and she made it a point not to worry about them. Judy could pin point the ones she had to worry about; Mr. Smiley with the huge set of choppers; a short fat Hispanic man eyeing her like she were a piece of meat; and a young white kid in the back, who looked like he had golden teeth.

I wonder how much that grill cost him and what he had to do to get it. I'm sure his parents must be proud.

And of course this handsome guy standing in front. Mr. Tattoo. He was the real threat. His good looks and sly smile probably drove the woman crazy.

Probably drove them broke too.

Half of them looked like they had a whole jewelry box full of woman's necklaces around their necks. The others were carrying duffle bags stuffed with only God knew what. They'd obviously been looting the apartments; the ones not occupied with creepy children. Judy quickly eyed each of the men. The ones in the front were smirking as if they were hyenas who had cornered a little snack. Something inside Judy hoped they were hungry.

The tall bearded one, 'Ben' they called him, took a few steps to the side, making his intention of blocking her path more obvious. He was big, looked like a biker and the only one not smiling. Judy glared at him.

Judy's demon spoke up.

You can take them; all of them, Judy. The voice sounded sinister and Judy's eyes narrowed.

"Move out of my way and let us by," she grumbled. Anger started to bubble up inside of her.

The rest of the men just snickered at the comment, but the one blocking her path fixed his eyes on her. Judy didn't take her eyes off his.

The voice spoke up in Judy's head again.

They're going to want the bag. One of them is already eyeing it. We should end them, but not that one.

Judy felt the voice gesture to Mr. Tattoo.

Save me that one. He would make a most satisfactory host.

Judy glanced at Mr. Tattoo.

I'm not helping you do jack shit! Get out of my head! I can take care of this myself.

Judy flexed her hands and could feel the tips of her fingers going numb as the peppermint mist sloshed around in her body. In a split second, she scanned the men again, almost as if she had high speed cameras under her eyelids. Bad Judy was right. Two of the guys in the back; Mr. Smiley and the young kid with the expensive grill, were staring at her back pack, as if they had superman's ex-ray vision and Pete's thirst for good cocaine.

Mr. Tattoo let out a sarcastic puff of breath through his nose and said, "Don't be like that, Chicka. We just want to—"

He was interrupted by Britney's voice as she casually strolled up to them, with Jamie close behind.

"Hey Victor, don't give her any shit, she's with me."

The look on Mr. Tattoo's face changed, as he looked Britney up and down. A sinister smile turned his face from a hyena looking at prey, to a lion looking at a forbidden lioness.

"Hey pretty girl. What are you doing out here? Isn't it past our bed time?"

The other guys snickered at this, but Judy clenched her jaw and moved her eyes to Victor.

After a tense moment, Britney relaxed. She knew Victor from the neighborhood. Not a 'nice guy' but at least he remembered her. He always talked nice to her and she thought his tattoo's made him kind of sexy, for an older guy. He was acquainted with her parents, sort of.

Britney's face brightened. "Na, I'm a night owl, you know that. This is my friend Judy, her son Tommy and my friend Jamie. We're getting out of here. This place has gone mad." She paused while the men looked at Judy and the children.

Before she could say anything else, one of the men in the back spoke up "Why aren't you on the buses?" Judy looked in the direction the voice came from. It came from the kid with the golden grill. He had his cap on sideways, making him look like a cocky little shit. Something inside Judy didn't like his tone, but before she could answer, Britney said, "Those buses look cramped. Besides, we have a car."

Judy's eyes shot to her. *Geeze Britney, why don't you just tell them everything. Do you want to invite them to come with us? Maybe this big bearded asshole in front of me can ride shotgun?*

Then the voice whispered in her ear.

Watch that one on your left.

Judy's eyes moved left and saw that the short, fat, Hispanic man was slowly moving down the alley behind Britney, clearly blocking that way as an escape.

These men mean to harm you. I would do something if I were you…If you can.

Judy knew the voice was right. She slowly adjusted Tommy in her arms. He was alert and watching Britney talk to the men. Judy could feel his little heart thumping in his chest, either from what was being said or from what he just heard the mean lady say. Judy centered her eyes on Mr. Tattoo as he continued to speak to Britney.

"So how's your daddy, Chakita? I haven't seen him since I got out. Seems like a long time ago. How much more time does he have?"

Victor talked in a taunting voice and Judy could see the other men smiling and whispering to each other.

Judy watched as Britney looked down at her feet, then heard her say in a deflated voice, "I haven't heard from him in a long time, but I think he still has like five or six years to go."

Victor had his eyes fixed on Britney.

"Is that so? Well, maybe he'll get out on good behavior, like I did." The other men snickered at the comment. Victor's eyes moved down Britney's body and Judy wished the teen had worn a better fitting top. Too much of her skin was showing and after all they had been through, the neckline was stretched out, reveling even more cleavage than it had when they first met. In the dark light of the alley, Britney looked like a hooker.

Victor's smooth voice drifted softly to Britney again.

"Dang girl, you're starting to look just like your mamma. Is she around? Don't tell me she has you working the streets too."

Britney shot a desperate glance to Judy, then her eyes went to her feet. She didn't answer the question.

Judy looked back to Mr. Tattoo and narrowed her eyes on him. He notice and gave her a questioning look.

Something festered inside Judy's body and she couldn't hold her tongue any longer. "Why aren't *you* on the buses? Afraid the army's looking for recruits or fresh assholes to beat?" she said, taunting him. "What are you doing hiding in this alley?"

A few of the men smiled at this and Victor didn't hesitate to answer. "We aren't hiding anywhere, nurse lady. Just waiting for things to calm down and doing a little window shopping. As soon as the army gets all the assholes out of the city, we'll be the only assholes left." After a pause, he added, "We'll be kings." He put his hand, palm up over his shoulder and one of the guys behind him obediently slapped it.

Victor looked at Judy from top to bottom. "And kings need their queens. I would hate for anything to happen to a couple of fine looking lady's like yourselves."

Before he could continue, the short, plump Hispanic man standing behind Britney said something. His accent was so thick, it was hard to put together what he was saying until he was finished.

"Hey, I knows who chu are! Chur Pete's wife."

Judy's eyes went wide at the sound of Pete's name. She looked over and saw that Britney was just as surprised.

"Chu guys knows Pete. He's da gringo that Alex gets de really good powders from."

Alex smiled, showing off his set of gold teeth and shook his head in agreement. Mr. Short Fat Man continued, "Chu knows, de power we sold to—"

Before he could continue, Mr. Tattoo put his hand up, cutting the man's comment short. Mr. Short Fat Man shrank back from the evil look Mr. Tattoo was giving him. When Victor turned back to Judy, the smooth smile was already back on his face.

"Pete the drug dealer's wife, hu? Ya, I know Pete. We go back a long way. Where is he? I could use some good stuff right about now." After a pause, he added, "You heading to meet him? Bringing him a package?" Victor said the last part eyeing the bag sling around Judy's shoulder.

Judy let out a sigh.

Tell them you killed him with a snow globe, Judy. That should send them running.

She couldn't tell if it was Bad Judy's voice or her own that said it. It was getting hard to tell the difference.

"He's gone. Skipped town." Judy said. "Left me and our son to fend for ourselves through this mess. He was always kind of a dirt bag. I'm not surprised you know him. He had a lot of dirt bag friends too."

All eyes went to Victor and his smile faltered slightly.

The bearded man barked, "What's in the pack?" clearly tired of the back and forth conversation.

Victor looked at the back pack slung over Judy's shoulder, then his eyes went to Tommy.

"What's your momma got in the back pack, big man? I doubt it's full of diapers."

Tommy raised his head slightly and said, "I don't wear diapers. I'm a big boy." He said the last part proudly and Judy's blood boiled.

The tall bearded man in front of her barked again, "Enough talk, just give us the bag and get the fuck out of here!"

Judy glared at him and slowly lowered Tommy to the ground. The bearded man watched her as she did.

Judy pushed a thought to her son.

Don't worry honey, everything's fine, but I need you to go over to Britney.

The thought drifted into Tommy's mind and he started to shake his head side to side before it finished.

"Mommy, I don't want to," Tommy said out loud. "Don't listen to the mean lady."

A couple of the brutes standing around them looked at each other, with questioning expressions, before snickering at the little boys comment.

Judy clenched her jaw. Suddenly her face felt hot, as if her brain were glowing red. She sent her next thought to Tommy as gently as she could manage.

Just go, my good Tommy. It's ok. The bad lady is gonna go bye, bye. And so are these creeps.

His mother's voice grumbled in Tommy's head and a sensation of fear shot through him. Her voice sounded like she was really angry. Tommy didn't like her to be angry with him and he knew better than to argue when she used the voice. He turned to Britney and quickly walked to her. She greeted him with open arms.

Judy waited for Britney to pick Tommy up, before looking back to Victor. She could see the bearded man glaring at her, but she ignored him. He was Victors muscle; no more than a dog and Judy knew he wouldn't bite without a nod from his keeper. She pulled the pack off her shoulder and let it fall, catching the strap in her hand before it hit the ground.

"If you want the pack, come and get it. I dare you," she said, in a dry tone, looking at Victor. He smiled, as the others behind him 'oohed' and 'awed', taunting the situation. Britney and Jamie's eyes went wide.

While the kings of the city were still registering what she said, Judy sent a thought to Jamie, hard enough for the little girl to skip a breath.

Jamie, I don't know if you can hear me, but I think you can. I need you and the others to run as soon as you see me throw the pack. Do you hear me? Just run like hell? If you can, grab the pack as you go by and keep running to your dads SUV.

Jamie looked and saw Judy was looking at her from the corner of her eye. Jamie shook her head up and down slowly. Tommy saw her do it, looked at his mother and shook his head in unison with Jamie. It registered that both kids heard the thought and Judy looked from them to Britney. The look on Britney's face changed, as if say 'What the hell are you doing, Judy, you crazy bitch?'

Judy gave her a sinister wink, wishing she could send the message to her as well. The look on Britney's face said the wink was enough. It told Britney 'The shi...*crap* was about to hit the fan'.

"Listen, nurse lady," Victor said, in his smooth tone. "Just hand over the bag and we'll let you little girls go."

As Victor looked at Judy's glare, her mouth curved into a smile and he saw a thin curl of green smoke float out of the left side of it. He narrowed his eyes on it a split second before Ben, his top muscle, went for the pack.

•••

Judy saw the big asshole coming at her out of the corner of her eye. He lunged forward and wrapped his huge hand around the strap of the pack. Without looking away from Victor, Judy brought her hand up, yanked it forward, causing bearded Ben to lose his grip. The next second she brought her elbow back and it connected with his nose, crushing the bones into his brain. His thick beard quickly became saturated in blood as it poured from his nostrils. His legs buckled and he went down hard, bouncing off the wall behind him before hitting the ground.

It all happened so fast, every person in the alley just stood and gawked for a few seconds. Judy scanned all of them and when her eyes met Jamie's, she threw the pack down the alley. The pack soared so far, the sound of it hitting the ground wasn't heard. She sent Jamie a push as soon as it landed. Not a thought, but a hard push.

Jamie flinched out of her mindlessness and instantly remembered what Judy had said. She broke free of Britney's hand and took off running down the alley.

"Jamie, wait!" Britney screamed. A second later, Tommy wiggled out of her arms and chased after Jamie. Britney watched the two of them for a few yards and her attention went back to Judy. Britney's mouth drop open at what she saw.

As the men were still looking at the bag make its final bounce, before settling, Judy lunged forward, bringing her right foot up between Mr. Tattoo's legs. The blow hit him hard enough to pick both of his feet off the ground and he let out a grunt. A second later, he went down to his knees and fell to his side, holding his crotch. Before Mr. Tattoo could catch his breath, three of the other men rushed forward at Judy.

Britney froze.

Holly shit! Oh crap, what do I do?

She looked back at the kids just as Jamie stopped to pick up the bag. The little girl looked back briefly, then turned and continue down the alley. Britney took a few unsteady steps in that direction and stopped as one of the men staggered toward her, holding the side of his face. His sideways cap had been knocked askew. Britney looked back in the direction he came from and saw Judy crack another man in his skull, sending him colliding into the wall behind him.

Oh crap! What do I do? Help her?

Britney watched the commotion for a moment. Just as the man hit the wall, Judy lunged at him and kicked him in the stomach, causing blood to explode from his mouth. He fell to the ground in a heap.

"What the hell?" Britney muttered. *She looks like she's kicking their asses,* she thought.

Britney started to look back to the kids, when she saw a gun appear in Mr. Askew Cap's hand. He pointed it in Judy's direction and hesitated. The barrel of the gun danced side to side as Judy bounced back and forth, delivering blows and kicks to the third man, almost as if she were toying with him. Britney stared at the gunman. The look on his face said that he was worried about missing and hitting one of his comrades or that he had never fired a gun at another person. Regardless of the look on his face or the reason for the look, the gun went off and Britney's eyes shot to Judy, just in time to see her jerk to the side, letting the bullet explode into the wall behind her. The movement had a familiar quickness to it. Britney had seen it before.

Holy shit! Is she one of those things? How the hell did that happen?

Images of Judy knocking Richard out flashed in Britney's mind. Then the way the coffee table had soared across the room from one simple kick from Judy's foot. The fact that she was able to carry Jamie's ten year old body so far, as if she were nothing more than a pair of jammies stuffed with straw.

If she's one of those things, what should I—

Before Britney could finish the thought, a flash of light lit up the alley and a second crack of thunder echo in her ears. This second shot made up Britney's mind. She turned and ran down the alley in the direction the kids went.

Judy paused for a split second and looked at her arm. A gash big enough to put a roll of pennies in appeared as if by magic and blood was oozing out of it. She realized her speed was nowhere as fast as Bad Jamie's had been. The bullet grazed her, either for this reason or because the shooter was a horrible shot and she'd ran into it.

She narrowed her eyes on the gunman. Before he could aim the gun again, Judy took the six steps between them and brought her hand up, knocking the gun out of his grip. It went flying to his right and Judy hit him in the throat with the fingers her other hand. He staggered backward and made a gasping attempt at a breath. As soon as he went to his knees, Judy kicked him in the side of the face, sending him the rest of the way to the ground.

"This is too easy," Judy whispered.

She smiled as a gall of laughter filled her head. Judy pushed a thought at the laugh.

I hope you're enjoying this, you nasty bitch.

When the laughter tapered off, Bad Judy's voice replied.

I know you are, Judy, I can smell it. Just remember, I want that one. Victor I believe he is called. Let me have him and I'll be out of your head.

Judy smiled and looked down at her handy work. She felt like a different person peering down at the bleeding man at her feet. Some of them were moaning and moving lazily around on the ground. In less than a few minutes, she had taken out six full grown men. She felt like an animal.

Six? There were seven of them, if you count the bearded one. Where did number seven go?

Suddenly Judy heard the rhythmic sound of running, glanced over and saw that Alex; the one with the expensive dental work and who liked to wear his cap sideways, was sprinting down the alley.

Aw, one got away, Judy thought. *And just when I was having some fun.*

"Come back, you forgot your friend!" Judy's voice echoed down the alley. "Some King you are!"

Judy looked at him longingly, as if he were a fast bottle of liquor running away from some lonely bum with a thirst. Just as her attention started to drift away from the runner, a flash of light from the military spotlights crept into the alley for a split second and she saw another figure running. The figure in the lead looked back and let out a female shriek. Judy's heart dropped. It was Britney. The punk wasn't running away, he was chasing Britney and gaining on her fast.

Oh shit!

Just when the muscles in Judy's legs flexed, preparing to move her in the runaway king's direction, something heavy collided with the back of her head. Judy legs buckled and everything went dark. When she opened her eyes, she was lying on the ground and small fireflies of light danced around the edges of her vision. She focused her eyes in time to see a mangled shopping cart land on the ground in front of her.

Bad Judy; or 'Sumonk' as it called itself, spoke up in her head.

Aw, you were doing so well, Judy. You should have watched your back instead of worrying about those worthless flesh bags.

Judy raised her head slightly. Before it got a few inches off the ground, she felt a hand grab the back of her hair and her face collided with the ground again. If it weren't for the influence of the mist, her cheek would have been broken.

"Fucking puta!" Victor barked. "You're going to pay for that, nurse lady!" Victor's accent was thicker when he was pissed. "No one kicks me!"

Judy could feel his breath on the back of her neck, as he bared down on top of her. She could feel his knee pushing into her spine. It didn't hurt, thanks to the mist, but the pressure of it made her feel like she was pinned under a truck.

You can't get out of this, Judy, the voice whispered. *I can help you if you let me in.*

Judy ignored the voice and started to move her limbs. Just as she started to thrash her body, she heard a second voice, followed by more weight being pushed down against her. She struggled, but had no leverage as a second pair of hands assisted in pinning her down.

"Dis bitch broked my nose and I tink I cracked a rib!" The second voice's accent was even thicker than Victor's and Judy knew it was the short fat man. From his tone, it didn't sound like he was excited to know her anymore. He stuck his nose in the air, pinching it with the fingers of his free hand, the other hand pressing down on the middle of Judy's back. Blood dripped down his chin, making a mess of his neck and the collar of his t-shirt.

"Victor, I tink che kilt Ben!" the fat man said, talking through his nose, making him even harder to understand.

Victor ignored the comment and sent his voice echoing down the alley. "Kill the bitch and bring the kids back!"

Judy heard Britney scream again and could picture her looking back at the man chasing her. Judy felt the muscles in her limbs begin to tighten and her dirty fingers went numb. In a burst of force, she used her arms to lift her body up off the ground, bringing her in a pushup position. Victor and the fat man clinched on to her tighter as she started to rise. Both men gaped at her sudden strength and movement.

"Wat de hell, Victor? Dis bitch is possessed or someting. I can not hold her!"

Victor said nothing, released his grip on Judy and glared at her savagely. His comrade gawked at him for a moment as Judy continued to move under his hands, until Victor stood back a few feet and positioned his body as if he were about to kick a field goal. The fat man smiled and braced himself.

Judy felt Mr. Tattoo's weight leave her and was just about to flick Mr. Broken Nose off of her like a fly, when Victor's foot connected with her stomach.

Judy's wind was knocked out of her in a gust of green mist. She went back down to the ground, bringing the fat man with her. As they settled, Judy rolled over under his arms and ended up face to face with the creep. She continued to gag and choke, fighting for a breath. The fat man watched as Judy burped up small puffs of green smoke, accompanied by droplets of spittle, which he could feel tickling his face. His eyes narrowed on her and a look terror crossed his eyes.

"Wat de hell? Wat are you?" he whispered, moving away from her. Just as he did a small gale of green mist escaped Judy's mouth, formed into a ring and drifted up toward him. He stopped and stared at it, momentarily mesmerized by its movements. It looked alive.

The ring gently drifted toward his face and he made no effort to move, as if he were a fat deer dumfounded by headlights. He closed his eyes and held his breath, just as the minty ring collided with his face. Judy looked up just as he started to scream. He toppled to the ground next to her, covering his face with his plump hands.

Victor's eyes moved from Judy, to the man squirming on the ground beside her.

"Sancho, what is it? What'd the bitch do to you?" Victor barked, in an annoyed tone.

The fat man didn't answer, but continued to squirm with his hands over his face. Victor watched him for a second, then focused back on Judy, as she made an attempt at crawling across the asphalt. She was suddenly aware that she had been shot. Her arm was numb and uncooperative and stung with every twitch of her muscles. Her elbow bumped along the ground, slowing her feeble attempt at an escape. Victor took a step toward her, brought his foot up and placed it in the middle of her back, pressing her weak body back to the ground. Judy didn't resist, she had no fight left. She continued to breathe in unsteady gasps, choking up puffs of her precious mist. She could feel her body weakening with every breath of fresh air she sucked in.

Bad Judy's voice spoke up again in her head, this time with a tinge of concern in it.

Look at you now, Judy. You have lost yourself again. You should have been able to take them out, but instead you've put your boy in jeopardy again. I can only imagine what they will do to him and the others. I can help you, if you let me.

Judy ignored the voice and continued to take huge breaths. She couldn't have spoken out loud if she wanted to. Next to her, the fat man continued to scream and kick his feet, with his hands over his face.

Under the fat man's chubby palms, a small amount of the mist darted back and forth across his skin and streamed in and out from between his fingers playfully. He could feel the bones in his nose shifting under his skin. In a painful crunch the cartilage and bone reconnected and he could feel the blood dripping down his face start to move upward and back into his nostrils. He started to gag and kicked his feet in all directions. Victor watched as the blood rolled up his chin and disappeared under his trembling hands.

"Sancho!" Victor barked. After a moment, Victor repeated the mans name, in a louder tone. "Sancho!" His voice echoed down the alley.

"Oh dios mio," Mr. Tattoo whispered, as he looked around him. The men that were left, were getting up off the ground, rubbing various parts of their bodies. They looked beat to hell. The big bearded one, Ben, was the only one who didn't stir at the sound of Victors voice. His head rested in a pool of blood. It looked black in the moonlight.

"Get up you pussies! Get over here and—"

Victor stopped talking mid-sentence and noticed a shift in the movement at his side. Sancho, the fat man, stopped kicking his feet. His screaming died down to a few muffled sobs from under his hands and his breath steadied. He took his hands down from his nose and looked up at Victor with a blank expression on his face. It looked as if he'd seen the devil itself. Carefully, he rose to a sitting position, his big belly hanging out of the bottom of his shirt. The rest of the men, including Victor, watched him without blinking. Judy watched him with one half closed eye. The other one was buried in the asphalt.

The fat man's blank eyes moved to the thugs around him. The only men left were Mr. Smiley, Victor and the two *nervous nellies*; who looked even more nervous now. The fat man barely seemed to notice any of them, brought his hand up and pinched his nose. It didn't hurt the slightest bit. His eyes moved down to Judy. She was lying flat on her belly, with her head turned to him. She was glaring at him and the instant his eyes met hers, a sinister grin surfaced on her face. To him, it looked like her eyes were glowing green. He suddenly scrambled to his feet.

"Demonio Blanco!" he blubbered, as he pointed at Judy. His eyes shot to the other men standing nearby and he said it again, with more emphasis and in English. "White She Devil!"

Without another word, the short, fat man turned and started to run down the alley, pushing two of the men out of his way as he went. They both stumbled and watched him go for a moment, before one of them, Mr. Smiley, called after him.

"Sancho! Brother, come back!"

Victor glared at the fat man for a moment, then back at the others. "Let him go! We don't need him!" He focused his attention to Mr. Smiley and snarled, "We don't need that fat piece of shit, right?"

Mr. Smiley didn't shrink back from Victor's glare, but returned it with trembling lips. Victor watched as his wide eyes moved down to Judy.

"What is she, Victor?" Mr. Smiley whispered. "Is she really the devil like he said?"

Victor hacked and spit close to Judy's body at his feet. "I'll tell you what this bitch is, amigo…dead!" He turned and addressed the other men gawking at him. "This bitch is dead! Just like all those freaky things in the windows. She's dead, amigos, just like this whole fucking city!"

The men watched, as Victor lifted his foot and delivered another kick to Judy's mid-section, letting loose another gust of green smoke from her mouth. The men saw the mist and looked at each other. One of the new guys crossed his chest with his finger and taped his forehead before bringing his hand to his lips, kissing it.

Before Judy sucked in a breath, Victor kicked her again. Then, again. Victor continued to kick Judy until Mr. Smiley joined in. The two nervous nellies glanced at each other in horror. One of them took a step back and gestured down the alley. Before the other guy could react to the gesture, Victor's eyes moved to them as he continued to kick. The look on his face flexed into a sneer with each strike of his foot and he didn't take his eyes off the two of them. Each kick and sneer seemed like an invitation to madness. Victors stare did just what he wanted it to. He had a way with people. A way of getting people to do what he wanted and after a moment, one of the guys stepped forward and joined in. Shortly after that, Judy felt all four men kicking her body. And without the mist surging through her, she could feel every kick.

Judy's body jerked and twisted with each blow. She waited for the voice in her head to say something; to taunt her on her present situation, but there was nothing. Not even a chuckle. For once, the voice was silent.

Images started to cascade through Judy's mind. She didn't know if the thing invading her head had anything to do with it or not, but they stung just the same. She saw Tommy as a toddler, taking his first steps. The first time she saw a look of pride in his eyes, when he drew her a picture of the puppy he wanted, which she never got around to getting for him. The loving way he used to sit by her side, with his hand resting on her leg. The thousands of times he smiled at her. Then as if knowing what she was thinking, she heard his small voice whisper in her ear— *"I love you too, Mommy, forever and ever."*

Something inside Judy broke. The boots and shoes thumping against her skin seemed to take a step back in her thoughts and she sent a message as clear as she could, hoping it would be heard through the chaos around her.

Ok, you win. I can't do this alone. Please, I have to make sure Tommy is safe.

After a second, the voice of Sumonk spoke up.

That's not good enough, Judy. I can't intervene if you don't ask me properly and by name, if you please. You have to submit to my being, if you want my help.

Judy had no pride left and sent her next thought back in a monotone voice.

I need your help. Please, do what you need to do and take what you want, as long as Tommy is safe. Sumonk, I submit to you. Please help me.

The second the words left Judy's thoughts, a clownish smile forced its way across her lips. She tried to stop it and realized she had no control over it or any other part of her body. The smile wasn't hers. It was Bad Judy's.

✧

Chapter 8.

Britney ran as fast as her sore legs would carry her. She heard Victor yell something behind her. It sounded like 'Bitch, bring the kids back'. She glanced back and let out a scream as she saw one of the thugs running after her. Ahead of her, she saw Jamie pause, causing Tommy to come to a stop just behind her. He looked close to collapsing.

Between gasps of breath, Britney yelled "No Jamie! Keep going! Tommy, please just run!"

Both kids looked back at Britney, then at the man running behind her. Jamie secured the back pack over her shoulder, grabbed Tommy's hand and pulled him back into a fast jog.

Britney spared a glance back and saw the thug they called 'Alex' had closed some distance. He was fast, probably not much older than she was. Britney could see the expression on his face now. Ironically, it was at this moment she realized she knew him. They had gone to school together. Not in the same grade; he was one or two grades ahead of her at the time, but you couldn't forget his smile. His golden teeth made him look like an animal. Britney looked back in front of her and picked up speed. She ran faster than she thought she could run. After a moment she spared another look behind her. The thug was a little further away this time and a feeling of relief washed over her. She looked past him, at the commotion going on at the end of the alley.

Judy and the other men were just oblong shadows against the alley wall, but Britney could make out which one was her friend. Just then, she saw Judy go down. Britney gasped and looked back in front of her. She saw the two children go around the corner and out of sight. A huge circle of light creeped across the sidewalk after them and disappeared in the direction they went, as if they were being stalked by a titan with a giant flashlight.

At that moment, Britney wished the light would see them. That it would find them, gather them up and take them to safety, ridding her of the grown up task.

I can't do this without Judy.

Her mind flashed back to seeing Judy punching and kicking Victor and his crew. Judy moved like she was one of the creatures and Britney swallowed hard.

Judy's gone. If she isn't one of those things, they'll kill her for what she just did. If she kicks their asses, then she has to be one of those things. It's up to me now. I have to be the adult and take care of Jamie and Tommy. I'm all they have now. Judy's gone either way...it's up to me.

The thought made her eyes narrow and she slowed her pace. She was nearing the end of the alley and scanned the area for anything she could use. She could hear the thug's foot falls behind her getting closer.

Just as she came around the last set of trashcans that littered the alley, she spotted what she needed. Changing direction slightly, she reached her hand out and snatched up a two by four piece of wood that was leaning up against one of the cans. She gripped it in both hands as she rounded the corner in the direction Jamie and Tommy went. As soon as she hit the sidewalk, she came to a clumsy halt, slammed her back against the wall and bit her bottom lip between her teeth, squeezing her eyes shut. She slowed her breath and listened. She started to raise the two by four over her shoulder, when something moved in the corner of her eye. Her eyes darted in that direction. A few feet away, stood Jamie and Tommy. They were wide eyed and staring at her. Britney cringed.

"What are you two doing? Why didn't you keep running?"

Jamie saw the frustration on Britney's face, opened her mouth to answer and closed it again when Britney put her finger in front of lips. The gesture said, 'be quiet' and Jamie obediently moved closer to the wall, bringing Tommy with her.

Through the commotion at the end of the alley, the three of them heard the thug's foot falls approaching the corner. Britney raised the piece of wood in her hand like a baseball bat and waited, with her heart thumping in her chest. She closed her eyes as Alex turned the corner. The second he did, Britney blindly swung the two by four at shoulder height. She heard a hollow slap, followed by a male scream. She was jerked from her place against the wall and saw that the kid caught the bat with his hand, almost as if he had known it was coming. He held on to it as she tugged, still screaming, as if the blow had hurt him badly. Britney never heard a man scream as shrill and the noise echoed down the alley.

Holly shit! I didn't hit him that hard! What the hell's going on? Let go...you fucker!

She gave the wood one final yank and it came free from the Alex's grip. He instantly cradled his hand against his chest and looked at it in horror. Before he had a chance to look up from it, Britney hit him with the piece of wood again, this time in his side, just below his ribs. Alex let out another cry, went to his knees, clawing at the make shift club. Britney tugged on it and was confused when it didn't come away from his body, almost as if it were metal being pulled from a magnet. Britney pulled harder, causing Alex to scream out. The wood separated from his side and Britney brought it up, preparing to swing again, paused and looked down at him. Alex had his hand up, in a pleading gesture.

"Please stop! I give up! Please don't hurt me!" he said in a desperate tone, sounding more like the kid he was.

Britney took huge gulps of air in through her nose, looked at him and sneered. Her eyes caught sight of a small wound in the middle of his outstretched hand. Blood was spilling out of it. She looked back to Alex's eyes and followed his gaze to the end of the piece of wood. A rusty, slightly bent nail protruded from the end of it and was dripping with blood. Her eyes went wide and snapped back to Alex.

"Get the hell out of here then…and don't come back!" Britney snarled, lunging at him again.

Alex jumped to his feet, turned and began running down the side walk, holding his side as he went. Before disappearing into the shadows, Britney saw the side of his t-shirt was dark with blood. She stepped away from the wall to watch him go. After a moment, she looked back at the bloody nail and shivered. She dropped the piece of wood on the sidewalk and it made a hollow *clunk* in the silence.

Silence? It's too quiet! Britney thought.

The commotion in the alley had stopped and Britney peered at the shadowy figures on the wall in the distance. They were silent and motionless, almost as if they were mere black smudges of graffiti. Britney feared the worse for Judy, until she saw the shadows spring to life and the so called kings began to scream.

•••

As if welcoming Sumonk to the situation, a scream echoed down the alley and the kicks to the nurse ladies body ceased. The smile on her face didn't falter. Her eyes looked up at the men standing over her and the smile widened mischievously. They were all looking to the distance, as Britney pulled the rusty nail from her pursuer's side. They could hear Alex mumbling; pleading, but could barely make out what was being said.

"What the fuck," Victor barked, out of breath. "He can't even take care of one little bitch and a couple of kids?" Victor glared at the other three men. "You all want to be lions, but no one wants to do lion shit!" The men said nothing in return and continued to stare down the alley, waiting for something reassuring to happen. Their eyes followed Alex's silhouette in unison, as the tinny figure fled, disappearing from their view. Next, the familiar sound of a two by four dropping to the ground echoed down the alley.

Clunk Clunk Clunk

The men glanced at each other, wide eyed. To Victor, they looked scared and his fists tightened.

Victor opened his mouth to roar at them, when he felt something brush his leg. He looked down and his face distorted into a sneer. The nurse ladies body was gone. He turned and scanned the ground around him, expecting to see the bitch crawling away, but there was nothing, aside from a few droplets of blood.

"What the hell? Where did she go?" he asked out loud, mostly talking to himself. The other men's attention snapped from the end of the alley, to the confused expression on Mr. Tattoo's face, to the empty spot on the ground.

Mr. Smiley let out a nervous babble of unrecognizable words and the others glanced at him. He stepped up to Victor and took the fabric of his shirt in his hands, pulling him closer. His next words were spoken an inch from Victor's face.

"Holly shit, man! This is some crazy shit!" The word 'shit' caused Victors face to be sprinkled with a small amount of spit. He flinched and pushed Mr. Smiley away from him, causing the man to trip and fall backwards. Mr. Smiley's fists kept hold of the fabric of Victor's shirt and ripped most of the buttons off the front on his way down, exposing his tattoo covered abs. Victor said nothing and continued to stare at Mr. Smiley, as he quickly got back to his feet and began taking steps backward. His wide eyes moved to each man as he continued to babble. "We got to get away from here, man…I mean, like far away. Fuck being kings. This place is—"

His words were cut short and he stared past the others, as if something were creeping up behind them. They looked over their shoulders, each man's heart pounding in their chest, only to find nothing but the brick wall casting their own shadows in a slant. Their eyes fell back on Mr. Smiley, as a gargling noise escaped his mouth.

Before any of them could speak, Mr. Smiley's body began to hunch forward and the top half of his torso slid off the bottom and fell to the pavement with a *splat*. The bottom half of his body, cut just above his navel, stood for a second, before its knees buckled and it followed the rest of the body to the ground. As if materializing from thin air, a woman's figure appeared behind the sprawled corpse. The men gasped and took a step back. It was the nurse lady, but none of them recognized the sly smile frozen across her lips. She didn't look like a woman who had just been on her way to being kicked to death. Her right arm was covered in blood from the elbow down and it only took them a second to realize that their comrade had just been sliced in two. The realization seemed to paralyze them and they stood staring, unable to move.

Bad Judy tilted her borrowed head to the side, causing it to make a loud cracking sound, stepped over the halved body in front of her and moved toward the men gawking at her. This broke the thugs paralyzed state and they scattered in a burst of noise that resembled teenage girls being chased by a prankster holding a dead rat. Victor watched as the nurse lady lunged at one of the fleeing men, moving an amazing fifteen feet in a few quick steps. She collided with him hard and the man went soaring through one of the apartment windows that lined the alley. Victor's eyes flinched shut as the glass shattered. When he opened them, his comrade's legs dangled motionless over the window sill. Victor watched for signs of movement. There was none. After a second, he heard childlike giggling followed by the man's screaming. The legs began to kick and in an instant they were sucked into the window. The screaming stopped after an abrupt crunching sound and Victor took a step back and looked around him.

After a second, he saw her a few yards away, crouched down with her knees bent and her hands on the pavement. Bad Judy looked from the window directly into his eyes and smiled. From the way her eyes were glowing, she looked like an animal with a light being shinned in its face. The green lights in her eyes seemed to vanish, as she turned her head and looked toward the other man running down the alley. Victor took the opportunity and scanned the ground for a weapon. He quickly spotted a gun a few feet away from him, lying in a clump of dirty snow; Alex's 9mm. He took a few steps toward it, picked it up and snapped his attention back to the woman crouched in the alley. When he did, there was nothing there. She was gone.

Victor fumbled the clip out, peered at it and snapped it back in place. He brought the gun up and pointed it down the alley. He moved the barrel side to side, looking for a target, but there was nothing. No nurse lady. No screaming. The alley was silent other than the muffled sound of something moving around in the apartment the legs had disappeared through. It sounded like a large animal tearing meat off of a bone and eating it eagerly. Victor waited, breathing in and out as quietly as he could, with his eye fixed along the sights of the gun barrel. To his credit, the gun was steady in his hand.

•••

Britney heard the sound of glass shattering and jumped as Jamie and Tommy filed in behind her, each looking down the alley at the commotion. Britney caught her breath and looked back in time to see a screaming man running toward her. Before she had time to move back around the corner and out of sight, they made eye contact with one another. Britney saw the relief in his face and cringed.

Damn it! Now what? Why does every one see me when I don't want to be seen? I am not helping him! I have enough to worry about.

Just as she finished the thought, the man went sprawling chest first on the icy pavement. When he hit the ground, he didn't slide as Britney would expect him too. His body stuck to the ground, as if he had a rope tied to his foot and had run the length of it. He looked back up at her with a terrified look on his face.

"Please help me! Something has my feet! Please, I'm not with those guys! I was just—" Suddenly he was yanked back into the darkness, screaming. The instant he was out of sight, his screams went silent, as if the alley itself had swallowed him up.

"Holy shit!" Britney shrieked. She turned to the kids. "We have to get out of here!" She took the two of them by the hands and started to move them away from the opening to the alley. Britney tightened her grip, as Tommy tried to wiggle free from her grasp.

"No! I got to help my mommy!" he screamed.

"We can't help her, Tommy! We have to—" Britney started, continuing to pull him along, until she felt his small arm slip away from her. She stopped, turned and saw him glaring at her. His face was set in an unhappy scowl and it reminded her of an expression the other Tommy would have made. It gave Britney the creeps. Before she could say anything, Jamie moved forward and began to talk to him softly.

Yes, Jamie, please talk some sense into this kid, Britney thought. She kept her mouth shut and looked in all directions as the children talked.

"Tommy, your mommy's gone," Jamie said. "The bad lady got her."

"No she didn't. My mommy said she wouldn't let her. She said there was no bad lady!" Tommy put his head down and rubbed his left eye with one of his dirty knuckles.

Jamie moved forward and gently put her hand on his shoulder. Tommy flinched away slightly and looked up at her. His eyes looked glossy. Jamie could tell he was trying hard not to cry.

"I know you heard the bad lady," she said. "I could hear her too."

Britney attention shifted back to the two small children. "What bad lady? What are you two talking about?"

Both kids looked at Britney, then to each other and hesitated, as if they were trying to hold back from sharing a secret. Britney said, in a slightly stern voice, "Tell me now! What bad lady?"

As Jamie started to talk, Tommy's eyes peered down the alley. At that same moment, Victor picked up the gun from the icy snow.

"When we were walking down the stairs after her apartment, was the first time I heard it." Jamie started. "It was a bad thing talking to her, just like one talked to me and Tommy before. It was trying to get Judy, but not like us or the rest of the kids."

Britney knelt down in front of Jamie. The little girl was talking too fast and not making any sense to her.

"Slow down and tell me what you mean, sweetie! Are you telling me that isn't Judy back there? Do you mean that one of those things killed her?"

As soon as the words left her lips, Britney's mind started to race at the thought of having to find Judy's body and bring her back like they had brought the kids back. She squeezed her eyes shut.

I don't think I can do that by myself. But if I have to, I'll try. I can't leave her after all she did for us.

Before her thoughts made it too far, she saw Jamie's head shaking side to side. "No, she didn't get killed. The bad thing got inside her head. It wanted her help finding a..." she paused, struggling to find the right word. Tommy's small voice found it for her.

"A host," he said, dryly, not taking his eyes off the alley.

"Ya, a host. I think the other things kill the kids, then take their place, but I don't think they can live here very long. They just wanted a vacation. This one wants a live body. One that it can keep. I guess it wants an adult, but not Judy because it said she was weak."

Britney narrowed her eyes.

Judy's not weak, she thought. *At least she didn't seem to be to me. She sure kicked Mr. Porter's ass good.*

"How do you know all this, Jamie?"

"Cause I could hear it talking to her. It's been messing with her since we left her apartment." Jamie pointed at Tommy and said, "He could hear it too. She told us to run as soon as she threw the pack. The voice told her the guys wanted what was inside. Judy told me to pick it up when I went by, so I did." Jamie brought the backpack up a little, to emphasize what she was saying.

Tommy looked at them and nodded his head in agreement.

Britney looked at the bag, stood up and peered at the mouth of the alley. "Well then, if that's true, then we really have to go. We can't stay here and just wait. If one of those things has Judy, I mean, is inside her, then I don't know what we can do about it."

Before she could say anything else, Tommy spoke up. "No, it said it wanted one of those guys, not my mommy. It said if she helped it, it would leave her alone and take them instead. I heard it."

Britney looked down at him. "Do you think it was telling your mommy the truth?"

He shook his head slowly up and down, with his bottom lip sticking out. Britney let out a sigh and looked to Jamie.

"What do you think?"

Jamie shrugged her shoulders. Britney brought her hands up and rubbed her temples.

I guess this is what it feels like to be the adult.

"Ok, we'll wait a few minutes, but be ready to run if we have too. We *do* have the army to worry about too, you know." Britney sighed and continued, "I don't know if I believe any of this, but after what I've seen, I'm giving you two the benefit of the doubt."

Britney spotted the piece of wood on the ground, walked over, snatched it up and walked back to the kids.

"But can we please wait over there?" she said, pointing across the street. The kids looked and saw she was gesturing to an oak tree, surrounded by a variety of shrubs; a perfect place to hide and watch both the alley and the streets.

A few moments later, they were huddled together surrounded by shrubbery. Tommy eyes were focused on the opening to the alley. In the silence, one of their stomachs made a loud growling sound and the three of them looked at each other and smiled.

Jamie whispered "I'm still hungry. I wish we had some food."

"We'll try to find something soon, honey bunny," Britney said. Then she thought to herself, *As long as it isn't raw meat.*

•••

Victor watched the alley for another moment and slowly lowered the gun. He didn't like being alone, in a smelly alley, without his entourage, waiting for some freak to show her face.

"Hey! Anyone there!"

He didn't expect to hear a voice answer him, but it was all he could think of to do.

Just as his nerves started to ease up, he heard a scuffle to his left. The gun in his hand jerked in that direction and he squinted his eyes, trying clear up his view of the dark corner. A second later a large rat emerged from a stack of old limp boxes. Victor exhaled as he grasped the gun in his hand. He watched the rat move along the bottom of the wall and a nervous chuckle escaped his lips. He followed the rat in the cross hairs of the gun.

"Fucking rat. I hate fucking rats," he mumbled to himself, squeezing the trigger almost to the point of firing.

A voice whispered in his ear, "They're not so bad."

Victor ducked, bringing one of his knees to the ground, turned and pointed the gun, expecting to see the nurse lady right behind him, but when his eyes caught sight of her, she was a good ten feet away.

He paused for a second, wondering how she had gotten by him. He brought the gun up, putting her chest in the cross hairs. It trembled for the first time in his hand, as she continued to speak.

"They're blood is bitter and lacks the sweetness of your own."

Her voice sounded more realistic, drifting across the air at a distance. He could tell she had somehow tricked him a moment ago. There was no way she moved away that fast.

As he made this conclusion, he noticed the top of her scrubs had been removed and she now wore a thin white tank top. The kind that was meant to be worn under your cloths. It was soaked with sweat and under the thin material, he could see the outline of a light blue bra. Some of the undergarment was poking from the edges of the neckline as well. His eyes focused on her breasts and he marveled for a second on how different she looked without the baggy scrub top on. The cold night air also caused the nurse lady's nipples to harden and they looked like they were ready to pierce through the thin material. Combined with the blood splattered scrub pants, the sight had an unexpected seductive quality to him. A naughty Halloween costume party vibe. The gun loosened in his hand for a second, before he tightened his grip on it and turned his attention back to her face.

"Shut up!" he barked, sounding a little more nervous than he intended. "I don't know who or what you are, lady, but I'm gonna blow you away this time, bitch!"

A seductive smile crossed nurse ladies lips and again, Victor felt an urge to loosen his grip on the gun.

Her voice seemed to caress his ears, causing him to doubt his intentions. "You don't want to waist the last bullet in that gun on *me* do you?" She had the scrub top in her hand. She slowly raised it and rubbed it down her neck. Victor watched as she continued the motion until the garment slid over the top of one of her breasts, pulling down the light blue bra slightly, before it snapped back into place. Victor's stern expression loosened, as if drugs suddenly flowed in his veins.

Without warning, the gun seemed to gain ten pounds in his hand and before he could stop himself, he lowered it until it was pointed at the ground beside him. He clenched his jaw and looked down at it and realized he couldn't bring it back up. He took in a deep breath and flexed his muscles, trying with all his mite to gain control of his actions. He let the breath out in a burst and brought his attention back to the woman standing in front of him as she spoke again.

"Maybe you want to use it on yourself?"

Before Victor could respond, he felt his arm begin to twist the gun around, until the end of the barrel was pressed against his crotch. He started to breath hard in and out and said his next words calmly between breaths.

"Please don't. What do you want? Anything, just please not that." He paused and added, with a nervous smile, "I can't go out like that, Chicka. It would disappoint a lot of ladies."

He felt the trigger finger start to tingle, as nurse lady looked at him from head to toe; checking him out as if he were a sexy new sports car she was thinking of purchasing. It was as if he could feel her eyes move across his body.

He looked down at the gun and focused, in one last attempt to pull it away from himself. It was no use. He had no control and the feeling infuriated him. He looked back to the figure across from him. His vision was a blur. He was concentrating on not pulling the trigger enough that his eyes were watering, causing the figure in front of him to shimmer, as if she were underwater.

"Kill me if you're going to, bitch, but do it all the way. If you don't, I'll make you wish you had."

A split second after he muttered the words, he felt his finger push down on the trigger and he closed his eyes hard, waiting for the explosion. There was a click and he felt something thump against his boot. He slowly opened his eyes and looked down. The top portion of the gun lay at his feet. Without realizing he had regained control of his limb, he brought the butt of the gun up and peered at it. The barrel portion of the gun had snapped in half just above the trigger. He let out a grunt and tossed the rest of the gun away from him, as if it were going to explode in his hand. He looked across the alley, unable to speak. His throat was in knots. He could see the female blur in front of him, still ten feet away, but heard a soft whisper in his ear. He could almost feel the brush of her lips.

"I don't want to kill you. You're too beautiful for that," the seductive voice whispered.

Victor cleared his throat and managed to push out a few words. "Then what the hell you do want?" He quickly wiped the liquid from his eyes and looked back in front of him. When he did, he saw nurse lady toss the scrub top to the ground and start to advance toward him. She moved slowly and with more grace than he expected. Her walk was even more seductive than her smile and when she answered him, it made him forget what he had asked. Her words made his mind go blank.

"I want you, Victor. Every inch of you."

Bad Judy cleared the last five feet between them in one effortless leap. She collided with Victor, knocking him to the ground. When they landed, his vision was jarred as the back of his head smacked against the pavement. The thump pulsed in his head, like an echo moving down a deep, endless shaft. Before it finished, he felt warm hands creep around the back of his neck and the familiar feeling of lips pressing to his mouth invaded his senses.

Victor struggled for a moment, until a thought crossed his mind and he relaxed.

Can this be happening? Does this crazy bitch really want me?

He felt her tongue push its way into his mouth and it tasted like peppermint gum, fresh and clean. Victor didn't stop it. Instead, he let his struggling body go limp and a boyish feeling of sexual bliss surfaced, as if it were the first time he had a woman on top of him. For once in his life, he really did feel like a king.

Damn, this feels good. Fuck it, I know it's crazy but I want her too.

He slipped his hands around her back and ran them down her spine, until they were moving over the curve of her ass. Nurse lady started to kiss him harder, her tongue making circles around his. Suddenly, Victor clenched his hands and squeezed the cheeks of her ass hard. He felt her fingers playfully dig into his neck and the sides of his head, just behind his ears. It hurt, but felt wonderful at the same time. He felt his crotch start to stiffen against the fabric of his jeans, as his hands pulled the nurse ladies hips into a dry hump motion.

Holy God damn! This is fucking amazing! I can't believe this shit's happening to—

The thought was suddenly cut short, as Victor realized he couldn't breathe. The crazy bitches tongue felt like it was going down his throat and into his stomach. Not only into his stomach, but through his entire body, like the roots of a tree burrowing through soil in fast forward. His eyes jerked open. He tried to push her off of him, but had no control of his limbs again. Even his hands had a mind of their own and continued to squeeze at her ass, pulling it tighter against him, as her hips moved. A few muffled moans escaped his lips and his feet began to jerk, as if an electric current was streaming through his body.

Nurse lady continued to kiss Victors twitching body, until his legs stopped moving and his hands fell off of her, thumping to the icy pavement. As if repulsed by Victor's sudden lack of movement, their lips parted and her body slumped over, rolling off of him, until she rested next to him on her back. Both of their chests heaved up and down as they sucked in gulps of air and their eyes stared up at the sky without blinking. Strings of green mist flowed out of Victor's nostrils, ears and mouth. Neither of them moved, as a rat scampered across the ground between them, giving them a sniff, before moving on its way across the alley.

Chapter 9.

Britney, Jamie and Tommy watched the opening to the alley for what seemed like forever, before the two girls attention began to wonder. Tommy's didn't wonder. He watched the alley adamantly, as if looking away would cause the opening to close up, trapping his mother inside. Britney glanced at him every so often; he looked ready to pounce.

They were in a good spot, hidden from whoever or whatever came out of the alley and the spot lights that circled the streets. Whatever happened, they had a straight shot from there, to the garage Jamie assured them was the building her father's Rover was parked in. At ten years old, she honestly never paid attention to what the structure looked like from every angle, but she was pretty sure.

"Are you positive that's the one?" Britney asked her, for the third time.

"Ya, I'm pretty sure," Jamie said, sick of the question.

Britney hopped she was right. She didn't want any more complications at this point.

Britney fiddled with the piece of wood, picking shards of it off and crumbling them into tiny pieces. She looked down and saw she had bits of the wood all over her lap and she brushed them onto the ground. Jamie glanced at her sudden movements and then back to the end of the street, where she had been watching a group of soldiers load up what looked like the last of the people waiting in the lines.

Britney's eyes fell back on the opening to the alley. Other than a few voices, there hadn't been any more commotion and she was starting to feel like they were wasting their time. She glanced at Tommy. The little boy hadn't taken his eyes off the alley. He looked anxious, tired and scared.

I can't blame him for wanting to wait, but damn, we can't sit here forever.

After ten minutes of waiting, Britney had attempted to move on, but Tommy wouldn't have it. She could tell that he had a way of getting what he wanted, so she gave him another ten minutes; which had ended four minutes ago and he still wouldn't budge. Jamie was no help either. It was as if the two kids could read each other minds or something. It made Britney feel like a third wheel. She decided to try another tactic. It was too quiet for her anyways.

"So, Tommy, what do you like to do?" Britney asked.

Jamie looked over at Tommy as he turned his head in Britney's direction. She smiled a second before her new friend answered.

"I like to watch cartoons," Tommy said, with no enthusiasm in his voice.

Britney flashed on the hours she spent watching cartoons with the other Jamie and shivered. Before she lost Tommy's attention, she pressed on.

"Really? What's your favorite cartoon?"

Tommy answered without giving it a second thought. "Mr. Crabs."

A questioning look surfaced on Britney's face. "Don't you mean Sponge Bob Square Pants?"

Tommy looked confused for a moment and shook his head side to side. "No, Mr. Crabs."

"Well, Sponge Bob Square Pants is the name of the cartoon that Mr. Crabs is in, isn't it?"

Tommy glanced back at the opening to the alley and said, "Mr. Crabs is the boss, so it should be his show. I don't like Sponge Bob. Mr. Crabs is funnier."

Britney stared at him for a moment.

God, this kid is kind of weird. This whole thing is weird.

Britney put a fake smile on her face. "Oh, I see. I guess that's true. Tommy, do you go to school?"

Without looking back at Britney, Tommy replied "No."

"Well, how old are you? Your five right?"

Tommy nodded, still looking at the alley.

"Well then why don't you go to school? You really should be in school. I mean, what do you do all day?"

The comment gave Britney an adult vibe when she said it and she waited for his response to her grown up question. Jamie waited for Tommy's response as well, somehow knowing it wasn't going to be what Britney expected.

Tommy glared back at Britney. "How old are you?" he asked.

"I'm seventeen."

Tommy continued giving her an unblinking stare. "Do *you* go to school?"

Britney was taken back by the question and fumbled her answer. She had dropped out her sophomore year of high school, for no reason other than she was sick of going and her parents didn't seem to care if she went or not. Before she answered the question, the adult feeling she had a moment ago waved bye bye.

"Well, no...no I don't."

Before she had a chance to prepare for another odd question, Tommy asked, "Shouldn't you be in school? What do *you* do all day?"

Britney gave him a blank look.

Jamie let out a giggle and turned her attention back to the soldiers down the street.

Britney stared at the five year old for a moment and couldn't think of anything to say. Tommy turned his head and went back to watching the alley, as if he knew the conversation was over.

Britney put her head down and continued to pick tiny pieces of wood from the plank laying across her lap.

God, this f-ing sucks. I wish Judy were here. I can't do this shit alone.

Suddenly Britney didn't mind waiting a few more minutes, in hopes that somehow Judy would walk out of the alley and take control of the situation again. She glanced at a clock across the street, in the window of a small post office. They had only been waiting for about twenty five minutes. She let out a sigh.

This is the longest half hour of my life. Five more minutes we go, even if I have to drag Tommy by his ears.

•••

Jamie watched the soldiers load up the last few people, not really paying attention at what was being said, although she could hear every word. It was as if she had super girl hearing. At first she thought it was a little strange, but now she was getting use to it.

As soon as the doors slide shut, the bus took off, heading straight a few yards before turning in the direction the other buses had gone. Usually another bus would be pulling up in its place, but now the spot sat empty and Jamie watched as the remaining soldiers quickly collected various gear scattered about and started to pile into a few large military SUV's parked on the curb. She focused and listened as one of the soldiers, holding a large riffle, address another taller man smoking a pipe.

"Major Massy, sir." The soldier saluted the taller man.

"Ok, ok, have out with it," Massy said, brushing off the salute as he re-lit the expensive looking pipe. It was a wonder how he got the thing to light in the cold wind, but smoke began puffing out of the left side of his mouth. Massy had been smoking for close to 50 years and considered himself an expert. He preferred a good pipe these days, but would smoke anything he could get his hands on; well, anything legal. The guys in his unit took to calling him 'Old Smokey', but never to his face.

The armed soldier lowered his hand and addressed the officer in a formal tone.

"That was the last of them. Civilian casualties should be down to a minim—"

Major Massy answered before the armed soldier finished what he was saying. It gave Jamie the impression the taller one with the pipe was in charge.

"That's fine, Parker. At least the media pricks can't say we didn't try. After all, the big boys upstairs didn't give us much time and it's not like we can chase all the normies out of hiding. 'Get them on the buses kicking and screaming if you have too,' they said, as if that's an easy task. All in all, I think we did fine."

The armed soldier obediently waited until he knew the major was done talking before he spoke again.

"We still have some foot patrols out on the streets. Should I call them in?"

"Hell yes, call them in. They should have been called in an hour ago. Some people don't want to be helped and we did what we could. We shouldn't even be loading these buses. Do you know what would happen if one of those things slipped through the cracks?"

After a silent moment, the armed soldier spoke up. "I hope they all fry!"

Major Massy eyed the man with one of his brows raised. He took another blast from his pipe and blew the smoke out in a gust rather than a savory trickle. He didn't wait for the smoke to vacate his mouth before speaking. "Have you ever heard the verse 'Love thine enemies, bless them that curse you, do good to them that hate you and pray for them which despitefully use you and persecute you...and hate thine neighbors, for they are your true pain in the ass."

The soldier swallowed hard. He knew it was a trick question and didn't know how to answer it. Instead he patiently waited for the major to continue, hopping the man didn't expect an actual answer.

131

Major Massy let the question linger for a moment, taking a long blast off his pipe and savoring the flavor before continuing.

"Look at all these people for instance. Martial law? They don't even know what those words mean. I have people threatening to sue me, for hecks sake. All this effort wasted on people who can't even follow a simple command without questioning it. Information, before evacuation, I always say, but no one listens. We should have waited. It's a horrible thing that happened here, but let us not forget we can learn from it."

The next words from his mouth had a grumble to them that made the soldier straighten his posture.

"Let them fry? Have you ever tried to get information from an enemy that's brunt to a crisp?" The majors voice settled back into a reasonable, almost gospel tone. "May God have mercy on the souls who are left." After a short pause, he added, "and to all the children who had to die, but we have a job to do. A long job that isn't finished yet. Tell the men to drop what they're doing and get to the trucks. We need to be as far from here as we can by twenty two hundred hours."

The armed soldier saluted the taller man and watched as he casually walked a few yards away, to a dark green Jeep that was parked half way on the curb. The Major boarded it, with the pipe clenched in his teeth. The jeep purred to life and pulled onto the road, heading the way the bus had gone.

Jamie glanced at the clock in the window across the street. The clock read eight thirty two p.m.

I wonder what he means by twenty two hundred hours. It's only half past eight. It must be a military thing.

Before Jamie had a chance to think too much about the difference in regular people time and military people time, Tommy let out a cry, stabbing the silence.

"Mommy!"

Britney and Jamie jumped and looked first at Tommy, then to the direction he was looking. A female figure stumbled out of the alley and stopped, looking up and down the street. Britney squinted her eyes, trying to get a good look. It was Judy, but she looked different. Britney quickly noticed she had taken off her scrub top and had a lot more blood on her than she did before. The thin tank top under shirt she wore showed all of her curves; more curves than Britney thought she had.

Wow, she looks 'brick house', she thought. I had no idea she looked like that, those scrubs were so baggy.

Before she finished the thought, Britney saw movement out of the corner of her eye. Tommy's small body jump to a standing position and start moving toward the alley. Britney's heart dropped into her stomach.

"Mommy!" Tommy yelled again, making the female figure take notice of them. It waved its hand and moved in their direction.

Britney bolted to her feet. "Tommy no! Wait!" She took a few steps and grabbed the small boy before he made it too far. When she looked up from him, she saw Judy lightly jogging toward them. She looked cold and exhausted, which gave Britney a shred of hope.

Please be Judy and not some freaky thing I have to clobber this this piece of wood. Please be normal.

As Judy approached them, Britney looked back and saw Jamie was keeping her distance, hanging back where they had been hiding. Britney adjusted the piece of wood in her hand, spinning it so that the nail at the end was facing forward. She hadn't realized the nail was there the last time she used the wood as a bat, but this time, she didn't intend on messing around. She raised the two by four over her shoulder.

A lot of good it will do if she is one of those things. With my luck, it will snatch it from me and beat the hell out of me with it.

Judy's face settled into a worried scowl as she stopped a few feet from them.

"Britney, what are you doing?"

"Stop right there!" Britney's voice sounded stern and the club was shaking in her hand. "Don't come any closer!"

Judy slowed her stride. "Britney, what's gotten into to you?"

"How do we know it's really you?" Britney sputtered. The closer Judy came, the more nervous she felt. "If you're the real Judy, then what's my name?"

Judy tilted her head, with a questioning look on her face. "What?"

"I said...tell me what my name is!" Britney barked, holding the piece of wood higher.

Judy gave her a comical look. "Your name is Britney. I've said it twice just now."

Britney's posture sagged and the club lowered slightly. "Oh...right," she said dumbly. After a second, the look on her face tightened. "How do we know it's you, Judy?" she asked. "How do we know you're not one of those things?"

Judy's expression softened, as she seemed to ignore the question. She looked down at Britney's side, where Tommy was smiling up at her.

"Hey, honey," Judy said softly.

Tommy answered, "Hey, Mommy."

Britney look back and forth between them for a second, letting the piece of wood in her hand sag lower. Before she spoke again, she tightened her grip and held it up higher above her shoulder. "Answer me! How do we no it's you! How do we know you're normal?" Britney barked.

Judy continued to smile at Tommy for another second, then looked back up at Britney. "Of course it's me, Britney. Why wouldn't it be?"

Britney stared at her for a few seconds, not knowing what to say. Her mind went blank and she slowly lowered the wood again, without noticing. Without warning, Jamie spoke, causing Britney to jump. The little girl was suddenly standing right behind her.

"We could hear the bad lady talking to you before," Jamie's voice had the slightest tremble to it. "We know she was trying to get inside you."

Judy stared at her for a moment and her face softened as she spoke. "Oh, honey, don't worry. It's me." Judy looked down at Tommy. "That bad lady is gone now."

Britney looked back and forth between Jamie and Judy. Her mind was still blank and she had forgotten all about the make shift weapon in her hand. She saw that Jamie had a skeptic eye on Judy and the little girl held it there until Judy spoke again.

"Jamie, don't worry. It's really me. You say you heard the bad lady before?" Judy turned her attention to Tommy and smiled. "Honey, you could hear her too, right?"

Tommy slowly shook his head up and down. The look on his face had changed from excitement, to worry.

Judy smiled and addressed the two of them. "Well, can you hear her now?"

Tommy and Jamie listened. Tommy's eyes squeezed shut. His nose wrinkled, as if keeping them shut took a lot of effort. Jamie's eyes narrowed on Judy, as if reading her. After a moment, Jamie's expression softened into a smile.

"No, she's gone. I don't hear her now. Not even her breathing. It's just you."

Tommy opened his eyes and smiled.

Britney let out a sigh at the same time Tommy took a few steps forward, wrapping his arms around Judy's legs, hugging her as tight as his weak muscles could squeeze. The sudden movement caused Judy to stumble backwards slightly. She steadied and began rubbing the top of his head with her bloody hand.

Tommy pulled his face away from her legs and looked at the other two girls. "See I told you! My mommy said the bad lady was gonna go and now she's gone! She left!"

Judy looked down at him, continuing to stroke his head. "That's right. No more bad lady!"

Britney lowered the piece of wood until the tip of it tapped the asphalt at her feet. "Holly crap, Judy. What the heck is going on? What happened in there?" she said, gesturing to the alley.

Without glancing in that direction, Judy said, "I don't think you would believe me if I told you. I'll tell you later, I think we should just get going. We've lingered here too long."

Britney smiled. *Yep, that's the same old Judy. Welcome back! And thank God. These kids were making me feel like a big, stupid, idiot.*

Judy reached down, put an arm around Tommy and hoisted him up to her hip. The little boy fit her body like a puzzle piece. He put his arms around her shoulder and pushed his face against her neck.

Jamie watched this with great interest. Jealousy reared its ugly face for a moment as she watched the display of infection.

Jamie sent a thought in Tommy's direction. *Good for you Tommy. You got your mommy back. I'm so happy for you.*

Tommy pulled his face from his mother's neck and gave Jamie a bright smile, as if to say 'thank you'.

The whole scene caused Jamie's mind to wonder to her own mother for a moment and her throat tightened against her breath. Her mind dwelled there for a second, until she looked up and saw Judy heading in her direction. Jamie straightened her posture as butterflies fluttered in her stomach.

"Hey, sweetie. So I guess you heard me when I told you to grab the bag?" Judy said in a soft voice. "Sorry if I scared you, but I had to distract those bad men."

"Ya, I heard you, but I wasn't scared of *you*. Those men didn't even scare me. It was the other one I was afraid of."

Judy smiled at the little girl for a moment, then her gaze moved to the back pack Jamie had slung over her shoulder.

"I'll take that now, if you want."

"Oh, ya, sure."

Jamie handed the pack over and Judy took it, brought it up and over her shoulder, flinching slightly as she did. Jamie noticed a smear of blood on her left arm, where flesh looked swollen and meaty underneath. Judy had so much blood smeared on her, it was hard to tell if this was an injury or not.

When Judy was done, she took a breath and looked back at the two girls, knowing they were both watching her.

"Well, let's go before someone see's us."

"Or something," Britney added, looking back at the mouth of the alley.

Judy started walking without following her gaze. "Yes…or something," she mumbled under her breath.

...

As the four of them moved down the sidewalk, toward the parking garage, voices started to drift down the alley. Had they lingered a few moments longer, Jamie's good ears would have heard them.

"Nick, come over here quick, take a look at this!"

Two more soldiers rounded the corner, stopping to gawk at the carnage.

"Holly shit, it looks like a massacre. This guy's cut in half at the waist," another soldier said, in a confused tone. He stood over the body of what was once a black man, wearing way too much bling.

"See, I told you I heard shots," the first soldier said, as he knelt down next to the bloody body, pulled out an instrument, running it over the top half of the corpse. "Clean. And this one wasn't shot either," After a short pause, he added, "Maybe he was the shooter, but not a very good one I guess." He looked at the other men. "Spread out and look around."

The other two men did as they were told. After a few seconds, one of them called down the alley. "Hey, there's another one over here! This ones decapitated!"

The first soldier looked in that direction and saw that the man was pointing the end of his riffle down towards the ground. In the dim light, the corps was barely visible.

"Check it. Hurry up though. We have to get out of here soon. We shouldn't even be here. We were told to come in." He looked down at the two halves of what used to be a human being at his feet and cringed.

One of the other two men settled in beside him and lit a smoke. He took a drag and blew it out as he spoke. "Do you think we should call this in to Old Smokey?"

The first soldier smiled and replied, "Na, he's probably smoking old butts out of an ashtray in front of a liquor store somewhere."

This got a chuckle out of the other man, as he took another drag. "What the hell do you think happened here?"

"I don't know. This is some crazy shit. It's like something from a bad horror novel. From the looks of it, both of these guys must have been—" suddenly he stopped talking, as both men caught movement out of the corner of their eyes. Without thinking, they both brought their rifles up. A large rat scampered across the ground, squealing, as if something had spooked it. Both men looked back in the direction it had come from and spotted a third body lying motionless on the ground. This one had his shirt opened, displaying a variety of tattoos on his chest and stomach. The first soldier lowered his rifle, pulled out the mechanism from his belt and approached the body. The other man kept his rifle pointed at the heap on the ground, with his cigarette clenched tightly between his teeth.

He waved the mechanism over the top of the body. Instantly, a high pitched whistling sound blared from the machine and he looked back at the other man.

"Looks like we have a live one." After a short pause he added, "Wait, this can't be right. This thing has to be broken."

A voice from behind, startled them both.

"What have you got there, soldier?"

Both men turned and saw Major Massy strolling toward them. Past him, across the street in the distance, his Jeep sat on the sidewalk under a large oak tree, with grey puffs of smoke exiting the tail pipe.

The two men looked at one another for a moment, then the first soldier addressed him.

"Major Sir, it looks like we have a live one here. Readings are off the charts, Sir, like nothing we've seen so far."

The Major took a few steps until he was standing next to the body. He looked down at it. "Is that so?"

The armed soldier kept his rifle pointed at the man on the ground and the cigarette clenched between his teeth. The first soldier continued to gawk at his scanner, tapping it lightly with his finger.

"Cuff his hands and feet and let's hope it's enough," Major Massy said. "Keep a gun on him too. You never know—"

The major stopped mid-sentence, as he spotted something lying on the ground a few feet from the body. He reached down and picked it up. It unfolded at the ends of his fingertips and appeared to be a woman's blouse. The kind a nurse would wear. It had smears of blood on it and felt heavy on one side. Major Massy dropped one end of it and fondled the front pocket with his hand. He reached inside and touched something familiar to him. He pulled out a pack of menthol cigarettes and a silver Zippo lighter. He looked at them for a moment, spinning the lighter in his hand.

'Peter'

He looked down at the man on the ground.

This guy doesn't look like a 'Peter', Massy thought. *A 'Pedro', maybe, but not a 'Peter'.*

His eyes went back to the piece of clothing, as he discreetly slipped the pack and lighter into his coat pocket.

The three men watching smirked at each other secretly. Then their eyes went back to the man lying at the major's feet.

Massy wadded up the scrub top and tossed it aside, as he pulled a walky talky from his belt. He hit the button on the side and spoke into it. "We have another one, McCain. An adult male. Come over to section eleven B, in the west alley and load him up with the other one we found earlier."

A robotic voice erupted from the hand set.

"Copy that. On my way."

Major Massy looked back down at the man at his feet and whispered, "Love thine enemy. Whoever you may be, no matter 'Peter' or 'Pedro', we're gonna take good care of you. Lots to learn. Lots to learn, indeed."

Victor's eyes moved back and forth under his lids and his pulse quickened a few beats.

Major Massy walked toward the other men, while they continued to gawk at the mystery man on the ground. Before they noticed he had approached them, the major reached out and snatched the cigarette out of the armed soldier's mouth, causing the extremely long ash on the end of it to flutter to the ground. They're eyes moved to the major, as he brought the cigarette up to his mouth and took a deep drag, squeezing the filter between his thick fingers.

"Waist not, want not, gentlemen," he said, as he strolled past them, in the direction of his idling Jeep.

•••

More steps, Britney sighed.

The Porter family Land Rover was located on the third level of the parking garage and Britney cringed when she saw the elevator was out.

The four of them ascended the stairs slowly, taking short breaks on the landings. Tommy smiled down on the two girls, still being carried by Judy. He marveled how the echoes of their footfalls and breathing bounced around in the small space. When they reached the third floor landing, they paused before opening the door.

"When we get out there, stick together and hope to God the tank is full," Britney said. She wanted nothing more than to be able to sit down for a while, give her legs a rest. Looking at the others, she could tell they were thinking the same thing.

Judy glanced at Britney after she made the comment. The thought of fuel never crossed her mind.

They opened the door to the parking level, walked out into the lot and looked around. At first, the lot seemed empty and Britney's heart dropped a few inches.

Britney looked down at Jamie. "Which way is your dads Rover?"

Jamie pointed a finger to their left. "It's usually parked around that corner."

As they rounded the corner, more vehicles came into view and they spotted Richard's Land Rover. Britney's face puckered up, as if she were looking at a piece of maggot infested meat. In all the time she had been watching Jamie for the Porters, she never seen Mr. Porters ride. If he were keeping it a secret, she could see why. It was an ugly color of gold, dented and scratched in half a dozen places. The aftermarket front bumper made it look like something out of 'Mad max and the Thunder Dome', except not in a cool way.

What a piece of shit, Britney thought.

Tommy looked at the vehicle in awe. His parents had never owned vehicle as far as he could remember. His transportation experiences mostly consisted of bus rides and the occasional taxi.

Judy walked to the passenger back side and tried the door. It opened. She put Tommy in the back seat, then unshouldered the back pack and placed it inside as well. Britney watched her for a moment before turning her attention to Jamie. The little girl was looking down the row of cars. She jumped when Britney spoke.

"That's your dads Land Rover?"

Jamie looked over at the SUV. "Ya, why?

"It looks like a piece of shi….I mean, *junk*," Britney mumbled as she reached in her pocket for the keys. Her jeans were tight and she had to shimmy her hand deep into her pocket. The action of getting the keys had made her forget what was coming out of her mouth.

Jamie snapped, "Well, he's had it for a long time. What did you expect it to look like?"

Britney could hear the offence in the little girl's voice and tried to back pedal. "I don't know? I'm not complaining, it's just, you think of a Land Rover and a luxury SUV pops into your head…ya, know?"

Jamie looked back to Britney just as she yanked the keys from her pocket. "Well, I like it!" Then after a short pause, she asked, "You've never seen it?"

"No, I guess I haven't," Britney answered. "Your mom usually picked me up or dropped me off in her Camaro."

Mrs. Porter's car was parked a few spots down from the Rover, crisp yellow paint, glimmering in the florescent lights. It looked brand new. It was a beautiful car.

"Boy, I wish we had ended up with the keys to that one instead," Britney said, still not really paying attention to what was coming out of her mouth. "I've always wanted to drive it. Your mom used to drive that thing like a maniac. You used to giggle so hard, I thought you were gonna hurl."

Britney looked back to Jamie, expecting her to be smiling at the memory, but she wasn't. The little girl's eyes were locked on her mothers car. Britney realized her friend was staring at the car before she had even started talking, probably missing her mother. Britney regretted mentioning Mrs. Porter.

Dammit, I have to learn when to keep my trap shut.

Before Britney had a chance to say anything more to Jamie, Judy strolled up to them and spoke.

"What's holding you two? Hop in and lets go."

Neither of the girls answered her. To Judy, they looked nervous and edgy. As soon as she was done talking, they headed toward the Rover without a glance at each other. Judy watched as Jamie got in the back seat and Britney slid into the front passenger seat. Judy scanned the parking lot for a second and walked to the Rover, opened the door and got behind the wheel, slamming the door shut as she did.

"I'm guessing you know how to drive a stick, right?" Britney said, with a hopeful look on her face.

Judy looked down at the shifter, then the petals on the floor by her feet. "No, but we're not going to let that stop us."

Britney gave her a doubtful look, before handing the keys over. A second later the Rover purred to life. Britney glanced at the fuel meter and let out a sigh of relief.

"At least the tanks full," she mumbled, as Judy struggled to put the SUV into gear. After a few seconds, the gear caught and Judy backed the beast out of its parking spot. Before she could stop, the back of the Rover collided with a sedan parked behind them. Judy let out a muffled giggle and fought to put the Rover into first gear. The look on her face caused Britney to smile and look back at the kids. They were both griming as well. The Rover made a few jolts forward, before smoothing out and moving down the lane, towards the exit.

As they rolled out of the garage, they all felt safe for the first time since meeting each other. The feeling only lasted about a block.

•••

The cars parked in the streets weren't much trouble; Judy could go on the side walk and creep around them easily. It was the intersections that were the problem. Each one they came to, seemed clogged with parked cars. Judy struggled with the gears every time they had to come to a stop, but after a couple of twists and turns, she seemed to be getting the hang of the gears. There were only four or five roads that would take the out of the city and they couldn't seem to find one that wasn't congested with abandoned vehicles. Britney fumbled with the radio tuner, turning it back and forth, looking for a station. There was nothing but static and after a moment, she abruptly clicked the power off.

"Dammit, this thing doesn't work."

Britney seemed to be the only one in the car surprised by this. After a couple of minutes, Judy noticed Jamie leaning forward, whispering something in Britney's ear. Britney turned and replied to her as quietly as she could.

"I know honey." Britney said, in a whisper. "But let's just get a little further, then I'll ask…ok?"

Judy heard Britney's reply and had an idea what the little girl was asking. Judy's next words were music to Britney, Tommy and Jamie's ears.

"Well, if were gonna stop for food, we better do it now. Anyone as hungry as I am?" Judy said, stinging the silence in the small space. The silence was further interrupted as both kids and Britney let out cheers of agreement.

After a moment, Britney asked, "Where we gonna to go to find food?" Just as the question left Britney's lips, Judy pulled the Rover down a dark alley and it came to a stop, casting them under the shadows of the surrounding buildings. She put it in park and turned off the engine. Before Britney could mutter a question, Judy spoke.

"You guys wait here. I'll be right back." Judy reached around the back of the seat and pulled the back pack into the front with her. Britney watched her, wide eyed.

"Wait! What are you doing?" Britney asked.

Judy stopped with her hand on the door handle and looked back to her. "I'm going to get food. Stay here with the kids, I'll be right back."

Judy motioned to the building next to the alley. Britney followed her gesture and calmed when she saw what it was. The place was called Grimaldi's Grocery and it was a small mom and pop store Britney had never been inside of. From where they were sitting, she could see that the front windows were busted through and somewhere inside, a light pulsed, on the verge of going out.

"You're going in without us?" Britney said, with a frown. "You're leaving us here? What if something happens?"

Judy opened the door and got out of the cab before Britney finished the comment. For a second, Britney held her breath, thinking she wasn't going to get an answer. That Judy was just going to take off again, like she had back in the stair well. Then Judy's face appeared in the doorway.

"I think you'll be fine for a few minutes," Judy said. "After all they've been through, I don't think we need to drag them out of the car again."

Britney looked back at the children. Tommy was watching them, but his eyes were far away, closer to sleep, than to anything going on around him. Jamie was staring out the window, in the direction of the pulsating light. Britney's attention snapped back to Judy, as she continued.

"Just lock the doors and keep a look out. I won't be too long." Then after a second, Judy added, "After all you've been through, I think you can handle anything that might come up."

Britney smiled and gave a nod. She knew Judy was right. They would be ok. It was just the thought of her going in that building and not coming out that made her nervous.

The door clicked shut and Britney reached across the driver's seat and pushed down the lock mechanism. She watched as Judy walked along the side of the building and disappeared through one of the ceiling to floor window without a pause.

Britney heard a shuffle in the rear of the car, looked back and saw Jamie shifting in her seat. The little girl was rubbing her hands together, either for warmth or sourness. Britney could relate to either reason. After a moment, she looked to Tommy. His eyes had finally given in. They were shut and his head was clocked at an uncomfortable looking angle, his cheek resting on his shoulder. Britney could hear him snoring lightly and it reminded her of a purring kitten. He looked tinny in the backseat.

He really should be in a car seat or whatever you call them. A booster seat thing. He looks so uncomfortable.

An image of Judy carrying the little boy's burnt, dangling corps from the hallway crept into her mind. Her body shivered.

Well, I guess he looks more comfortable in the back seat than he was in the dryer. Poor little guy.

Britney shifted around in her seat and climbed into the back. Jamie scooched over, giving the teen room to sit between them. Britney carefully adjusted Tommy, placing his head in her lap. He let out a tired sigh and continued to sleep deeply.

Britney looked over at Jamie and smiled. "There, that's better. Poor little guy looked like his neck was broken."

Jamie didn't respond and shifted her glance back out the window, where Judy had entered the building and the light continued to pulse.

Britney followed her gaze for a moment, then glanced back to the sleeping boy in her lap. Before her mind could linger on

Tommy too long, Jamie spoke without taking her eyes off the store window.

"Do you think we'll be ok?"

Britney looked at her and without hesitation, she answered, "Yes, we're gonna be fine."

Jamie shifted and looked to the front of the car, near the steering column. She settled back in her seat and looked down at her hands. Britney had the feeling she was about to spill something and patiently waited for it.

"She took the keys," Jamie said. "Why did she have to take the keys?"

Britney glanced at the ignition and saw Jamie was right. Judy had taken the keys. At that moment it dawned on her that Jamie wished they could take off and leave Judy behind.

"What's wrong Jamie? Do you not think Judy's not ok now? I mean, you guys said you didn't hear the bad lady in her or whatever."

Before Britney could finish, Jamie's head started to shake side to side. Britney stopped talking and waited.

"No, it's not that. It's not that I think there's anything wrong with her. She seems really nice, but…" Jamie's words drifted away, as if she didn't want to finish.

"But what?" Britney pressed. "Go ahead and say it. It's Britney. You know you can tell me anything. Do you know something?"

Jamie glanced back out the window. No Judy in sight. Then she glanced at Tommy's sleeping face a second before returning her eyes to her lap. Her next words were spoken in a whisper.

"It's just that, do you know she killed that guy in the apartment. She bashed him to death with that snow globe."

Britney's eyes narrowed on her. "How do you know that, Jamie?"

The little girl's hands started to roll around themselves as she continued to speak in a whisper. "When we were in the apartment and the thing on the floor was trying to get at me, I think it showed me somethings to try to make me feel weak or maybe not to trust you guys. Some messed up things. That was one of the things it showed me, her…you know." Jamie let out a puff of air through her nose. "I was hoping it wasn't true…But it looked kinda true when we left that guy behind."

Britney watched her for a moment, not knowing what she should say or if the little girl would see through a lie if she told it. Something told her the little girl would, so she told the truth. As bad as it sounded, it felt better coming out of her moth than the lie would have.

143

"She did have to kill that man." Britney said. "She told me about it. She thought he was going to hurt Tommy. She didn't know it wasn't the real Tommy, when she did it."

The scenario sounded familiar to Jamie.

"Then why did she just leave the man there?" she asked.

Britney thought about that question for a second. There wasn't an easy way to answer it, because she didn't know the answer entirely herself. From what Judy told her, she knew Pete was a drug addict and kind of a dick, but that still didn't justify leaving him behind in her opinion. It had been Judy's choice.

"I'm sure she had her reasons. Sometimes people, even grownups, do thing that don't seem like they make sense. And sometimes they don't make sense. Sometimes you just don't understand the reason, but that doesn't mean it isn't there."

Jamie looked up from her hands and her eyes met Britney's. The clarity in them made Britney want to look away, especial when the little girl asked her next question.

"Do *you* think we should have left him?"

Britney let out a low breath. "As messed up as it seems, no, I don't think we should have left him, but it was Judy's choice. You're too young to understand everything you saw, but believe me, that thing only showed you what it wanted you to see. I'm sure Judy had her reasons for leaving him."

Jamie reflected for a moment. She could see how Britney was right. When she wanted to shove memories back at the thing, she made sure the memories were unpleasant ones. Of course it was easier for her to pick the bad ones. That thing in the apartment didn't seem to have any good memories, except for ones from its vacation on the couch.

Jamie spoke again. "So, does that mean everything I saw is true?"

Britney could feel her head start to thump in her skull.

God, why do conversations with little kids have to suck sometimes!

"I don't know, Jamie. I have no idea what you saw or if it made things up or what."

Then a dreadful idea popped into Britney's mind.

I wonder if that damn thing showed her stuff about me too.

A hundred things she wouldn't want Jamie to know flashed across her mind, making her temples hurt even more. The look on her face must have shown her frustration, because next she felt Jamie's small hand caress her shoulder.

"It's ok, Britney. I wasn't trying to say anything bad. I just don't know. I'm scared. We could have been killed when we went back to the apartment. And in the alley. It just seems like Judy is kind of…risky."

That word 'risky' perplexed Britney. She could have finished the comment with the same word if Jamie hadn't said it first. Judy was risky.

She's right. Judy takes risks, but if she didn't, I'd still be stuck in that bedroom with pervert Porter and the children would still be dead.

Britney swallowed hard. "Ya, you're right, she does take risks, but where would we be without her? I mean, we went back to that apartment to save Tommy. We didn't know what to expect when we got there. She didn't even want us to go in with her, but we did. We took the risk. If we hadn't, I don't think she would have come out. You saved all of us in there, didn't you Jamie?"

Britney felt Jamie's hand tighten against her shoulder. The little girl didn't answer her.

"I know you did," Britney whispered. "I'm sorry you had to do what you did, but I'm *glad* you did it. You risked your life for us and saved us."

Jamie's small voice whispered, "Ya, I guess. But what do we do now?"

Just as Jamie asked the question, Britney saw Judy step out of the window, carrying two armloads of grocery bags. It was a lot of stuff, more than it seemed like she should be able to carry with the ground as slippery as it looked. As Judy got closer, Britney saw the strain on her face and the way she was taking short, carful steps. Even the back pack slung over her shoulder looked stuffed with food.

Jamie looked out the window and noticed Judy, just as Britney answered her. "We trust that Judy will get us out of here, no matter what the risk. She's done good by us so far, right?"

"Ya, she has." Jamie added a hint of amusement to her voice and said, "She just scars me a little."

The teen smiled at her and whispered playfully, "Me too. Let's hope she scares anyone else that comes along too." They both giggled as Judy approached the Rover. Jamie leaned forward and slid her hand beside the front seat, unlocking the door. Britney looked back down at Tommy as Jamie leaned back and settled in her seat. Just before Judy opened the door, Britney heard Jamie say something in a hushed tone.

"Oh…and Judy has drugs in her back pack."

Britney's attention snapped back to Jamie and her eyes went wide. She opened her mouth to say something when, a second later, the inside of the car was filled with a chilly breeze as Judy opened the door and slid into the front seat.

"Who's hungry? I've got snacks galore," Judy said, as she clicked the door shut. She tossed the bags in the passenger seat, turned and glanced in the back. Tommy was sleeping peacefully with his head in Britney's lap. His mouth was gapped open and his small hand had hold of the fabric of the teen's shirt. It was a habit he had growing up and Judy smiled at him. The smile lingered on her face as she looked up at Britney. The look on the teens face seemed expressionless.

"Everything ok?" Judy asked, looking from Britney to Jamie.

"Yep, everything's fine," Jamie said, as cheerful as she could manage. Britney glanced at her and the little girl gave her a discreet look. A look that said told Britney she had better wipe the guilty look off her face. A look that said 'act natural, stupid'.

Britney gave Judy her best fake smile and hopped it was convincing enough.

Judy smiled back and grabbed one of the bags from the seat and passed it back.

Britney let out a breath she didn't realize she was holding.

Jamie took the bag and looked inside at the assortment of snacks. Chips. Candy bars. A few Slim Jims. Her eyes focused on a bag of cheese puffs. She reached her hand in and pulled them out and passed them to Britney. Her seventeen year old eyes lit up.

"Sweet, my favorite!" Britney blurted. "Thanks Jamie. And thank *you* Judy."

"Ya, thanks Judy. I'm so hungry," Jamie added as she ripped the wrapper off a chocolate bar.

"No Problem. Hope I got some good stuff. There wasn't a lot to choose from in there. Someone got there first and I think they were hungrier than us."

As Judy finished her sentence, she pulled the backpack off her shoulder and tossed it in the floorboard. Britney followed it with her eyes.

Why would she have brought drugs? It was kinda weird she took the pack in there with her, like she didn't want to leave it with us.

Then after a second, she thought, *I hope Pete was the only drug addict. I mean, why would Judy even marry him or even talk to him unless... I mean, she doesn't seem like she would be that kind of...*

Britney shook her head slightly.

Whatever. I don't care. It's Judy. I'm sure she knows what she's doing. Maybe Jamie's just confused.

Britney was staring at the back of Judy's head, when the keys appeared in the woman's hand. She slid them into the ignition, gave them a twist and the Rover purred to life. As soon as the headlights lit up the alley, Judy shifted the engine into reverse and the Rover made a few quick jerks backwards and onto the street. After some grinding of the gears, they began moving forward.

"Hey Judy, do you want something to eat?" Jamie said, through a mouth full of chocolate.

"No, I'm fine for now. I had something when I was in there. I just get the feeling we need to get out of ...oh shit!"

Britney and Jamie froze at Judy's sudden outburst and followed her gaze out the window. They were passing an intersection and to their left a group of soldiers stood in front of two large military SUV's blocking the road. The roadblock was far enough away, that Judy stepped on the gas and the Rover sailed across the intersection, unnoticed.

Britney turned her head, following the roadblock as it went by. As soon as it disappeared behind the buildings, she said, "Holy crap! How the hell did they not see us?"

Judy kept her foot on the gas, accelerating, steering around obstacles in their path with more urgency. The Rover jerked from side to side, causing Britney to put her arm across Tommy's back, holding him steady.

As they passed the next intersection, Judy slowed, contemplating making the turn. It looked clear at first glance, but Jamie was the first to see them.

"Look! Way down there. I can see soldiers...and more trucks," Jamie said, pointing down the street. Britney squeezed her eyes into slits and after a second, saw them as well.

"She's right. I see them too."

About three blocks down that way, another road block sat, waiting. Britney let out a silent sigh.

Judy kept her eyes straight ahead and drove them casually across the intersection.

Britney watched this one go by and turned her attention to Judy. "Shit! What are we going to do now? Could they be blocking every way out?"

"Of course they are," Judy said in a dry tone, with a hint of contempt in it. "It's a *quarantine*...remember? They're probably covering every road out of town."

The comment snapped Jamie out of a daze of worry and before she knew what she was saying, words started to blather out of her mouth.

"The rich bitches!"

Britney snapped her attention to Jamie with a comical look of surprise on her face. "What? The rich what?"

"The rich bitches in Snobsdale!" Jamie struggled to connect the words in her head. "The airport!"

Britney saw the strain showing on her face and spoke in a clam voice. "Jamie, slow down. Tell us what you're feaking talking about...slowly."

Jamie took a few breaths and started talking rapidly, but with more control of her words.

"Earlier, when we were in the lobby, looking out at the soldiers, I heard one of them say they were letting the rich bitches take their own cars out of the city. I guess they didn't want to leave them or they didn't want to ride the buses. I don't know, but they said they were letting them drive through as long as they were clean."

Judy was coming up to another intersection when she spoke. "So you're saying they are letting people go through at the airport? You positive?"

Jamie looked at the skeptical look on Britney's face, then answered timidly, "Yes that's what I heard them say." Then a second of doubt engulfed her and she added, "But I don't know for sure. They also said something about this place frying at twenty two hundred or something, but I don't know what they meant."

Britney's eyes widened and she glanced at the clock on the dash. "Holy crap, twenty two hundred hours is ten p.m. It's already after nine. Did they really say that?" Her tone had a hint of unintentional rudeness in it.

Jamie looked down at her hands and to Britney, it didn't seem like the little girl was sure of anything. What Judy said next made Jamie stop fiddling with her hands and the look on her face brightened.

"Jamie, if you say they said it, then I believe you. Let's just hope it's still open that way. Britney, how do I get to the airport?"

Britney looked around for a second before answering. "Make the next left, then a right at the park." Then in a burst of emotion she added, "Right here! I mean...make a left here! Don't pass it or we have to go all the way around!"

Without taking her foot off the accelerator, Judy turned the wheel, sending Britney's weight shifting in Jamie's direction. The ten year old was pinned against the door. She let out a deep grunt that reminded Britney of her father baritone voice. Britney pushed her hand against the window, releasing some of the pressure between them and Jamie squirmed to adjust herself.

When Judy turned the wheel, they were already part way passed the intersection, but the Rover fish tailed on the icy road just enough to point them in the right direction. After a few spins of the wheel, the tires grabbed and they were moving along the street coming up to the park on the right. The intersection was clogged with cars, so Judy cut the wheel and the Rover bumped onto the sidewalk. Britney and Jamie looked at each other and smiled nervously.

Britney let out a sigh. "That was close. Sorry about—"

As soon as they made the turn, bright light poured into the cab, causing the four of them to flinch and block their eyes.

Spot lights, Britney thought. *No, headlights!*

And not just the headlights of another car. These where blindingly bright and way too high from the ground to be on anything other than the military vehicles they had seen around the city.

Britney let out a scream. "Quick, turn into the park!"

Without a second's hesitation, Judy turned the wheel, sending the Rover across the street and cutting off the military truck. The breaks on the large truck locked and it slid sideways to avoid the collision. There was a hard jolt as the Rovers tires connected with the curb adjacent to the park. It jumped the sidewalk, causing the three of their butts to become airborne for a second. Tommy shifted under Britney's arm. She reinforced her grip on him, holding him in place. He continued to sleep as the Rover flattened a pair of bushes lining the sidewalk and continued across the snow covered grass.

Jamie turned around, placing her knees in the seat and gawked out the back window at the large truck.

In a calm voice, Judy asked, "Are they coming after us?"

In an equally calm voice, Jamie responded, "Yep."

Britney turned her head enough to see that the truck was rolling over the sidewalk after them.

Judy adjusted the rear view mirror and said, in a grumble, "Well, let's see what this thing can do." She down shifted and hit the accelerator.

The Rover launched over a small hill and crossed over a brick walking path, barely avoiding a snow covered park bench. Less than thirty seconds later, the bench was flattened by the massive rubber tires of the M939 truck.

✧

Chapter 10.

Britney tugged on Jamie's shirt for the third time. "Jamie, sit down and put your seat belt on!" The Rover was jerking all over the place and Britney had her other arm in a death grip around Tommy. "I hate this shit! Slow down or we're gonna crash!"

Judy ignored Britney's pleas and Jamie didn't move from her backward position in the seat.

"Are they still back there?" Judy asked, as she made another hard left turn, avoiding a tree.

"Oh, ya, they are! They're coming fast!" Jamie answered.

The excitement in the little girl's voice made Britney feel like screaming at them both. She squeezed her eyes shut.

These two seem like they're having a blast. I feel like I'm gonna piss myself again. We're flying through the park in a stolen car, being chased by the army and they're both smiling. That truck's so big, it could flatten us like—

Britney's eyes shot open. She glanced around at the snowy park around them.

That truck is big. Really big. Too big to fit through—

Britney's thought was cut off by her own voice. She knew this park well and saw an opportunity coming up.

"Judy, veer right and go down that hill!" she said, hopping one of them would pay attention to her. Sense entering the park, they both seemed like they were in their own little world.

Judy veered right and shot down the hill. Britney relaxed a bit and leaned forward, hopping she was right about what was ahead. Jamie turned and looked out the front window with her.

Through the foggy front window of the Rover, a small black dot came into view. As they got closer, it started to resemble what it was. A tunnel.

"Go in there! That tunnel! Go through it!" Britney said, pointing dead ahead of them. "The airport is just on the other side."

Jamie squinted her eyes. "That tunnel looks too small. Will we fit?"

They were going so fast, that seeing the small opening made Jamie turn around and sit in her seat. Britney watched as she fumbled to fasten her seatbelt.

Judy had her eyes fixed straight ahead, with her hands gripping the steering wheel tight. "We will. Just barely."

"But they won't," Britney added. A smile crease Judy's face, as she gave the Rover more gas.

Britney felt Jamie grab ahold of her hand as they neared the tunnel. As they got closer, it started to appear lager than it looked a moment ago, but Judy was right, they were barely going to fit.

Judy looked in the rear view mirror, just as the truck came over the top of the hill. The size and speed of it made it look out of control, like a huge dead tree sliding down the hill after them.

"Look out!"

The scream could have been either one of the girls sitting in the back seat. It sounded shrill and snapped Judy's attention from the truck, to the black hole in front of her.

Britney's voice erupted from the back seat. "Judy, slow down!"

Judy ignored her and pushed the gas petal to the floor just as they entered. They slid in like a freight train following rails, instead of four rubber tires on slick, icy cement. The inside of the Rover dimmed and the only light they could see was at the end of the tunnel, about a quarter mile in front of them. From this distance, the exit looked as small as the entrance had.

Judy spared a look in the rear view mirror. Before she could focus on anything, the wheel jerked out of her hand, causing the Rover to skim the side of the tunnel. Sparks filled the windows as the side view mirror was ripped off by the cement walls.

"Judy, Please watch were you're going for Christ sake!" Britney pleaded.

Judy's eyes shot back ahead of her. "What are they doing back there? Did they stop?"

Jamie unbuckled her seat belt and quickly turn around, peering out the back window. She could see the headlights of the truck. They looked like they were only a few feet below the roof of the tunnel. They began to move, slanting together and Jamie knew they were backing up and away from the opening.

"They won't fit!" Jamie shrieked. "They stopped! It worked!"

Britney let out a sigh of relief. "Thank God, that's over. I feel like I'm in an Indian Jones movie."

Jamie let out a muffled giggle. "Ya, I know. Too cool!"

Britney rolled her eyes and unclenched her hand from the 'oh shit' handle above Jamie's head.

•••

As they approached the exit to the tunnel, Judy slowed the Rover to a crawl. They crept out looking in both directions to make sure there wasn't another truck waiting for them. They saw nothing in either direction.

Britney broke the silence. "See, I told you. They have to go all the way around. There's a metal railing, fence thingy across the top of the tunnel and I don't think that thing could even make it over it. Hit the gas, we're home free!"

Judy smile at her in the mirror. "Which way?"

Britney pointed slightly to their left, toward a large flat looking building. "That way. That's the south gate parking lot. If we drive around the side of it, there's a fence that leads to the runway." Britney looked at Jamie. "You said the soldier guys said at the end of the runway right?"

Jamie nodded her head. "Yep."

Britney continued, "I know just what they are talking about. Me and my friends used to go park in the woods at the end of the runway and watch the planes take off. Seriously, it looked like they were gonna run right into us. It was crazy! Then there was this one time, my friend Brad actually climbed up in a tree and almost got blown right out of it…"

Jamie mused at the way Britney was jabbering on like normal, even though a few minutes ago she was winning like a baby.

And to think, this is the creature my parents hired to watch me.

Jamie smiled, as Britney's continued jabbering faded into the back of her mind. She looked out the front window. Judy turned the wheel and took the Rover across the snow covered grass, in the direction of the building Britney pointed out. Soon they were thumping across another side walk and back on the street.

As Jamie watched out the window, she saw something in the distance. At first glance it looked like a train traveling across the intersection. She squinted her good eyes and focused them on the spot. When she did, she saw that it wasn't a train at all. It was a line of military vehicles. It looked like they were leaving the city and in a rush. She glanced at the clock on the dash and wondered if it was close to twenty two hundred o'clock yet.

•••

The Rover rolled up to the gate Britney had described.

"Damn it! It's locked," Britney said, as their headlight illuminated a stern looking chain and padlock. "Well I guess it would be. I mean, why wouldn't it, right?"

Jamie grabbed the back of Judy's seat and pulled herself forward, bringing her face next to Judy's ear. "Do you think we can ram it?" The comment had a childish excitement to it.

Judy didn't answer her. Instead, she put the Rover in first gear and revved the engine. Jamie noticed the sinister smile on Judy's face in the rear view mirror and smiled back as she clinched her fingers tighter around the seat and prepared for the maneuver. The Rovers tires chirped slightly and they lunged forward.

As soon as the aftermarket bumper connected with the fence, both sides swung open and the SUV cruised through with little trouble. Jamie unclenched her fingers and looked back as the gates rebounded. She was hoping it would be more of a dramatic entrance. She glanced around as the Rover slowly moved along.

The airport was usually a busy place, twenty four hours a day, seven days a week. That didn't seem to be the case tonight. It seemed like a ghost town. The only sign of life was a lit up room at the top of a tower in the distance.

Jamie thought, *That must be the...control tower?*

Her good eyes could see several figures moving around up there. She looked to the others and saw that they didn't seem to notice it. Before she could point it out, they rounded a corner and Britney saw something more malicious.

"Holy shit!" Britney blurted out. "We're busted for sure! Judy, turn us around or something!"

Judy shushed her quietly and continued to drive despite the soldiers lingering about. A half dozen huge helicopters were scattered around the open area. A few of the men looked in their direction, but continued to go about their business. Two of the choppers in the distance were running and Judy could hear the hum of the blades as they sliced through the air. Bright lights were set up and it felt like the Rover was on display all of a sudden.

Judy narrowed her eyes on the men stirring about.

They look like they're in a hurry. Good, just mind your business and don't worry about us. Nothing but innocent women and children here. We want the same thing you want. To get the fuck out of here in one piece.

"Crap, Judy. What are you doing?" Britney whispered. "They can totally see us. Is this cool?"

Judy sighed. "Britney, did you think there wouldn't be any soldiers here and we would drive right up and off the runway? We're supposed to be here, remember?"

Britney caught sight of Judy's eyes in the mirror and gave her a nod.

In a calm voice Judy added, "For all they know, we are just the last few rich bitches wanting out."

This comment got a smile out of Jamie, but Britney kept a stern look on her face and glanced back at the men. One of them was defiantly curious about the banged up Rover. He stopped what he was doing and pulled a radio from his belt and spoke into it as he watched them roll by.

Britney tensed. *Shit! Could that other truck have told them about us? They would all have radios on them I bet. This doesn't feel right.*

The thought made Britney's mind settle on something Jamie had said earlier, when she was sputtering out sentence fragments.

"Judy, what if they really do scan us? Do you think the kids will come up clean? Or what about you? You had that thing or whatever in you right? What if you guys are dirty? Besides, you're covered in blood, Judy!"

Judy didn't reply and glanced down at her bloody arms. Britney was right, they didn't look very inconspicuous, but there was nothing to be done about it now.

"I guess we're gonna find out, aren't we?" Judy said, softly, almost to herself.

It wasn't the answer Britney wanted to hear. It wasn't much of an answer at all, but then again, it was just the answer she expected from Judy.

Britney looked back at the man with the radio. He had replaced it on his belt and continued to watch them go by, with his hands placed on his hips. Somehow the stance made him seem knowing and Britney swallowed hard and moved her eyes forward, not wanting to make eye contact with him.

Jamie was watching out the window as well and made eye contact with the soldier just as Britney looked away. Jamie smiled and gave the man a little wave.

We need to find our way out of here, Mr. Soldier, She thought. *Can you help us?*

Jamie absently had the thought and was surprised when the look on the man's face faltered slightly. His right hand came up from his hip and Jamie thought he was going to wave back, but his arm continued to rise, until he was pointing in the direction they were headed. He gave her a nod, as he continued to point.

"There, look. That man is telling us to go ahead," Jamie said, casually. Then to herself, she thought, *Wow, did he just hear me or something. It felt like he did. That's weird.*

Britney looked out the window and saw that Jamie was right. The man did seem to be leading them to the exit. She relaxed her breathing and took her attention back out the front window of the Rover. As they came around another corner, the busy parade of soldiers and aircraft disappeared behind the buildings and again, it felt as if they were sneaking undetected.

Britney and Jamie looked back out the window, as one of the choppers slowly rose from behind the buildings. It lingered for a moment, then turned and headed north and Britney got the feeling it would never come back to this airport again.

They're out. God I wish I were with them.

She looked back at Judy.

"Maybe that was it? Maybe we lucked out and they were just too busy to bother with us. It looked like they were getting ready to leave." She paused to glance at the clock on the radio. "It's almost ten. They have to get out of here too, right? I think that was it. I think we're good."

Judy didn't reply and Britney looked to Jamie. Britney's eyes seemed to plead for a response. Something encouraging. The little girl shrugged her shoulders. It wasn't the response Britney hoped for.

•••

Britney soon saw she was wrong. A hundred years ahead of them, they got their first glance at the road block at the end of the runway. It was only two men and a couple of trucks, but both men were armed, riffles in hand. Worse than that, there was a dog. For some reason, seeing the dog made Britney even more nervous.

Shit, that dog's going to tip them off. Judy has enough blood on her; this whole car probably smells like a dog treat.

Somehow in the moonlight, Judy, Britney and Jamie could even make out the looks on the soldiers faces as they noticed the vehicle rolling up on them. They looked either pissed, scared, confused or all three combined. One of them started to walk forward, into their path. Judy slowed the Rover to a crawl.

Judy spoke without taking her eyes off the man. "Maybe you guys should act like your sleeping. Just close your eyes and let me handle this."

Jamie looked at Britney. The seventeen year old had her head back against the headrest, her eyes closed. Her lips were clinched shut, causing the edges to look whitish. Her hand was stroking Tommy's back as he continued to sleep. Jamie looked back out the window at the soldiers.

I wish they would just let us by. Please just let us by.

Jamie remembered her encounter in the apartment with the other Tommy. She was able to push thoughts at the thing. A second ago, when she pushed a thought at the soldier, he seemed to do what she wanted; he seemed to hear her, so she started to push thoughts at this man as well.

Please let us by.

Please let us by.

We just want to leave without hurting anyone.

Please let us by.

They were ten feet from the soldier and Jamie saw the dog tighten up on its leash. She could tell it was about to bark.

She started to push her thoughts at the dog as well.

We don't want to hurt anyone.

We just want to leave, Mr. Doggy.

Please let us by.

The dog started to wine and back up as the Rover crept closer. It looked scared. The soldier holding the dog, tugged on the leash, said something to the animal and looked back at the vehicle. Jamie watched his free hand go to the side arm on his belt and she willed him not to pull it. His hand seemed to relax, hovering over the gun. Jamie saw this and continued to push for another moment, until Judy spoke.

"You guys hold back there. We may have to ram them if they don't let us by. There's no way I'm stopping this car."

Britney's eyes opened when she heard the comment. Her next words had a hopeless tone to them.

"Well then just ram them, Judy. You know they are going to stop us."

Jamie's eyes went from Britney to Judy's reflection in the mirror. Judy had a smirk on her face that made Jamie skip a breath.

She's going to ram them. Then they will shoot at us and chase us. Please don't do it, Judy.

Jamie closed her eyes and continued to chant silently in her mind.

Please let us by.

Please don't bark at us, doggy. We don't want to hurt anyone.

Please let us by.

Britney's voice broke Jamie's concentration.

"Holy shit! This can't be happening. Is he letting us go?"

Jamie opened her eyes and gawked out the window. The soldier was waving them through. He wasn't even going to stop them to ask any questions. He was in fact rushing them through, with quick waves of his hand.

"My God, go, Judy!" Britney urged. "Hurry, before he changes his mind!"

Judy made eye contact with the soldier, as she pressed on the gas. She was surprised when he looked away and continued to wave, as if he didn't want to look at her. The Rover rolled between the two trucks, off the pavement and onto a gravel road.

Judy narrowed her eyes as she looked at the two men in the rear view. They were getting in one of the trucks and in a hurry. In the distance, a few more of the helicopters were rising from behind the buildings and heading north. Before they were out of sight, Judy watched as the lights on the truck illuminated. A second later, it sped away in the direction of the choppers.

Judy sneered. Deep down, she really wanted to run over the soldier that waved them through, while the other one watched his friends legs flatten under the tires.

Why did you let us pass? Why didn't you stop us like you were supposed to? It makes no sense.

Britney's voice broke the silence in the cab. "Holy shit, Judy! That was awesome. I don't know how we made it, but you rocked that. I would have flipped out. Way to keep your cool! I freaking love you, Judy!"

Jamie wanted to butt in right there. Tell them she thought it was her that made the men let them through. That she had some sort of power that enabled her to go into the man's mind. That even the dog seemed to hear her. But something inside her told her to keep her mouth shut about it, for now.

I don't know it was me. It felt like it was but I'm not sure. I kind of hope it wasn't. I don't want them to think I'm a freak again. I just want to be normal.

Jamie reached forward and pulled herself up to Judy's ear again. "Ya, Judy. That was awesome. You're too cool."

Judy smiled and said, "Thank you. Thank you. I don't know what happened back there, but at least we're out." Then after a second, she added, "I couldn't have done any of this without you two. We make a good team."

Jamie released her grip on the seat and let herself fall back into her spot in the back. Britney put her hand on Jamie's leg and Jamie covered it with her own. They both looked at Tommy. He hadn't seen any of it. He twitched in his sleep, as if he were having

a bad dream and Britney returned her hand to his back and started
to rub it lightly. Just looking at him was making her tired. A huge
yawn escaped her mouth. Jamie watched Britney and waited. Her
mother used to always say that yawns were contagious. After a
second Jamie felt her own yawn coming. She let it come. A deep
moan escape her at the end of it. Britney looked at her and smiled.
Jamie slouched toward the middle and rested her head against
Britney's shoulder and closed her eyes.

Britney looked out the front window of the Rover just as
they entered the tree line. They rocked gently back and forth as the
gravel road gave way to a rut infested dirt road. The motions of the
slow moving vehicle were soothing, as if they were in a boat
drifting over waves.

"So what are we going to do now?" Britney asked. "I mean,
where are we gonna to go?"

Judy looked at her in the rear view. "I don't know. I just
feel like driving as far as I can. Maybe you two should get some
sleep, like the little man there."

Judy's eyes gestured to Tommy. Britney looked at him,
then to Jamie. The little girl was breathing heavy, with her mouth
gapped open.

"I think Jamie's already there," Britney said, with a smile.

Judy watched the winding dirt road appear from the
darkness in front of her. There were trees to avoid now and it was
hard to see, so she drove slowly. The last thing they needed was to
wreck the Rover.

"Well maybe you should join her," Judy said, softly. Her
stomach grumbled and she eyed the backpack as Britney spoke.

"You don't have to tell me twice," the seventeen year old
said, as she laid her head back against the seat and let her heavy
eyes fall shut. After a pause, she added, "Tell me if anything
happens."

"I will."

"And thank you, Judy. I'm so glad it was you that walked
out of that alley. I don't think I could have gotten these guys out of
there by myself."

Judy looked at her in the mirror. Britney still had her eyes
closed. "Yes you would have, but you're welcome anyways."

Judy waited for a reply, but instead Britney's head slumped
to one side and she started to breathe deeply through her nose.
Judy watched her for a second. Britney hadn't heard what she said.
Sleep had taken her somewhere in the middle of the comment.

As Judy's eyes drifted from Britney, she felt her stomach
gurgle again and a loud, animal like growl rattled her insides. It
was loud enough that Judy's eyes shot back to Britney, afraid the

unexpected sound would wake her. Britney didn't stir and Judy relaxed.

Wow, I guess I am hungry after all.

Judy's eyes fell to the passenger side of the car. Just as she started to reach her hand, she heard another sound, but it didn't come from her stomach this time. Several sharp popping sounds echoed through the trees, almost as if someone were slapping two wood planks together in the distance. Her eyes shot to the rear view mirror.

Behind them, toward the city, a blast of bright light filled the sky for a moment, barely visible through the trees. A second later, Judy felt a vibration on the floorboard of the Rover and the gearshift shook in her hand. A strong gust of wind blew the branched of the trees forward, in the direction she was driving, as if waving her through, like the soldier had. After a few seconds, everything settled again and a smile blessed Judy's lips.

She looked at the clock on the dash. Ten p.m. on the dot.

Her eyes shifted to the kids. They didn't stir. They hadn't felt it. They didn't get to see it.

I wonder if they would have wanted too, she thought. *I wonder if they would have smiled or frowned. We made it after all.*

Then after a moment.

No, it's good they didn't see it. The brats probably wouldn't have appreciated it, as close minded as they are.

Her stomach growled again and she eyed the back pack on the floor. Her hand left the shifter and fiddled with the zipper until she was able to open the top of the bag. Next she shoved her hand inside and rooted around at the contents. Several low grunts escaped her mouth, as she did.

She pulled a package of hamburger meat out of pack and tore a hole in the plastic. She didn't want to make a mess that Britney and the others would notice, but it was hard. In the grocery store, the meat had tasted so good, that it was clear why the others had been so carless and greedy. So content to slumber and eat mindlessly, with no true agenda.

She pushed her fingers into the meat, scooped up a large, soft wad and popped it in her mouth. The mineral taste of blood practically made Bad Judy's body go week and she had to fight to keep her eyes from rolling back in her head. As she chewed and savored the slimy constancy of the ground beef, her guard dropped just enough for the real Judy's horrified face to materialize in the mirror. It was only a matter of time before it happened. The damn bitch had been buzzing in her ear like a fly since she walked out of that alley. Bad Judy could feel Judy's presents before she glanced in the mirrors direction.

*So you finally managed to show yourself, Judy. And I see
you waited until the heroic deeds were done.*

In the mirror, Judy's face looked frantic and scared. Her
lips moved, but the volume was turned down in Bad Judy's head.
She smiled at Judy efforts tauntingly.

*What's that, Judy? I can't hear you. You see, I can chose to
listen to you or chose not to. So you better watch what you say,
considering I just saved your brats for you.*

Bad Judy put her hand up and placed her fingers around an
imaginary knob in the air. As she turned the imaginary knob, Judy
voice slowly gained tone and flowed into Sumonk's mind.

"You nasty bitch," Judy screamed. *"You tricked me! Why
didn't you take that ignorant fucks body and leave me in piece like
you said? We had a deal!"*

Judy's eyes moved past Sumonk, to the back seat, where
the children sat sleeping.

*"Jamie! Wake up! I need you to wake up! You're being
tricked!"*

A cackle erupted in Judy's mind. She looked back to
Sumonk as she continued to chew the meat in her mouth.

*She can't hear your pathetic pleas, idiot woman! Our
conversation remains between us. No matter how much you
scream, they can't hear you.*

Then after a pause, Sumonk smiled and added though her
mouthful, *And I told you to be nice. I could very easily slit their
throats right now as they sleep.*

The comment was spoken sweetly, as if being conveyed to
a child. It made Judy stop her raving. She had been cursing and
screaming at Sumonk and the kids for hours, ever since leaving
Victor's body in the alley. The moment Sumonk stood up and
walked away, Judy knew she had been double crossed, but could
do nothing about it.

Judy bit her bottom lip and tried to control herself, despite
the fact that she was naked and freezing in some sort of cave or
hole in the ground, looking through what seemed like a reflection
off of a rock in front of her. She had been looking through it for
hours and could see everything that had happened since the alley.
Bits and pieces of it anyways, mostly though the rear view mirror.

Sumonk sent another thought her way and Judy knew she
had no choice but to shut her mouth and listen.

*But to answer your question, I saw the way Victor looked at
me. The female form has power that I did not understand until I
saw the way he drooled. He would have given me anything, before
looking past his own selfish lust. When you let me in, he wanted me
in a way I did not know existed. I have never been lusted after like
that. It was wonderful. It made my mind up. I decided to keep you*

*as my host. Victor, as beautiful a specimen as he was, did not have
your power. Too bad he probably did not survive the blast. He was
cruel. The one trait you lack.*

Judy paused for a moment, thinking. The thing wasn't
wrong. Men were puppets sometimes. Especially when some evil
bitch was tugging at the strings. Then another thought surfaced.

*The blast. Pete! If the city blew, he didn't survive the blast
either. I left him and now he's probably dead because of me...for
the second time.*

Judy's eyes lowered and she stared off into space for a
moment.

*No, that's not my fault! This whole thing is her fault. These
things caused all of this and the military followed right along with
it, another puppet with strings to pull. Pete's death isn't on my
hands.*

Sumonk snickered and a voice whispered in Judy's ear.
Believe whatever you want to believe, Judy.

Judy looked back up at the things reflection and narrowed
her eyes.

"Where the hell am I?"

Judy could hear her voice echoing, making the seemingly
small space appear larger. It was an eerie feeling. If there was
anything else in here with her, she was sure it would be able to
hear her for miles. Sumonk's voice didn't echo like her own and
Judy knew it was in her head. She listened as the thing answered.

*You're in your new home. The catacombs. Of course, I'm
not sure how long you will last. As I said before, our bodies can
not survive in the above and I do not think you're going to do very
well below. Though, it will be interesting to find out. Do let me
know how you're doing from time to time, will you?*

When Sumonk sent her thoughts, it sounded like it was
coming from an old, blown radio speaker, but Judy could still hear
the taunting tone she was using.

Somewhere behind Judy, an eerie dripping noise echoed
through the corridor, like a clock ticking, keeping track of the
seconds she was stranded. It echoed in her mind, making it hard for
her to think.

Drip Drip Drip

If she had to stay here with it much longer, Judy was sure it
was one of the things that would drive her mad. The sound was
mind numbing.

"How do I get out of here?"

Sumonk answered her in a more serious tone and Judy got
the feeling she was telling the truth for once.

*That I don't know. I know how I got out. You let me out and
into your body. But I have to say I'm not sure how it works for you.*

161

But it's no matter. All I know is…you are there and I am here. Your brats are my new family.

Judy blood boiled. She forgot about her nakedness and unfolded her arms from her cold body. She wanted to bang her fists on the reflective rock, but refrained herself at the last moment.

"If you hurt them, I'll kill you!" She grumbled.

I do not want to hurt them. I didn't think I needed them, but now I see that I do. I doubt I would have escaped as easily without their help. They need me too, as you have probably seen. I am not used to companionship. The others and I are a solitary group, spending years upon years avoiding each other. Love and friendship have never existed for me, but now that I have it, I can see how it can be useful. They love me. I can feel it radiating off of your Tommy even as he sleeps. He loves me now and eventually, I may love him too, as long as he remains useful. After all, I am his mother.

Judy's mind went blank and she stared back, silently. The comment cut her deep. It might as well been a sharpened blade.

Nothing I say is going to help anything anyways. I'm trapped again and for good this time.

Judy crossed her arms over her naked chest again and shifted her feet. Every extremity of her body was shaking and she could see the breath exiting her mouth from the light the image coming off the rock in front of her gave off. Suddenly she had an overwhelming feeling of loneliness. A loneliness that seemed like a wet blanket being thrown over a fire.

The dripping continued, counting away her existence.

Drip Drip Drip

She could feel how this place's solitude could make something turn evil. Uncaring. She had only been there a few hours and already felt her fire going out. She missed Tommy, but already had trouble remembering what his face looked like. The other Tommy's face kept creeping into her mind instead. The bad one seemed to be more familiar all of a sudden. The feeling perplexed her.

How can I forget my good Tommy's face?

Bad Judy picked up on this simply by the look on Judy's expression in the mirror. Could feel Judy's loneliness. She didn't even have to read her mind.

But do not worry, Judy. In the catacombs, we are solitary by choice, but not alone. There are still many others down there, but I'm not sure how they will take to you. They may rip you to threads or ignore you all together, leaving you to wonder until your end.

Sumonk caught sight of something lingering in the back ground behind Judy and smiled. It was an unexpected surprise even to her.

I believe there's someone there who may pay you some attention. Someone who misses you. Someone who loves you.

Judy looked up at the reflection, with a confused expression on her face. Just as she prepared to question the comment, the dripping sound stopped and the silence dug the knife in deeper. She held her breath and listened. She suddenly got the feeling she wasn't alone. She turned her head slightly and said, in a soft voice, "Hello?"

Judy's word echoed three times and then seemed to fall short, as if something snatched it out of the air before it could continue. She waited for an answer, hoping she wouldn't hear one.

Please let there not be anything there. If something there, I might go insane right now.

Then after a second.

Or have gone insane already...It feels like I have.

Just as she finished the thought, out of the corner of her eye, Judy started to see a green misty light radiating from somewhere behind her. Her body stiffened and she turn her head. Her eyes went wide at what she saw.

Standing less than five feet away from her, was a creature, hairless and white, standing about four and a half feet tall. An aura of glowing, green mist hovered and shifted around its body, giving it the appearance of movement despite the fact it was standing perfectly still and staring at her with blank eyes. Its legs were short compared to its long arms. It didn't look like it could be real. It looked like something out of a cheesy horror movie or a wax statue that had seen too much sun. Judy focused her eyes and it dawned on her that she had seen one of these things before, for a split second in Jamie's apartment, before the TV blew. But this one had something familiar about it. Judy unwillingly looked at its eyes. They were hard to look away from, milky whitish, with a grey center. They seemed to suck her into them. The looks of them made her wonder if it could see her at all. She was afraid to find out. She was afraid to move.

She held in a whimper, as she took a step to her right. Without warning, the thing side stepped, following her movements. Its feet made a wet slapping sound on the rock floor as its shuffled. Its steps were short and quick, as if it were wearing ankle cuffs. The mist circling its body quickened it movements and settled as the thing stopped. It stood silent and motionless, as if it had never moved.

Judy stumbled and moved back where she was. Without thinking, she pleaded with the creature.

"What do you want? Please, leave me alone!"

The things pink lips puckered and Judy thought it was going to speak. Instead its lips parted, a single dripping sound echoed in the space. Judy let out a nervous cackle, as she held back a cry. The thing tilted its head and the repetitive dripping sound commenced. As the things lips opened and closed, it looked like it was giving kisses. Judy stared, horrified.

Has this thing been in here with me the whole time, making that damn noise?

Judy shrieked, "Stop!" She covered her ears with her trembling hands.

The dripping stopped and the things lips curled into a smile. A familiar smile. One she would never forget.

Judy gasped.

She knew this thing. She had seen it before. She had listened to it giggle. Listened to it tell her it loved her. She had sat with it in her own apartment. She had also killed it. Or at least she thought she did.

"No! This can't be real!" Judy shrieked. "I beat you!"

The thing stared at her for a moment, before a childlike voice filled the cavern. "Mommy, you came back. Do you wanna watch cartoons wif me? They're funny."

Judy let out a silent gasp and brought her hand up over her mouth. The thing spoke in Tommy voice, just as it had before.

"You still love me don't you?" it said.

Judy started at the creature and her hands began to shake. A second later, Judy screamed out in surprise, as the thing took several steps in her direction with unnatural quickness. It stopped just as fast and was still again, as if it had never moved. Judy backed up a few steps, until her back bumped the rocky wall behind her. Her hands came down and grasped the stone. Her naked chest heaved up and down, as she sucked in gulps of air. She began to weep between breaths.

"Please, I just want my son back. I was just trying to be a good mother. I just want my Tommy to be sa—"

Judy's pleas were cut short, as a childish giggle erupted in the small cavern a second before Bad Tommy lunged at her. Judy turned and clawed at the walls, as she felt its clammy hands creep around her waist. She made eye contact with Sumonk's smiling reflection on the rocks before her vision clouded over in a green misty haze.

•••

A final scream tore through Bad Judy's head, causing her to squeeze her eyes shut with a smile. She brought her hand up again and tuned the imaginary knob in front of her. Judy's screams faded until the image in the rearview mirror clicked off completely, as if it were a picture tube. Bad Judy opened her eyes and glanced back at Britney and the kids. They were still fast asleep.

Sleep on, my pets. It's been a long day for us all, especially pathetic Judy.

Next, she looked at the radio.

It's too quiet in here. I've suffered the quiet too long already.

Bad Judy leaned forward facing the radio, took a deep breath, puckered her lips and blew. A stream of green mist exited her mouth. It curled and twisted, drifting toward the dash, as if it were alive. It collided with the radio in a smoky splash and after a few burps of static, whimsical music started to play from the speakers. The volume was low enough that it wouldn't disturb the children, but distracting enough that it would cover up the sound of something being devoured.

Bad Judy looked down at the package of ground beef sitting on the passenger seat, reached her hand out and tore the plastic off the top. She grabbed a heaping handful of the meat and shoved it in her mouth, using her fingers to cram every bit in until her cheeks were bulging.

As she chewed, with bits of fat dripping from the corners of her mouth, she hummed and grunted along with the music.

Tommy would have recognized the tune as the theme song to one of his favorite cartoons, although the fact they would never play it on the radio wouldn't have crossed his five year old mind.

Above the Rover, came a break in the trees. The moon was full, casting a soft white light across the forest, causing the snow to glow white under what looked like a thousand sparkles. Bad Judy stopped humming, looked up at it and her chewing slowed. She had never seen the moon before. It was a spooky sight and made her feel uneasy.

Such a big place. So big, it makes me feel small, she thought. Strangely, the thought made her mind wonder to Victor. His image flashed in her mind and something inside her quivered, causing the corner of her mouth to raise into a smirk. She quickly shook the feeling off.

Worthless creature, stay out of my thoughts. Your just a memory and memories are for the weak!

Just as she began to look away from the moon, her eyes moved back, as a green haze drifted over the front of it, flowing from the direction of the city. The white light dimmed and the moon glimmered green, with a familiar aura around it. The image reminded Sumonk of her old home, her old life. She cringed at the memory, looked away and stuffed more meat into her mouth.

In the back seat, Tommy sat awake staring out the window at the sky. The green moon reminded him of something as well. Something he would rather forget. A nightmare; one that had startled him awake moments ago. It seemed so real. In it, some monster, with the same colored aura around it, chased his mother into dark places. She ran and it followed her. She screamed and it laughed. Even now, half awake, he felt like he could still hear echoes of her screaming in his head. He tried to squeeze his eyes shut to make it stop.

It's not scary.

It's not real.

My mommy beat the bad thing.

When he opened them, he slowly looked to the driver seat of the car, where his mother sat, safe and sound. He relaxed and the whispering of her screams dimmed in his ears.

Bad Judy swallowed the last bit of meat in her mouth, when Tommy's small voice startled her.

"Mommy?" Tommy said.

Sumonk quickly covered what she had in the seat next to her, looked at him through the rear view mirror and said, "Yes, boy, what is it? Are you ok?"

"Ya, I'm ok. I had a bad dream...*You* ok, Mommy?" He said the last part with a tinge of skepticism in his voice.

"Yes, I'm fine," Sumonk said, trying not to show her frustration. "You go back to sleep now, ok?"

After a short pause, Tommy spoke again. His eyes were getting heavy already.

"Mommy?"

"Yes, Boy? What is it?" Sumonk's eye twitched and she fought the urge to turn and give the little boy and evil glare, one that would stop his mindless yapping.

"You won't let the bad lady get you, right?"

"No, the bad thing can't get me," she said. *Because, I am the bad lady*, she thought.

Tommy's voice drifted again, sounding tired. "You beat the bad thing, right Momma?"

"Yes, I beat it. Now hush and go back to sleep."

Tommy was silent for a moment. Sumonk thought he had drifted to sleep. After a moment, she cringed as his small voice came from behind her again.

"Mommy?"

"Yes?" A sigh escaped her mouth.

"I love you, Mommy. Forever and ever."

A sinister smile crossed her face and she forced the bitter tasting words, "I love you too, boy."

Tommy's tired eyes jerked open slightly, with one of his eye brows raised. "Forever and ever, Momma?"

Bad Judy's jaw clinched and she forced a smile. "Oh yes, of course...forever and ever and ever."

Made in the USA
San Bernardino, CA
14 March 2016